THE WOODEN KING

THE WOODEN KING

THOMAS MCCONNELL

HUB CITY PRESS

SPARTANBURG, SC

McConnell

Library of Congress Cataloging-in-Publication Data

Names: McConnell, Thomas, author.
Title: The wooden king / Thomas McConnell.
Description: Spartanburg, SC : Hub City Press, 2018.
Identifiers: LCCN 2017032054| ISBN 9781938235375 (hardcover)
  ISBN 9781938235368 (Ebook)
Subjects: LCSH: World War, 1939-1945–Czechoslovakia–Fiction.
  Domestic fiction. | GSAFD: Historical fiction. | War stories.
Classification: LCC PS3613.C3817 W66 2018 | DDC 813/.6–dc23
LC record available at https://lccn.loc.gov/2017032054

Cover images: ©Shutterstock / Peter Vrabel; Elizabeth Addie Becker
Book design: Meg Reid
Copy editor: Kalee Lineberger
Proofreader: Megan DeMoss

HUB CITY PRESS
186 W. Main Street
Spartanburg, SC 29306
864.327.8515
www.hubcity.org

*This book is for John Abraham McConnell
and all my Czech friends.*

15 MARCH 1939

They came through the snow, trucks of infantry, motorcycles with men in trench coats riding the sidecars, platoons by bicycle hurling back the barriers at the frontiers for half-tracks, a few tanks, armored cars. A dress rehearsal for Poland six months later. Hitler himself came in the secure evening and the next day processed through the cities in his bullet-proof Mercedes. In the clamorous squares children peeked out from forests of legs to glimpse him, to wave little red flags with broken crosses while their cheering parents among the German minority gave the salute. The Ides of March, 1939. Their infamous day.

In Munich the fall before, Chamberlain and Daladier had cast the die, assigned to Hitler all he needed to render the country indefensible. Across the table the statesmen shook hands over the dissected map of what had been Czechoslovakia. No Czech was in the room while their nation was dismembered. Hungary hacked away a whole province. Poland gouged its portion. Slovakia was amputated into independence but might as well have been kept in a jar in Berlin.

So under a March snow their republic melted into the haze of the past and a new word came into the language for Hitler's man in the castle: Reichsprotektor. A new word for the land he ruled: Protektorate. Czechs had known twenty years as a free people since that day in Philadelphia at the end of the Great War when their liberator, their first president, Thomas Masaryk, had declared their birth in a street beside Independence Hall. For the rest of his life Masaryk reasoned with his countrymen, goaded them together toward middle Europe's first democracy until, exhausted at eighty-seven, he died when they needed his wisdom most. He was spared the fate of his country as his two successors were not. The bookish one, Benes, resigned after the disaster at Munich and went into exile. The old judge, Hacha, the last alternative, a grandfather doting on senility, collapsed across a carpet in Hitler's chancellery the night of the invasion. He had to be revived with an injection so he could sign the death warrant for the corpse that remained. And the assassination was complete.

What the people inherited was the gun and the Gestapo, the parading field gray of the Wehrmacht and thugs on the corners. Jews lost their jobs. The universities, except the ones for Germans, were closed. The blackouts began and the whispering. Schools became jails, the palaces of Bohemian kings became prisons, beams in their cellars hung with nooses of wire. So the people waited in line for black bread and bits of meat, for the will to go on and whatever the gods of fate or the lords of war would bring them.

Watching the great wet flakes descend on the eve of spring they parted their lace curtains with almost steady hands and looked out at the boots and tires splashing through their streets. Breaths misting on the pane, they murmured to one another, "It's bad."

1940

Now that the history of their country had come to an end he told the boy stories of the brave little Czech nation, and night after night Aleks listened, though the hour stretched his mouth into yawns. When the time came to switch off the light the boy delayed the dark with questions. Trn listened to them all.

"This morning, when we were walking to school? Remember? Why did you pull me over the ice, like I was skiing?"

"Because I thought it might make you laugh."

"Oh." In his fist he tried to hide a long yawn.

"Why don't you teach me German?"

"You don't need German."

"But you know German."

"I had to study it in school."

"When you were as old as me? In the empire?"

"Yes. Under the empire."

"Viktor?"

"Mother's calling you," the boy said.

"I will go in a moment."

"Mr. Director says that we will all begin to learn German next year."

"We will see," Trn said.

Aleks turned his face away, his head deep in the pillow.

"Will there be aeroplanes tonight?"

"No. No aeroplanes tonight."

"In Poland they had aeroplanes."

"That's true. But we're a long distance from Poland."

"The windows are covered?"

"You saw me hang the blankets, remember?"

He laid a hand at the boy's elbow, reached and found his hand.

"Viktor. Let him go to sleep now."

"Should you make sure? At the edges?"

"I will. I promise. As soon as you're asleep."

The clock spent its seconds. A January wind from Siberia shouldered snow against the windows. The boy's breath eased and Trn leaned for the lamp.

"Daddy, will I be alive in the year 2050?"

"Do you ask your mother these questions, or only me?"

"Only you."

"Why? What is going to happen in 2050?"

"I don't know what will happen. Will I be alive?"

"You will live a long time."

"Like Grandfather?"

"Like Grandfather. Yes."

"How old will I be?"

"In 2050? One hundred and sixteen."

What current ran through this boy that his little hands should always feel so fevered?

"Time for sleep now."

As Trn rose for the lamp the boy huddled into the back of the couch, tugged the covers over his head. As he did every night now, this metamorphosis, nature inverted, a chrysalis of bedclothes. You could have said anything else. You could have said that was a problem of subtraction you couldn't do in your head.

"I hope you're not chewing your nails there."

"No."

"What's that squelching sound I hear?"

"My tongue's feeling for my spit makers."

Trn stayed his hand, prolonged the light for them both a few moments more. No map in the world had a place for their country now. Vague beneath the blanket he felt the knots tight in the rope of the little spine, the unfledged blade of the shoulder. In the dark he sat a while longer, a hand at rest over this spare cradle of bones. How could anything I might ever do possibly be enough?

He whispered, "Good dreams, I love you," and rose to leave in the dark.

They were the same flight of seventeen he'd trudged up all winter but he counted them nevertheless, a hollow series in the dark of the well, as if each scuff of his soles were over empty stone. He pulled his fingers one by one out of the gloves, on the landing unlaced his boots, came in quietly shutting the door.

From the kitchen Alena leaned into the hall, her eyes bearing on his.

"He went in good order," Trn said.

She pursed her lips and was gone. He hooked his coat, scarf over the collar, hat last, coupled gloves in the coat pocket. At the counter she was rolling dough.

"Is your father up? "

"I don't know," she said.

"We talked on the way again about Adam," Trn said. "I believe he'll be fine."

"And what makes you believe that?"

"I told him Adam was upset about his father."

Her shoulders worked her elbows like pistons, the red embroidered hem of the apron leaping.

"And when we are upset, I told him, angry at the world because we can't be angry with the person who's upset us, we often launch our anger anywhere because we hurt everywhere, so we think it doesn't matter."

"And what did Aleks say to this?"

"He listened," Trn said. "He didn't say much but I think he understood."

She glanced over her shoulder to roll her eyes.

"And the next time Adam pushes him to the ground and kicks him," she said, "all will be well."

"I told him to keep away from Adam."

"But who's going to tell Adam to keep away from Aleks? Tell Adam that he's only angry with the world?"

"If it happens again I will speak to the teacher."

She slapped the dough against the counter, arched her weight to flatten it with the heels of both hands.

"'I will speak with the teacher,'" she said. "Just like you did about those German hoodlums last year. And if that doesn't work you will speak to the director again, I suppose."

"Yes."

Her eyes came round to bore on his again.

"And this will make Adam Svoboda conduct himself in a more civilized fashion. This will make Aleks grow ten centimeters over one night so he'll be bigger than Adam and Adam will suddenly leave him alone. Swing his kicks at another boy who will turn the other cheek."

"Aleks must learn to exhaust all the possibilities before pummeling back. I know that's what you want, for him to return every blow, but he must learn."

"And why? Because it's the honorable thing? Because it's what you wish him to do, to learn? Adam Svoboda's father went to Poland so he could go on fighting Germans. That's the lesson Adam Svoboda learned."

"And now he's probably dead and his son draws the blood from smaller boys because his father is not here to teach Adam the difference."

"The difference between what?"

"The simple difference between what we do and what we ought to do. Perhaps the difference isn't so simple but it must be learned."

She turned to the counter again, fingers clenching so the dough escaped them. She gripped at it again and never looked back.

"If you won't teach him to fight," she said, "I will. I'll find someone."

The muscle stood from her jaw, the tendons taut inside her neck.

"Thank you for making dumplings. We all like them so much."

She pounded the dough, set pale clumps aside on waxed paper.

"We have dumplings twice a week," she said. "It's nothing."

He closed the lavatory door, rolled his cuffs. The water purled in the stoppered sink and a vapor fumed over it. He undid two shirt buttons, folded in his collar. Be glad for hot water. The brush grew the lather in the cup and he spread it along his jaw, under his chin, toward the cheekbones. He put a new blade into the razor, glanced up at the face with its white beard in the mirror. An ersatz Saint Mikulas. The rasp of the blade took the soap and left behind the familiar stare puzzled in the cloudy glass, the eyes always set too close together. The razor dripped, her wedding gift all those years before. No one uses a straight razor anymore, she said. The scrape up the neck, the jawline. Not so many years before. Through the fog of the mirror a small rain coursed, blurred the lather, blurred the face. I could grow a beard for winter, a winter beard for warmth. Save time mornings. He lengthened his lip and razed the lather there. Save water. Save the gas to heat it. He stirred the suds in the basin, lifted the blade and blinked the fog away before cutting at the little that remained.

Winding west and south instead of east to the nearest tram stop he took in the houses on this long avenue of the quarter, ornamented with towers and oriel windows, pinnacles with weathervanes shaped like pennants that bore the year of their construction. 1906. MCMII. 1918. The last throes of a realm that couldn't hear its own death rattle, when the best fancied they were a suburb of old Vienna. Chandeliers hung behind the leaded panes, the street lined with weeping cherries naked to the weather. Hands in pockets he walked on, his breath scouting before him, the old leather case slung from his shoulder beating at his hip the time of his strides. Between the houses painted yellow or gray, pale green and white plaster, he glimpsed the bare trees on the hills that shaped the valley, snow powdered on the forest floors. To the west, just piercing the haze, the twin spires of the cathedral rose over the city.

At the bottom of the hill he waited to cross, an old man stooped in his heavy clothes beside him, looking right for the traffic.

"Sir? Sir? Now you should look the other way first."

"Why did they have to change everything?" the man said under his visible breath, under the drooping eyelids. "What was wrong driving on the left I would like to know?"

Trn smiled, nodded. The wattles of the man's neck shook in his sagging collar as he looked the wrong way again, his foot searching from the curb. He shuffled across the street as if his ankles were shackled.

Not many waited for the tram. A mother cooing into a blanket, a sturdy woman with her shopping netted in each hand, two men with silent eyes in the shadows of their hat brims. Through the trees on its long ridge the ancient hulk of the castle spied out beneath the scarlet flag, the crooked cross unfurled over its keep. A number fourteen drew up and paused and departed. An eleven rattled down the line, squealing to a stop on the rails, and Trn took the steps after the woman and her shopping. The two men behind their brims stood together in the aisle not talking and the mother whispered into the crying blanket until a man rose and she heaved down beside a woman with a round hat angled over chestnut hair fanning across the shoulder of her coat. He could see nothing of her face, but the hair, the brightest object in the tram, was lustrous, washed today, this morning. Dried before the fire, swung limp and wet to be treated to the rough toweling while she wore her slip. The tram lurched to a stop and Trn sighed at the interference of passengers. When they all swayed at the bend he stepped to the other side of the aisle but still she was out of his sight. A man with a toothbrush mustache read a newspaper, another little Hitler with his homage neatly trimmed. The headline declared the French had been repulsed again. Through one stop and another Trn gazed past the news for a glimpse of the chestnut hair. He consulted his watch. When the door folded open he took the steps to the street, a vain glance back for the luster, and then the tram jolted and left him behind. He would have a long extra block to the library, down another street fretted with bloodred banners, but today he had the time.

Under the cold sunshine he waited, cold but still sun revolving them into a new season. He unbuttoned his coat. The first boys came out putting on caps, swinging satchels. One slung his into the back of another boy and ran on, a gaggle joining him down the sidewalk, all of them laughing except the target, his knees jogging further and further behind. Finally he stood and watched, shrugged one shoulder and plodded on. Aleks was among the last. He took Trn's reaching hand, gave up his satchel to the other.

"How was your day today?"

"It was good."

"That's good. Do you have much homework?"

"It's Friday."

"That's right."

"What will we do tomorrow?"

"I thought we'd go hiking. Would you like that?"

The boy nodded.

"Look at that sun." Trn settled back his hat. "Won't it be fine shining through the needles tomorrow?"

"If it doesn't rain."

"What's wrong?" Trn asked.

"I don't know."

"Is it Adam?"

They were stopped at a corner for a staff car with the WH license plate of the Wehrmacht to thrush over the pavement. The boy watched the gutter.

"Yes."

"Did he hit you? I thought that ended some time ago."

"No. It's not about hitting."

"What then?"

Aleks shrugged. They crossed and climbed on. The shadow of one great cloud rolled over a far wooded hill and Trn squinted to see the sun blinded behind it.

"Tell me what happened. I thought this was all resolved."

"Adam is a kind of hero."

"How is he a hero? Because he bullies the other boys?"

"No. Because of his father."

Trn said, "I see."

"His father was in the army. Then he went to Poland to be in another army. Then he died."

"So now Adam is a hero for having such a father?"

Aleks said, "Were you in the army?"

"We all had to be for a time."

"But you weren't in a war."

"My father was. The last war. I know you know that already."

"And he was hurt."

"That's so."

"He had to have a plate of metal in his head for the rest of his life but you couldn't see it. But you could see the surgeon's scar when he lost his hair."

"You have a good memory."

They made the top of the hill, kept the gymnazium to their left on the crescent road round it.

"That's where you went to school."

"Secondary school. That's right."

An iron-gray van drew up to the iron gate, gray smoke choking from the tailpipe until two guards swung the gate.

"It's kind of you to walk me to school every day. And home."

"Do you like it?"

He shrugged.

"I like it," Trn said. "It's the best part of my day."

"But you don't have to anymore. I know the way now."

"I know you do."

"And the German boys, they don't push us into the street now. Not really. They don't shove us down. We can walk on the sidewalk."

"If you would like to take yourself to school we could arrange that. Or I could go only part of the way. What would you like best?"

"I don't know."

"Or we could go on as we do now."

Trn squeezed and a warm hand squeezed back.

"Alena, you know I don't have the English for that."

"But you do," she said. "You had that time in London. And Oxford. You used to talk about the library there, the round one. I'm sure universities in England and America would be—" Her eyes searched at two corners of the ceiling for a term. "Very excited to have a Czech scholar of history on their faculty." Her teeth smiled at the idea.

Trn glanced to the clock on the sideboard.

"First of all how can a professor who doesn't have a position in his own country get one in another? And who would want to study the history of a lost tribe?"

"It's not your fault the Germans closed the universities. You can explain it all in a letter. Benes taught in America."

"Benes was president, Alena. Of course he found a job."

"He believes he's president still to listen to him on the wireless, even though he ran away."

He could say, "You want us to run away," but he only watched her standing there in her white dress. Woven into the hair at her temples a few white threads. The war or life with him?

"So. Let's say then that I could get a position, though I couldn't. How are we to travel, even as far as England?"

She waved a hand. "I've thought of that. We cross into Slovakia. They haven't been independent long, their borders won't be fast. And besides, Slovaks are still our brothers. We can talk to the guard. Maybe bribe him. Then on to Yugoslavia. From there we take a train."

"A train to where, Alena? Yugoslavia and Slovakia don't have a common frontier. They don't meet. And what about papers? The Gestapo won't knock on our door with exit permits."

She concentrated on a fingernail, bit. She inspected the floor.

"Well first to another country, then Yugoslavia. Hungary, Bulgaria?"

"Hungary."

"I don't carry a map in my head like some bus driver. Hungary then, then Yugoslavia and a train through Italy to France. Won't that work? From there a boat to England. Or America. It's as simple as that."

He said, "You know the Slovaks are evicting Czechs," but her hands were already dusting him from their palms. She twirled toward the window so her skirts flared.

"Look, Viktor, a beautiful spring. It's only beginning and already the sun's brilliant."

The same flare, the smile beaming as she whirled to face him, leaned back into the sill. Her teeth were graying.

Yesterday was cold rain. He didn't say that either, didn't say that cold rain would settle over them again before they had spring in earnest.

"What will we do for money, Alena?"

"We have what we saved for a cottage and can borrow the rest. I'll earn some." Her fingertips played against one another. "Sewing, and cakes." She bit at the nail again. "Everyone on the street loves my pastries."

"The sugar you'll buy on the black market," he said. "And the flour."

"I'll set some aside from our ration every week."

Trn spanned his brow with a hand.

"How much sugar will you need to bake a bridge for us all to England?"

"Maybe the Overseas Service," she said.

"I'm sure the BBC have all the Czechs they need."

"You won't even write to England, will you? Not even to save your own son."

"I no longer know anyone there. And letters don't go to England from here anymore." Just behind the clenched eyes he felt the skull. The temple bones grown close under the skin. He dropped his hand to look at her across the room. "And what about your father? Even if we had the money, if I had the slightest promise of a job, is he well enough to travel?"

"I've thought of that too," she said. Her gaze examined the floor. "Father will have to stay here. We'll get someone to look after him, Mrs. Asterova will look after him, and then after we're settled we'll send for him. Send someone to bring him."

"Who, Alena? Mrs. Asterova is older than your father."

"Dita will help her."

"Dita has all that she can bear with Mrs. Asterova."

She glared so long and blue that he faced the radio, huddled his hands in his lap. He heard a long sigh.

"Why do you always have to paint the devil on the wall?" she said. "I see leaving this country as our only hope."

"I don't see that as a hope, Alena. It's a dream."

The squares of parquetry cracked under her heels. The dress flounced toward him.

"Another man would do something."

The dress passed on. Across the hall the door to the bedroom shut. The key rattled and shot the bolt. Since he was not another man.

Her prettiest dress. His favorite. Bleached for the occasion.

When Aleks was finished with his breakfast they asked but Alena frowned and shook her head and Miroslav said he didn't feel quite up to it today even though the sky through the window looked fair. The old man discomposed the boy's bangs and told him to enjoy his holiday and Aleks smoothed them right again, wincing. They heard the Steinhardt boys stomp down the stairs, waited for quiet, and then went out and followed the street and the path that left the street and went in under the pines. The ground dropped steeply and they held to roots and striplings to slide down the clay and then the slope gave way to flat ground again on the valley floor, the sound of water not far off. Ravens overhead croaked through the cool of the morning.

"Look, Daddy. Just like a tomahawk."

Aleks flung a stick wapping through the air and smiled and Trn smiled down.

They parted hands round a solitary oak and joined on the other side. A bleak sun gleamed off needles, broke among the branches to dapple the leafmeal, the soft straw. A dove cooed and they stopped to listen till its thin throat went quiet. Others moaned unseen in distant trees. A black beetle stumbled over a dead branch and they knelt to watch the legs strive with the air. As Trn reached it righted and disappeared without a sound they could hear beneath a crumbling log. They came to the freshet trundling over rocks in the steep groin between two pine hills and Aleks leaped out to a rounded stone.

"The snows are melting in the highlands," Trn said. The boy vaulted to the far bank, dropped to his knees and fashioned a sloop from an oak leaf, a smaller leaf for sail. He set it into the current and watched it ride, spoke across the water.

"Once more?"

Aleks made a horn of his hands. "Will my boat?"

Trn crossed with two long strides, crouched beside the boy.

"Will it sail to the lake and go over the dam?"

"We're south of the dam, downstream. So I'm afraid your little boat is destined to float past wide fields and under the bridges of beautiful cities and into the Danube and then the Black Sea."

"Is the sea really black?"

"I think it is."

"Will I see the sea one day?"

"I'm sure you'll cross many seas."

"Someday we're going to build a boat and sail it on the lake, aren't we? Only a little boat. Will it be as long as this?" He stretched his arms. "I want it to be blue. With red sails and white lines. Can it be blue?"

"Wouldn't that be wonderful?" Trn said.

They spoke of squirrels that barked lies about the humans crossing their forest down below and the different shapes of leaves they trod and the four black birds that scurried into the air after Aleks charged their bush. The birds had been eating red berries and Trn plucked a few that rolled together in his palm. They marveled how birds had stomachs that could swallow them but boys must never because they were poison. They looked for hedgehogs balled in the underbrush but none showed themselves and Aleks talked of the two new boys from somewhere in Slovakia whom he was helping with the routines of school. Next week was his mark on the calendar to feed the mouse in his cage and he wouldn't forget but Franto would sing every morning, "Aleks, mouse, Aleks, mouse." He picked a stick and whipped it to break against a trunk.

"How do you know Franto will do this?"

"He does it every time."

"If he does it to everyone try not to worry over it."

Aleks flung the remnant of stick. Trn looked at the sky.

"We should start home."

"I don't like the climb back."

"I know. It's not easy but it's good for us. To work to get back home."

The last stretches on the street in the unshaded noon were thirsty. He held the hose in the garden for Aleks while the boy slurped and then he drank. They trooped upstairs. Seeing Alena and Miroslav in the sitting room Trn said, "What's wrong?"

Miroslav pointed to the radio.

"Norway, and Denmark."

The newspapers next morning told stories of the Danes' feeble resistance. Black arrows on a gray map speared the Norse coast above the Arctic Circle.

"They couldn't possibly mean Narvik, could they?" Trn got down the atlas and Miroslav looked over the page with him. "Surely they mean Larvik."

"They mean both," Miroslav said.

A mild May day a month later and the same papers said the Wehrmacht had broken the frontier of the low countries. The fanfare from the radio one afternoon heralded an announcement of victory from the front: the armies of Italy had joined with those of the Reich and crossed into France. A crackling through the ether brought them the stamp of German boots parading past the Arc de Triomphe. Miroslav held his head. "Who would have thought those bastards could demolish in four weeks what they couldn't touch before in four years?" From the Eiffel Tower a red flag lashed the wind. Hitler was driven through the empty city to see it.

They sat on the couch listening, he and Miroslav. Alena paced with folded arms. Trn looked at the clock. The city's church bells rang.

"They'll burn London now," Miroslav said. "Like they did Rotterdam. Like Warsaw."

"Is there not one man in Paris with a rifle and a rooftop?" Alena said. "I would like to know that." The toes of her shoes pointed at him. "And you. When they came here all you could do was tell me to fill the tub with water while you ran to the shop for bread."

The joints of the parquet resumed their cracking.

"A historian, a student of history, that's what you call yourself, and that's all you could think to do."

"What would you have him do?" Miroslav said. "Even the president said don't resist."

Trn looked at his watch. "I must leave to get Aleks."

"Hacha is an ass," she said. "And look where it's got us, such strategy. At least that regiment in Silesia resisted."

"And now they're all dead," Miroslav said. "Is that what you want, the whole country burning? Every city a smoking ruin? The hospitals and schools hulks of rubble and the people inside too?"

Alena's face crimped. "Miroslav," Trn said, laid a hand on the old man's shoulder. She wiped at both eyes.

"No," Miroslav said. "Listen. Have you not heard what this Luftwaffe does to bodies of flesh and bone? Do you need to thrust your hand into a charcoaled corpse? Had their bombers flown here you would have been the first one weeping like a Magdalene."

"Why do you never do anything?" Her voice trembled toward Trn. "You sit there and you sit there and you never do anything."

The chair she flung herself into screeched upon the floor and they each stared at a different pattern in the rug and there were no more trains west.

When Trn opened the door to Miroslav's room, Aleks twisted in the chair, something in his hands on the desk.

"Are you ready for our walk?"

"But it's raining."

"It's clearing now. What's that?"

The boy frowned at the wooden box clasped in his palm.

"Only my treasures."

"Where did you get it?"

"Grandfather gave it to me. He found it in his wardrobe."

"What do you have inside?"

The boy raised his vast eyes and held out the box to Trn.

"Is it all right?"

Aleks shrugged, nodded. "It doesn't hold much. It's small."

When Trn slid back the lid a marble swirled blue beside a round cedar cone, a pigeon feather with a broken shaft. A ten heller coin. Two crude lumpish things that Trn fingered out to shake like dice in his hand.

"Where did you find these, Aleks?"

"On the street."

"Not our street?"

"Nearby. In the gutter."

"When did you find them?"

"I don't know. Sometime."

"Why do you keep them?"

"They're interesting. I found them and they're interesting."

Trn stared at the yellowed enamel, the rotted pith.

"I'll give you a crown for each of them."

"Two crowns?"

"Yes, two crowns."

"Two crowns each?"

"I didn't realize I was dealing with a banker."

"I'm not a banker."

"Very well. Four crowns altogether."

Aleks raised his hand.

"Is that to shake across our bargain or to take the money?"

Aleks grinned. "Both."

Trn took the coins from his pocket, replaced them with the molars.

"Get your shoes and coat and I'll meet you at the gate."

Since their weight might rest in the neck of the toilet and even in the bin they might be rediscovered he went into the back garden and pressed a crescent grave deep into the soft earth with his heel, let the teeth drop there and stamped them back out of sight.

The dial on the radio ran like a scale climbing all the frequencies their range once took in. Zürich, Preßburg, Rome. Athens and Warsaw. Trn watched the boy run his forefinger along the names.

"I smell cabbage. Are you hungry?"

Aleks wrinkled his nose away and said, "I don't really like cabbage."

"I know."

"We always have the aftermath of cabbage."

"What's that?"

"That's what Grandfather calls the smell."

"The smell of cooked cabbage?"

"No. The smell after. After we eat it."

Trn laughed and the boy did too.

"But Grandfather says he can always light his pipe to dispense with the aftermath of cabbage."

Back and forth, still the finger of a child, pale and tapering. Bucharest, Vilnius. Alexandria. Paris, Kiev, Stockholm.

"Do you want to get the atlas? We can find them all there."

Amsterdam, Lisbon, Algiers. It always stopped at Alexandria. The boy liked this best because it looked like his name.

"Now we listen only to Vienna."

"That's right. And Prague."

"And some others. But only when you and Grandfather put in the Churchillka."

"Viktor?" Alena called.

"Remember. We shouldn't talk about the Churchillka."

"We used to listen to so many. In the evenings. Even if we didn't understand the words. Once we listened to someone in Albania."

Trn smoothed a hand over the boy's hair. "That's right."

"Viktor. I need you in the kitchen."

"But now we listen only to Vienna. Mostly."

"I'm coming," Trn called.

"Because the penalty for listening to the foreign broadcasts is death."

"Where did you hear that?"

"Viktor!"

The boy lifted his eyes so they roamed over the far angles of the room. He shrugged.

"It says so there around the knob," and he pointed at the paper notice warning in Czech and German what Trn had thought the boy's mind too young to read.

Before he could hang his coat Alena called from the kitchen, "Did you get the sugar?"

"Yes. They had sugar."

He took the box from his case and stood it on the table, sat.

"There is a God," said Miroslav, "and just in time too."

"Father."

Frowning, she clinked a cup and saucer on the table before the old man, the little tongs already waiting in his hand for the bowl to be filled with cubes.

"Do you want coffee?"

"Yes. Please."

"What's wrong?" Miroslav said. "What's happened?"

"I just saw a dead man."

"A dead man? Where?"

"There was a crowd around him, staring." Trn watched the steam laze from Miroslav's cup. "On Udolni. On the way back to the tram."

"But that's just the other side of the hill," Alena said.

Trn traced a stain on the table.

"He was stretched across the sidewalk. His head was almost in the gutter."

"How do you know he was dead?" Alena said.

"He was dead. There were two policemen with their backs to

him, keeping people away. Around his head the blood had pooled, like a dark glue."

"So it only just happened," Miroslav said.

Trn shrugged.

"Probably one of those gangs," Alena said, "those little fascists running around."

"They put that rabble down last year," Miroslav said. "You didn't know him, did you?"

"I didn't recognize him."

"Maybe the SS. He might have been with the resistance."

"Or the Gestapo," Alena said. "He might have been a Jew."

"Or he might have been a collaborator," Miroslav said, "and the resistance left him as a warning. Broad daylight, you know. Gutsy people, those." He nodded to himself, sipped and set his cup down. "God this is awful coffee."

"He looked so ordinary," Trn said. "Dark pants, a black sweater. He lay there on his back in the sun. You might have thought him drunk."

"Except for the price of beer," Miroslav said.

"His feet, they splayed out flat, as if his ankles were broken. The wind blew his hair into the blood and it stuck there. He still had on his shoes."

"That's what the police were after. As soon as the crowd departs they cleverly grab the shoes. One each."

"May I have that coffee, Alena?"

She brought it, sat herself.

"He looked so like anyone," Trn said.

"Probably a collaborator," Miroslav said. "They're everywhere now, top to bottom. Did you hear that Göring was in Prague the other evening? Called on Hacha and invited him to dinner. When the waiter handed Hacha the menu our president opened his pen and said, 'Now, where do I sign?'"

Miroslav laughed and clapped the table so the spoon jumped in the saucer.

In the stairwell they could hear the shouting. The boy looked up and said, "Is that Grandfather?" Trn took the steps two at a time.

He was in the sitting room with the neck of a bottle in his fist still raving over Alena's pleas to be quiet. Trn laid a hand on Miroslav's shoulder and the old man looked at him like a stranger had put a finger in his face.

"Fifteen million," Miroslav said. "They mutilated a country of fifteen million."

"What began this?"

"He heard Benes from London," Alena said. "Father, you must be quiet." She scowled at Trn. "Why do we even have that machine here? It causes nothing but grief. It was better when they took the shortwave away."

"How could they allow that to happen? Civilization. Ha." Miroslav slapped the table and a pencil leaped to the floor. "The whole of Europe has abandoned us."

The boy picked up the pencil and stood holding it.

"Aleks, why don't you go out onto the balcony."

"It's almost dark."

"You've got a while. Go count the swallows. Take Grandfather's spyglass so you can see better."

"About us without us. That's all Munich was. About us without us." The old man slapped the table again and the empty bottle wobbled till Trn set it right. "Bastards."

"Where is the spyglass?"

"Goddamn them all."

"I'm sure it's in his desk where it always is."

"They've consigned us to a German hell." The bleared eyes looked up at Trn. "To make life gentler for them. And you know it too." He looked at Alena. "You know it. Chamberlain, that ass. A far away people of whom we know nothing. At least the bastard knows he's ignorant."

"And before the radio?" Trn said.

"The Asterovi had been in the country," Alena said. "They came back."

"Did he finish all of it?" Trn said.

"What do you think?" Alena said. "He stinks of plum slivovitz."

"I mean was it just the one bottle."

"If it had been more he'd be asleep by now. But that would be too much to ask."

"The sons of bitches. The whole thing is so utterly stupid. Austria was one thing. A different thing entirely. If that was rape then the Austrians liked being raped. But we cried for justice and not a soul in the world bothered to look us in the face."

"Father." She shook his shoulder and the old man smacked his lips. "Father. If you don't shut up they'll call the police. They'll bring the Gestapo."

"Who will call? The Steinhardts? Let them. I pay their goddamn rent but they're not my overlord and master, those traitorous bastards. Imagine Czechs flying that blood flag. On Hitler's birthday. And for ten days ringing every church bell after France pisses her pants and falls over." He lifted his wet eyes to Trn again. "We were the eighth largest economy in the world. Not Europe. The world."

"I know," Trn whispered. "The crown was a respected currency the whole continent over."

"That's it. You could spend the crown in Paris. In the Rotonde you could buy a cup of coffee with the crown."

"All we needed was fifty years of peaceful evolution."

"That's what Masaryk said. And we didn't have it. Goddamnit we didn't have half that." His eyes leaked at all four corners and Trn offered the handkerchief from his trouser pocket. The old man took it, brushed it over his face and tossed it on the table.

"Masaryk was so wise," Trn said. "Did it come to him with age?"

"No." The old man shook his bald head. "Masaryk was always wise. He was born wise. He wasn't just a president, he was a prince. A philosopher-prince like Plato dreamed of but better than Plato dreamed because the people elected him. We don't know that world anymore. All we have now are goose-stepping charlatans and toffee-nosed appeasers."

By the hand Trn began to draw the old man toward his room and said over his shoulder, "Alena, would you bring us a glass of water please?"

They sat later listening to waves of snores crest against the door. On the table Trn laid out the cards for solitaire and Aleks in his lap helped him spot the combinations.

"I guess he'll rumble on like that all night," Alena said in her chair.

Without looking from the cards Trn said, "Did Mrs. Asterova say how things were in the countryside when she brought the slivovitz?"

"How would I know?" Alena said. "I was out."

The raids worsened with the summer. Miroslav drummed his fingers beside the radio while Trn pondered the chessboard. "Human beings used to live on Earth," the old man said. "Now we live in it. In the future we'll all lead underground lives." Trn moved and they paused to listen. London said that Czech pilots in exile were bringing down their share of the Luftwaffe, more than their share. Vienna said the docks of London were a useless wreckage. "Troglodytes," the old man said. "That's us."

"Why do they always begin the broadcasts with such nonsense?" Alena said.

"What nonsense?"

"It's like French poetry. 'The pen is green.' 'Memory is watchful.' 'Delta to the Nile.'"

"That's not nonsense," Miroslav said. "It's code. Coded messages."

"Coded for whom?"

"The resistance."

"We certainly won't need to hear that here then," she said.

In the cool of an evening rain while Miroslav watched the boy, he and Alena went to the cinema like they used to do except now the newsreel with brass blaring spun up the monumental eagle of Die Deutsche Wochenschau. The spectators rose to salute and shouted "Sieg Heil!" and more than half the theatre was standing. When the Führer appeared such applause erupted that no one could hear his speech. After the torchlit parades other fires. British bombs on an oil depot in Lorient, on a Belgian hospital demarked with the red cross, the work of the war criminal Churchill. Wehrmacht soldiers in their coal scuttle helmets trained hoses on the flames. Goebbels said the whole of the Thames would not suffice to quench the fires begun by the Luftwaffe in retaliation and it looked so. Aerial footage of the Tilbury docks ablaze in the night, the Thames Haven petrol tanks. St. Paul's and Westminster shrouded in a cerecloth of smoke. He could imagine the Tube tunnels, the oily grit of their angles where Londoners crouched in their long coats, the tang of piss. Crying babies and the little children staring round for what they should do next, big eyes cringing at each detonation. When Trn looked up again they were all somewhere in arid Africa, an Italian tank geysering sand behind its treads.

The projector clattered and trumpeted the studio theme and the house dimmed. No cartoons to laugh at. The cone of light shot blue through the cigarette smoke and began to speak its German. She was quite beautiful, the heroine, lips as glossy as her haloed eyes in the unfocused close up, great lashes slumbering closed before the one permitted kiss. A single kiss, all that could be bestowed in wartime.

Once UFA had made wonderful films. As a boy, he would leave the cinema after the matinee blinking into daylight again, half in love with all the perfect faces. More than half.

The night was cold when they came out. Arms folded, Alena said while he looked out into the black rain, "Aren't you going to put up the umbrella?"

She hung a hand at his elbow and they looked down into puddles like tar. "They don't even know to turn off the lights during the newsreel," she said.

"They want to see who misbehaves before the Führer. That's why the policeman's there."

He could feel his trouser cuffs go sodden round his ankles, the water squeezed from his shoes at every step. Hulks of cars with their hooded headlamps crept along the street with goats' eyes, the slur of rainwater behind their tires.

"Do you want to wait under an awning for it to let up? Or we could have a coffee. Or a drink."

"I want to get the next tram," she said. "I'm soaked through already."

"It wasn't very good, I'm afraid. I'm sorry."

Her shoulder shrugged at his. "You're the one who wanted to go to the cinema."

"What's the matter?" He put his hand on the boy's shoulder. "Are you thinking about that letter again?"

"Why do I have to go to another school? I was just getting used to this one."

"Going to school will be an adventure now. We'll take the tram every morning."

"The Steinhardts still get to walk to school. Why is it only for German boys now?"

They approached a poster pillar, pasted there at eye-level a large red placard bordered in black and presided over by an eagle clawing a wreath. Below the talons the black columns of those most recently sentenced by the special court for unfriendly behavior toward the Reich. The parallel text in Czech, the same names to be hanged and the towns where they had lived, the days upon which they had been born.

Aleks glumly stuffed his fists in his pockets.

They passed Mrs. Zigismundova in the window of her vegetable stand and said good day as she smiled and nodded. Trn snapped his fingers and went back and asked for two onions and put them in his coat pocket with the newspaper. He took Aleks's shoulder and they made way for a lady with a baby carriage as Trn doffed his hat.

Aleks kicked a stone tumbling over the paving.

"I still don't understand why I have to go to a new school."

"Let's see what's in the paper, shall we?"

Trn took it from his pocket and unscrolled it before them as they walked more slowly.

"Why is he in the newspaper?" Aleks said.

"This man? Because the Germans and Japan have signed a treaty. An agreement between two nations about certain things."

"What do they agree on?"

"Practically everything."

"He's the führer of Japan."

"Yes. The emperor."

"The Japanese believe he is a god."

"That's right. Where did you learn that?"

"From you."

"Oh."

Their steps had come to a halt. Together they stared at the emperor in plumed shako, long black coat with its tails parted neatly and trailing over the haunches of the white horse on which he sat.

"Do you know his name?"

Aleks shook his head. "I don't remember. It's too hard."

"Hirohito."

"That's funny to say."

Trn began to read.

"Daddy?"

"Yes?"

"Do the Japanese never wonder why God needs glasses?"

At the square table in the front room he read over his history until his eyes winced at the page. Beyond the panes spires of spruce wavered over the roofs of houses scaled with tiles like red fish. Morning smoke from a scatter of brick chimneys ran before the wind. At the very crown of the hill sat the solid and foursquare gymnazium, the steep roof shingled with pigeons. What the stone of those walls hoarded now, the echoes they confined. All the dormer windows were barred and painted black. Some pigeons gathered themselves and heaved into the air, wheeled about and settled among the same slates. A few more stirred and then the whole flock suddenly vaulted and swept away into the dark of the trees before the echoing report penetrated the glass, followed instantly by two others. A space of time and then three more deliberate shots. The chimney smoke trailed toward him. Three more to make sure. He closed his book.

In that courtyard he'd kicked at footballs. The classrooms made over into cells now where they counted the prisoners' bones with their fists. Three roped bodies slumped from three posts driven into the ground where Pavel and Tomas had shouted at him, the ball bounding off the wall and the monitors admonishing them about the refectory windows. Rough triangles of cloth knotted at the back to blind the final seconds. What the red eyes of those pigeons witnessed. Blood and gore pulsing over the knots.

The lessons they handed out there now. The instruction the Gestapo trafficked in. Selling tickets to those with German names who wanted to watch the hanged man swing by his crooked neck from the arm of the gallows.

In the men's room of the library he felt himself retracting from the world, had the sensation of cowering, turtled away inside. He had difficulty finding it, his coward sex, cowled, shrinking as if all the world were tundra. Finally he brought out enough to pee, shook himself, buttoned again and went back to the library table. With Miroslav's magnifying glass he examined a photograph, leafed back several pages to stare again at a string of six men reined together at the neck, crossed wrists bound before them. A warrior stood to the side, chin lifted, his spear and proud shield. Only he looked into the magic box. The others gazed each at a different patch of dirt in the jungle and waited for the word of this new master, this latest sword. The legend read CAPTIVES OF THE SLAVE TRADE. Under the glass the gray and grainy day of their humiliation. What looked like a gash on the left shoulder of the second man. Wound sustained in a losing cause. You could not see them with a magnifier but flies gathered there, creeping to the shore of blood to sip, the flesh creeping away in defense. You could see the raised tattoos, the striations of scarified cheeks. Chronicle of their tribe, now ended. Neighbor plunders neighbor and the spoils of war go under the hammer. In ancient Rome the market bustled and in Africa it goes on still. And here. It continues here.

"Sir?" The clerk smiled with her mouthful of teeth. "Sir. We can't locate that other volume."

He smiled in return. Poor girl. Incisors jutting as in the American cartoons they used to show.

"I'm terribly sorry. It must have been misshelved."

"I understand."

She smiled again, so sad, and he felt his own smile sadden and depart.

"We will search for it, however."

"Thank you very much."

She left for her counter, plump behind shifting beneath her skirt. He thumbed some pages, glanced over random passages, at his watch.

"Trn."

He looked up at Dolezal taking a last step forward.

"I see you're hard at it."

Trn shrugged. Dolezal leaned over his paunch to raise the book, examine its spine.

"Come on, man. You're not still on this? Now's the time to get on with all that research we've longed after. A state salary and no teaching to be done."

"At any rate," Trn said, "some still draw a salary."

"I heard." Dolezal stroked his walrus mustache. "Sad business about Miroslav's pension."

"Especially sad for Miroslav."

"Why did they drop him, do you know?"

"I suspect someone lied."

"Well," Dolezal said, "good thing he has a son-in-law to look after him. Kupka has finished his book and begun another. I saw him here last week. I've an article on political economy coming out next quarter."

"Congratulations."

"Did you hear they're organizing a conference after the new year, in Prague? At the German university."

"Who's organized it?"

"You know who. They'll pay train fare. Free trip to the capital.

Might inspire you to other work." Dolezal removed his glasses, gasped on the lenses, plucked up the sweater stretched over his belly to wipe them. Squinting at the book he said, "I really thought you would have moved on to something else by now."

"What could be more appropriate?"

"How so?"

"Five trains left yesterday for the interior of the Reich. I'm sure you saw it in the papers. Five special trains in a single day."

"But that was voluntary. They raised their hands to go. They'll be well paid."

"Isn't voluntary an ambiguous term under the circumstances? And more importantly, from the standpoint of political economy, if the Reich's so desperately overcrowded and requires Lebensraum why do they need foreign labor?"

Still squinting Dolezal replaced his glasses, his nose wrinkling to set them right as he glanced about with round walrus eyes.

"You should be careful," he said.

Trn lifted his cuff, closed the book as he stood.

"So. I must be off. Goodbye, Trn."

"Goodbye, Dolezal. Congratulations again."

At the counter the clerk asked, "Will you be taking it with you, sir?"

"No. No thank you."

"Thank you for returning it to the desk, sir. You're always very kind to do that."

"The least I can do."

"We're so shorthanded now that—"

She looked left, right. The German swivel.

"I suppose," Trn said, "we should be grateful they've allowed the libraries to remain open."

"Thank you again, sir."

The wind was down and he carried his hat, paused to look back at the torsos of the four titans shouldering the library porch, the tension received down their shoulders from their bowed necks. He overtook the bearded kino man limping behind his piping cart, scanned the posters of an American Western, "Stagecoach," and wondered if Aleks might like to see it, John Wayne and Geronimo. In the next block the tram drew up with a blonde in one window. He eased into the bench directly behind her, the whorls of her ear, the fresh blush of autumn in her cheek. Mirrored in the glass her lashes blinked sleepily. Blonde, Germanizable. Twenty-seven minutes according to his watch. He crossed his legs and gazed at the window. Just time to ride the way north and walk to get the boy from school.

They left Horst-Wessel-Allee for Hermann-Göring-Strasse and took the slope rising slowly toward the square, the street so busy they could not walk abreast, Aleks in the middle with a hand for Alena, a hand for Trn, leading them through the jostle, the songs. The way widened into Wehrmacht-Platz, the second Christmas of the war, their second German Christmas. In their staved pools round the old public well the black carp drifted through cold water. The buyers peered over, considered, pointed, the men in long rubber gloves reached to haul out the Christmas feast. "O Tannenbaum" from a chorus in one corner of the square, "Stille Nacht" from the competing steps of St. Jakub. All the towered clocks said afternoon but the light failed in the sky, the square so crowded, as if each cobblestone must be occupied.

From wooden stalls like old barns, gaps between the rough and warped boards, the merchants hawked their grog and sweaters and wooden tops, fur caps and mufflers. A trio of policemen in black rounded helmets extended their fingers over a fire in a barrel. Smoke or steam or the fogs of breath everywhere rising. Aleks reached into a basket of stuffed animals guarded by a stout woman in an apron that fell to her muddy boots. She gummed a smile. Two of his fingers strayed over the rough fur, the leather patch of a nose.

"Look. Here they come already," Trn said bending to be heard. "Are you prepared?"

A girl and a boy in their teens, the first in pure white, came to look down at Aleks and the angel said, "Have you been a good boy or a naughty one?"

"Yes," Aleks said, "very good."

The devil brandished a black cloth sack. "If he's been naughty," he growled, "he'll be on his way to Hell in my bag." His voice took a sudden hurdle at "Hell" and overturned like a cart cracking at the joints. The angel laughed and covered her smile after. He had black powder on his face, a hat with horns of black paper. Aleks wouldn't look at him.

The devil lowered his chin and coughed in his throat and tried once more. "Can you sing us a song, little boy?"

"Yes, I can sing a song."

Aleks began, his voice thin and falling like his face till at the end only with his eyes did he glance at the angel, who smiled and kept smiling because now Aleks's face was hidden behind his brim and no one could be sure if he'd finished or not.

Trn looked under the cap. "Are you done?"

The cap nodded.

"Very good," said the angel. She handed her staff to the devil and put a hand into her basket.

Alena nudged the boy's shoulder. "It's over. You can look up now."

The angel held out her fist and Aleks put his palm beneath it. She placed a candy there in a bright red wrapping and before Aleks could say thank you they were gone on to another family.

"God I wish he weren't so timid," Alena muttered.

"That was better than last year wasn't it, Daddy?"

"That was so good, Aleks, there's no comparison. Your practice worked very well." He whispered, "He's still a little boy. He's gentle. That's his nature."

"May I have it now?"

"Ask your mother if it will undo your dinner."

"I suppose not." She fixed a smile on the boy, looked up at Trn. "No, he's timid. He's entirely too timid."

"He'll grow."

"When?"

"He's growing all the time."

Aleks drifted toward other stalls, trains and blue birds and a tin auto on cut tin wheels flanked by wooden tanks painted with the balken cross.

Trn said, "At least he's not looking at the dolls," but Alena could not smile.

"Has Baby Jesus already decided what I'm getting?" Aleks asked.

A man fisting a stein reeled into the corner of the stall and shook the toys on the shelves and caromed toward Trn. The beer sloshed on the stones and the man grumbled on.

"That was a near miss," Aleks said.

Trn raised his eyebrows.

"So has he? Has Baby Jesus decided?"

"Yes," Alena said, "he decided long ago."

"That's a pretty auto, don't you think? The blue one." He reached with two fingers and rolled it a short way along the plank. "But I can't have it, can I?"

The stall man eyed them through the steam of his cup, drank, lipped his mustache.

"It's very nice," Trn said. "Best not touch it though."

"How many crowns is it?" Aleks said looking at Trn. "I don't want Baby Jesus to have to spend all the money from Saint Mikulas's church box. Or is it only for German boys?"

"We need to find something for Grandfather," Alena said. "Let's look over there."

"Watch it," Trn said. "Some dog has left an early Christmas gift."

"So you're going to get it for him."

"Soon enough there won't be any more toys made of tin. You can count on that."

She sighed. "You're going to spoil him."

"Is that possible? In these times?"

"He'll have two shoes full of candy tonight and on Christmas Eve two books and a sweater and a drawing book with pencils. No other boy on the street will have as much."

"Some will. Some will have more. The Steinhardt twins will have much more."

"You know I mean Czech boys. The Steinhardts have family in Germany to send them things. The Steinhardts own the building."

Trn surveyed the crowd. "How many more Christmases will there be?"

"Don't talk that way."

She looked down at the cobbles, away to the farthest corner of the square where the chorus in white collars addressed themselves to "Adeste Fideles."

"You know as well as I do," he said. "How many more even like this will we have?"

Aleks was watching their whispers. A woman too was looking from the stall of carved pipes they stood before.

"Do you think Grandfather wants a new pipe?" Aleks asked.

"I don't know," Alena said. "No. He doesn't."

"What about that one? That's a pretty one." Aleks fisted his pocket, revealed in his palm a red candy wrapper and a small coin. "I have ten hellers. Will ten hellers help buy Grandfather a pipe? I don't know either if he wants one. I know ten hellers, it's not much. It's not enough."

"Perhaps we should try to find some tobacco to go in the pipes he has," Trn said.

"We need the coupons for that," Aleks said. "Did you bring the ration book?"

The boy pinched up the coin from his palm and held it toward them but Alena was looking at Trn. Her eyes darted over his shoulder.

"I'll take him by the plague column then. While you go get the toy."

Trn smiled. "He's scared of the plague column, some of the figures in it, you know."

"It's stone. It's just stone." She sighed heavily. "Then to a stall near the plague column. Come to find us there. Maybe they won't be selling monsters." She shook her head. "God."

1941

"What besides the contact lens?" Aleks asked.

"The sugar cube," Trn said. "That was invented by a Czech too."

Aleks stuffed back a yawn with his little wrist.

"Sugar came in loaves that had to be sliced with a knife and once this man's wife cut herself badly so he devised a method for portioning the block by machine into cubes. Clever, isn't it?"

"He wouldn't have to worry now."

"Why?"

"There's no sugar and so she wouldn't have cut herself."

"There's still sugar."

"Not very much. Not enough to need cutting."

Trn watched the face, the sleepy blink of both eyes. Eyes dark like mine.

"In the morning," he whispered, "you will have sugar for your tea."

"Mother says soon there won't be any tea. Or coffee, or anything else. She says it is all too expensive and becoming more so."

He knuckled at an eye.

"She is worried but we will have enough."

"You don't have a job. Grandfather doesn't have his pension. We all live together now. There won't be enough sugar for Saint Mikulas to leave candy in my shoes next Christmastime."

"But I am paid as if I did have my work. And on his day I'm sure Saint Mikulas will find some sugar for candy."

Gentle with sleep the boy's eyes gazed at the ceiling.

"Do you understand? It is important that you understand."

"Why is it important?"

"So that you won't worry. Agreed?"

Aleks nodded, eyes closing.

"Good. Sleep well. I love you."

The boy turned to the wall.

"Pardon? I didn't hear."

"I said I don't believe there is a Saint Mikulas." The blanket tugged up twice over the shoulder.

"You will when December comes again. Listen. Tomorrow night I'll tell you of Tycho Brahe and Johannes Kepler. From their observatory near Prague they were the greatest astronomers of their day. There are craters on the moon named in their honor. Their patron was Rudolf the Second, Holy Roman Emperor and King of Bohemia."

The blanket said nothing.

"And the cathedral spires here, above the old town, Saints Peter and Pavel, did you know they are the tallest twin spires in Europe? And when Mozart was your age he came here from Vienna and lived and wrote for a time. I can show you the building where he lodged."

The silence didn't move even when he laid a hand there. Let me not seem to have lived in vain. Brahe's last words, recorded by the hand of Kepler himself. Last words uttered at the end of eleven days spent thrashing in a deathbed. The chapters of life that are not for telling. That Holy Roman Emperor was an empty title. That Rudolf ended in disgrace. Let me not seem to have lived in vain.

"You've had a long day," Trn whispered. "I know you're tired." But before he could kiss the cheek he leaned for the covers rose and all the rest was hidden.

*
*

As they climbed the steps from the street Alena said, "I don't see then why I should have come at all."

"You'll feel better for having done a good deed."

Trn pressed the button on the panel.

"I hardly know her. What if she's not even here?"

"Where could she go?"

He stepped back from the door to look up.

"They're not my friends."

"You've known them for years."

"I've known the baker for years but he's not my friend. You could have brought the cake. All she will do is put it away."

A face appeared over the wall of the second balcony but said nothing.

"Anamaria? Good day, Anamaria. It's Viktor, and Alena."

"Oh. Good day, Viktor."

"Do you have a few moments? We came by to see you. Alena's brought you something."

"Let me get the key. Yes."

She reappeared and against the blank sky a dark object dropped from her hand and Trn let it fall into both of his.

"It's the largest," Anamaria said.

"We'll be up in just a moment."

"She didn't even say hello."

"She will when she sees you, I'm sure."

At the landing she met them, arms folded so her hands disappeared at the sharp angles of her elbows. She wore black so only the pall of her face appeared in the stairwell.

"Viktor, what a surprise. And Alena, thank you."

"It's just a little cake," Alena said, "for an evening, some evening."

Anamaria set a hand on Trn's shoulder, took the ring of keys, leaned to press her cheek to Alena's.

"I'm sorry I didn't come down. I don't feel capable of all those stairs." She led them up the flight. "We so rarely have company that I've become unused to them."

"Of course," Trn said. "We're glad we found you in."

Her hall was dark and she took them down its narrow passage, opened a door.

"I'll put this away. Please go in."

She sighed with both shoulders. "Or shall we have it now? You see. So little company I hardly know how to behave." She looked from one to the other of them and Alena looked at Trn.

"We've just had lunch," he said. "Please save it for an occasion."

"I don't know who will eat it then. Here we don't have occasions anymore." She heaved both shoulders as heavily again. "Put your coats anywhere. I'll be back in a moment."

"I'm keeping mine on," Alena said. "You're not?"

"No. I'm not."

"You can see your breath in here." She put her hands in her pockets. "I'm glad I put it on a chipped plate. I'm sure I'll never see it again."

Trn took from his pocket a folded note of a hundred crowns, slid his hand under the cushion as he sat, his coat over the arm of the chair.

Anamaria came in, said, "Sit, Viktor. Sit. Alena, here's your plate. Thank you so much for the cake. It's so nice of you to come."

She took a place at the end of the couch and smoothed her black dress over her knees, pulled tighter the black sweater round her shoulders.

"It's been such a long time. How long has it been?"

She looked from Alena to Trn and back, the skin below her eyes twin bruises.

"How is your father, Alena? How is Aleks?"

"Both as troublesome as ever. As men are."

Trn said, "How is Jakub? He's not in?"

Her right hand jumped in her lap as if the wrist were jerked on a string.

"He's studying. Studying German. That's what he does now."

She looked at the floor.

"It's the only way he can talk to Pavel, you see. If you want to write to anyone at Buchenwald you must write in German."

"Has Pavel written recently?"

"He's getting quite good at it now. He studies all the time. I worry he's neglecting school but what can we do? You know he wants to be an engineer. Wanted to be. Maybe he does still. We don't talk of such things now. We don't speak much, of the future. He said to me just the other day, he said, 'Mama, should I learn the future in German? What do you think?' And 'Jakub,' I said, 'Jakub, why are you asking me? What do I know of these things?' And he said, 'I don't know if I ought to spend the time to learn the constructions to make the future. I can't decide if it would be good for Papa to think about the future or not.'"

She closed her eyes and the bruises were all she had to see with. When she opened them toward the window they shone like little disks of glass. At her side the hand leaped, the thumb needling the flesh of her thigh through her dress before it retracted into the palm and went quiet among the other fingers.

"What do you think, Viktor?" She turned the disks on him. "Pavel always thought so highly of your opinion. 'We must ask Viktor about that when he visits.' That's what he would say. So what do you think, Viktor. Should he learn the future?"

Alena took a hand from her pocket, examined her nails while the pendulum ticked in the clock on the mantel.

"Yes, Anamaria, definitely. Jakub can always tell Pavel his plans for the next day. Learning all he can learn will be good for Jakub, good for his mind. I never heard anyone regret learning."

"I do," Anamaria said. "I have regretted much that I had to learn." She leaned toward him and the disks were eclipsed under the shadow of her brow. "But that's not what I mean. I mean should Pavel learn the future?"

"I should think it would give him hope, Anamaria. That would be quite a gift."

Her eyes blinked and went back to the window and she said, "I wonder if all gifts are only cruelty now."

Alena examined the other set of nails and put her hands in her pockets again.

"We send him parcels when we're allowed. You must get permission, a release. Of course we haven't much to send. The last time we had a round of pork with a nice bit of fat to it, I thought he would need that, I'm sure he's getting thin. The butcher passes us some cuts when he can. But please don't tell anyone. Please. In the gymnazium when I saw him the last time before the transfer he was already going thin on that gruel."

The thumb spiked into her thigh again more deeply. "I didn't know it was to be the last time." Her face fell so low that her eyes disappeared. "What date is today?"

Alena was already looking at him.

"The twenty-second," Trn said.

"The twenty-second."

"Yes, Anamaria."

"He never got the pork. I received the receipt for the parcel but weeks and weeks later when we had a card from him he said thank you for everything else so he never got the pork. I guess a guard sluiced it, they did that in the gymnazium too after I wasn't permitted to give him the box directly." She spoke as one murmuring in her sleep. "Today is our wedding anniversary. You stood by his side, didn't you, Viktor, all those years ago?"

Trn nodded but she still looked down and then the bruises started open on him.

"Viktor, I often wonder. I wonder why they took him. Do you know, Viktor, do you know why they should take Pavel?"

"They took him because he was brave, Anamaria. Because he would write the truth."

"They took a lot of them," Alena said.

"I used to get so angry at him. He'd leave in the middle of the night to talk to someone about things he couldn't tell me. He couldn't tell me but he could write them in the paper."

Trn leaned at the edge of his chair and on the couch Anamaria collected herself into a corner.

"That was to protect you, Anamaria. You and Jakub."

"Or stay late because he had some midnight deadline. How I hated that newspaper in our box every morning. After he would read it I would take it and burn it up in the stove even in summer. But now I like to think he's started a paper in the camp. The Prisoners Daily or something similar, I don't know. It would give him work to do with his hands, his mind, it would give him something to endure with. His hands were always alive here. But what could he write that they don't all already know. And they would never let that happen. I tell myself that too. That it would never happen.

"Now I like to think that if they let him come home I'll never burn his paper again."

Her eyes were staring at the thumbnail stabbed into her thigh. She jointed her hands in her lap, looked up into the window, spoke to the dim light.

"But he was taking care. I begged him to be careful and I convinced him to be more correct in what he wrote and what he was. The censors hardly struck anything anymore, not like in the beginning, even the German censor left him alone. And then all of a sudden on that day they should come here, just as the bombs are falling on Poland, the sun barely up and Pavel still in his pajamas. He hasn't even got the paper yet, Viktor. And they stand outside the bedroom door while he puts on his pants and while he's buttoning his shirt and buckling his belt. And I looked at his buttons and I said to myself, 'See, he doesn't need any help, his fingers aren't even trembling.'"

"I know, Anamaria. I know that morning was terrible."

Her hands came undone and she reached to move a small china plate on the end table. The nail of her long finger scratched at the paint on the plate and then her hands came together again.

"I'm holding his coat for him and he says, 'If you need anything go to Viktor.' Because he's known you all these years, in school and university and even before. And he doesn't even have his tie on and they're one on each side of him, their hands on his arms, fat hands, and they say, 'You won't need a tie,' and Jakub comes up behind me at the door, rubbing his eyes, and he says, 'Mama, where is Papa going?' and I say I don't know and I hurry to the balcony so down the street I can watch the van, just a gray van with gray doors and they open them and they hold him while he steps up and bends his head and I can see another man in there on the bench, I can see the hat on his head as he leans forward, his elbow on his knee and suddenly it comes to me. 'What if that's Viktor in there too?' And I think that will be good for Pavel, but you weren't, Viktor, they never picked you up even when they closed the universities. And so in all these months, in these years, I've begun to wonder. They've arrested a lot of professors but they've never rounded up Viktor. Why is that? They took Pavel with the neighbors watching, with Mrs. Krupkova and her puny dog staring at him herded down the street between two strangers and her dog squatting to shit in the gutter and then I hear he's in the castle where the stone drips and then in the gymnazium and after the gymnazium they took him to Buchenwald, one day I get a note with the Gestapo eagle at the top telling me Pavel's been transported to Buchenwald, it doesn't say why, it doesn't say when. Nothing ever says why. And so I wonder, Viktor, I wonder why they took Pavel and never took you?'"

The thumb worked her flesh but she was watching him. The bruises did not blink. He looked down at the carpet.

"Did you inform on him, Viktor? Did you tell them to lock him away?"

"Anamaria, you know that I didn't."

"I don't know anything, Viktor. You saw him only the week before. I remember you were here. I know you were the last friend to see him. You went to that pub. He told me."

"I don't know why they arrested him, Anamaria, other than the fact that they took a lot of brave people that day. All over the country."

"I remember, Viktor, I remember that day so well. Jakub's first day of secondary school and the pants and shirt I had ironed still hanging in the kitchen from the night before. And they hung there all day because I didn't let Jakub go because I didn't know what would happen to him without his father. His father taken with a lot of other men but not you, Viktor. Never you."

"They don't explain these things, Anamaria, as you know. They just do them."

"Perhaps your time will come then."

The room was so dim he could not tell the pattern in the carpet. A burgundy swirl in the dark, a dried blood. He stood and lifted his coat and his hat. Alena took up her plate. Anamaria watched them and finally rose. Alena went into the passage and he followed, turned back.

"I'm sorry you feel this way, Anamaria. I would like to help."

"The only help I need, Viktor, is my husband out of Buchenwald. Can you do that?"

Trn opened the door and Alena walked out. From the landing he said, "Perhaps there is something I can do for Jakub. Help him with his studies perhaps."

"He's too busy studying German."

"Perhaps I could move his mind back to engineering."

"I think his mind is unmovable at this point, Viktor."

Even now the thumb scissored out from her hand, pinning the dress against her.

"Goodbye then, Anamaria." He looked at her a last time. "I'm sorry you feel this way."

"I'm sorry about a great many things, Viktor. The outer door will lock behind you."

They went down the stairs and into the cold again. He checked the knob twice. Alena passed through the gate he held for her and they took their way down the sidewalk.

"So," Alena said. "That wasn't so bad as last time."

The frame of her bed creaked and her feet brushed the two steps across the rug and cold air swept his arm as the covers lifted and his mattress gave in to a warmth returning. Her touch drifted, raised his shirt, glided over his naked chest. Breath at his neck, humid, stale. Beyond the black curtain a tram down on the avenue clanged up the morning through the cold dawn. Her fingers traced the hair of his belly, glanced, glanced and stayed, the cup of her fingers. "It's time." A whisper dry as dust in the dark. "The right time." Deeply he breathed, the weight of her head on his shoulder, her sigh at his neck. Her hair grazed his cheek and the warmth of the cup drew away. She rolled onto her back.

"Why don't you ever want me anymore?"

"I do. But I must use the toilet."

"No. You don't want me."

He kissed where he thought the cheek might be and kissed a tear. "Alena."

"I don't know what you want but it isn't me."

"I'm doing all I can."

"Don't blame it on the war again."

He was taking breath to speak when she said, "I know. It's time for you to take Aleks to school," and tore the covers open to the cold.

*
*

In Wilson Wood they talked of Trn's boyhood in the country, of walks he'd taken, wheat to his shoulder and lowing cow heads over the fences with their wet tongues and furry chins and once in winter a man with reins skiing behind a black horse in a pasture of snow. Gypsy wagons on lost roads bending through the forest and trampers on holiday dressed as cowboys and Indians because of books by a man named Karl May. Hitler had read Karl May but Trn didn't add this. Before them like crystalline gossamer in the morning sun a great web loomed and they waited silently for its maker to appear till the air erupted among the trees. Nations of birds struggled from their branches and cried to escape but before they could take flight another report disturbed every leaf. Trn reached for Aleks already reaching for him and huddled the boy behind a pine, bark bristling at his shoulder, Aleks panting under his chin, resin and spring's sweet decay and a burn that scorched the sunbeams slanting through the wood where smoke coiled the trees.

A fourth or fifth shot cracked before they heard the voices, the laughing. Aleks whispered, "Is it cowboys?"

"Hurra!"

"Feuerfrei!" one of them cried and shouldered his rifle and fired and the bark of the pine next to them splintered into yellow meat. Another clapped the rifleman on the back, "Nein, nein, nein," and chuckled and shouldered his own weapon.

Trn waved out one arm. They were only twenty paces away now. "Bitte, bitte, meine Herren. Wir sind zwei Zivilisten."

They all had their tunic collars undone in the heat, cloth caps folded in their belts, sweat standing their hair. Six, seven, laughing. A day in the wood, away from the sentry box or the drillplatz. They came forward in their tall boots as Aleks left the tree and one of them made much of him, ruffled his hair, brushed some straw from his shoulder.

"Ach, mein Bruder," he said, smiling as he looked at Trn. "Ich habe einen Bruder, der sechs Jahre alt ist."

He held Aleks's chin, asked how old he was and Aleks looked at Trn. Trn said the boy was six now and the soldier roughed Aleks's hair again. With a rifle butt one of them shattered the spider's web and had to pick the filaments from the stock while the others laughed. The one with the younger brother apologized when Trn explained that families often walked the valley floor, picnicked here. They slung their rifles and went the way they'd come, began to sing.

"Dear Fatherland, put your mind at rest."

"Are you all right?"

"Did you see their guns?"

"I did."

"Firm stands and true the watch, the watch on the Rhine."

"He let me touch it."

"I know."

"It felt hot. The metal felt hot when I put my finger on it."

"I'm sure it did." Trn pulled crumbs of bark from the boy's dark hair, gave him a good brushing down to his brown knees. "You look almost like you did when we set out. Almost presentable."

He brought him near inside one arm before standing.

"What a story I have for Grandfather and Mother now," his eyes agleam, his cheeks glowing. Miroslav asked what sort of rifle was it and said perhaps it came from the gun works across the city and was forged by Czech hands and how even in wartime irony took no holiday and Alena said they were both fools ever to go into the woods anyway and could not go again.

The match flame disappeared into the bowl of the pipe and reappeared amid the gray smoke. Miroslav shook it out and tossed the matchstick into the ashes in the tray. Trn began to replace the pieces on the chessboard.

"And so," Miroslav said, "after a long time in the antechamber circling his thumbs Hess was brought before Churchill and Churchill said, 'So you're the madman.' 'Oh no,' Hess replied, 'only his deputy.'"

Trn laughed with him.

"You know," the old man said, "now that Hess has flown the coop to Scotland the thousand-year Reich has become the hundred-year Reich."

"How is that?"

"A zero has been subtracted."

Trn smiled and the old man drew on his pipe and said through the curls of smoke, "I see someone who is tired."

Aleks took his hand from his eye.

"I'm not tired."

"Come on, young man," Trn said. "Stand and we'll make ready your couch."

The boy strained his jaw to hold his lips together but a yawn stuttered through.

"Good night, gentlemen. I'll see you in the morning."

"Good night, Grandfather."

"Good night to you, Grandson."

In the bedroom Trn gathered up the armload of bedding from his wardrobe, the boy's pajamas folded on top.

"Be sure he brushes his teeth properly," Alena said from her book. "And we're almost out of toothpaste."

"I'll get some."

He lowered the music to a whisper, switched off the second lamp, tucked the sheet round the cushions while Aleks dressed for sleep. He had unfolded the blanket when the cuckoo came over the radio from Vienna, four notes that instantly widened the boy's eyes.

"That's the highest state of alarm," Aleks said. "That means they're almost here."

"We've got time. Just put on your clothes over your pajamas. Maybe we won't be down long."

He opened the bedroom door again.

"There's a warning."

She rolled her eyes toward the laundry on the rack in the corner, her underthings, some handkerchiefs of his. "I'll have to get dressed again."

He went back through the sitting room, nodding at Aleks's progress—"Hurry, Daddy"—knocked at Miroslav's door.

"Yes?"

On his bed the old man sat with ankles crossed, pipe cupped in his hand.

"Air raid."

"I'd like to get my hands around that cuckoo's neck. Won't they leave us in peace?"

Feet thudded down the stairs and a voice laughed, "Schnell, schnell." A weight leaped onto the landing so that their door shook in the jamb. The old man raised his eyebrows.

Trn said, "I'll go see if the Asterovi need help and meet you there."

Aleks in the hall looked up at him.

"Shall I get my coat?"

"Yes, it will be cool."

"Where are you going?"

"Upstairs for Mrs. Asterova. Why don't you get Mother's and Grandfather's coats for them. I'll see you downstairs in a moment."

"The twins have already gone down."

"Haven't they though."

The eyes peered dark and large from the pale face.

"Did you get my mask?"

"Tell Mother. I'll be with you in the cellar."

He smoothed over the boy's hair and shut the door behind him as the Steinhardts reached the landing.

"Are you going for Frau Asterova, Herr Trn?"

"Yes, Herr Steinhardt, I am."

"Good, good."

Mrs. Steinhardt held her husband's elbow. That this pair could spawn such boys, not one but two in the same clutch. Trn pressed the wall for them to shuffle past, Mrs. Steinhardt's spectacled eyes watching as her husband took the stairs one by one, always the right foot first, her hair white as his.

"We must hurry," she said.

"I know it, I know it."

"Have you the key?"

"I told you that I have it, here in my pocket."

Trn jogged up the stairs, knocked as the door opened.

"Oh. Viktor." Dita's hand went to her throat. "We thought you'd be coming. I had the radio off but I heard the others coming down the stairs."

"We have time, Dita. The sirens haven't even started yet. Do you want a wrap, Mrs. Asterova?"

"Oh," Dita said. "I'm forgetting again."

"You shouldn't have to do this, Mr. Trn. I believe with my hand on the rail I would be able."

"We're fine, Mrs. Asterova. We'll be there in a moment."

A distant wail began to climb nearer before he could support Mrs.

Asterova as far as his own door, his arm around her, a hand on the knob of each elbow. Dita looked back at them, at the scuff of her mother-in-law's slippers on the stairs, went down a few steps and looked back again.

"Thank you, thank you, Viktor. We don't know what we'd do without you."

"It's nothing, Dita. We're almost there."

Steinhardt was jangling the keys at the lock in the cellar door, the others gathered and watching. Miroslav leaned toward Havlicek and Trn heard him whispering, "Alles ist in ordnung."

"Mein Gott, Herrmann," Mrs. Steinhardt said.

"Try that one, Father," one of the twins said.

"I tried that one already."

"Mein Gott. I thought you sorted all those after the last time."

"There it is," he said. "That's what I thought."

He went first down the stairs, twisted a switch on the wall that lit two dim bulbs hanging in the cellar. "Quickly, Father," one of the boys shouted. The stairs creaked under them all, Alena holding Aleks's hand and Miroslav handling the wooden rail with Havlicek hobbling behind on his crooked foot and Trn last with Mrs. Asterova following Dita.

"You secured the door, Herr Trn?"

"I did, Herr Steinhardt."

"That is good."

The Steinhardts shared an old settee along the inner wall, gazed up at the narrow cellar window black with painted panes. There were stuffed chairs for the two boys and a straight chair for Mrs. Asterova. Miroslav and Alena and Dita perched on the crate of an old trunk. Aleks made himself small on a folded blanket in the corner.

"Mr. Havlicek, won't you have a seat?" Trn said. "Aleks."

"I'll stand," Havlicek said.

The twins gripped hands and grimaced to make the other surrender. Such bold health from exhausted loins. Beyond the zone of light the smells of damped clay, spades, dead grass, patches of fungus molding on block and mortar. One of the twins cried out and the other strained all the muscles in his arm the harder.

"Boys," Steinhardt said.

The one who suffered balled his free fist and punched his brother on the neck. The brother cried out and struck back with a blow that landed squarely on the Hitler-Jugend armband.

"Erwin. Erich."

They smirked together. Not identical but nearly. Not the same egg but two clearly allied. The Steinhardt-Steinhardt Axis.

"I hope there isn't a power cut," Mrs. Asterova said. "I wouldn't like to be down here in the dark. Do you have candles, Herr Steinhardt?"

"It would be better than being upstairs, don't you think?" Mrs. Steinhardt said.

"Oh yes, Frau Steinhardt. I didn't mean that. Yes."

"We have flashlights," one boy said. He brought it from his pocket, played an oval of light across the floor and conjured weird shadows among the beams of the ceiling strung with webs, motes suspended in the sudden light as if surprised. The light winced through Trn's eyes and moved on. He loosened his tie, undid the collar button.

"The batteries, Erich."

He flashed it in his brother's face and the boy threw his arm across his eyes, the other hand slapping out blindly. It struck an ear and the flashlight fell and rolled its beam across the floor.

Aleks watched from his corner, rubbed his nose, the canister across his lap. The Steinhardts gazed over the heads of those on the crate. Alena and Dita sometimes whispered. Trn's eyes met Havlicek's and they each looked at the concrete floor again.

Steinhardt said, "I suppose we will have more of these nights now. The British will be desperate to disrupt the invasion in any way they think possible. Rail lines, supplies. But it will in the end make no difference."

Trn glanced at Miroslav's appraising frown. Aleks unbuckled the canister and pulled out the mask, spread the straps and drew the rubber hood over this head, surveyed the room through the round goggle lenses, over the snout of the filter.

"The Wehrmacht says every stage of the offensive goes according to plan. After Minsk, Smolensk. You can see it all unfolding in the papers. Moscow is next, that's where Army Group Center is directed."

"Across the River Nieman," Miroslav said, "and down the same high road taken by Napoleon and his Grande Armée."

Steinhardt looked across the gloom with narrowed eyes.

"But with this great difference, Herr Vesely. This army does not retreat. Where the Wehrmacht soldier once sets his boot there it remains."

"I was merely observing the historical parallel," Miroslav said.

"Here history will not repeat itself," Steinhardt said. "Here all parallels end."

The boys were locked in the vise of their handshake again. One reached to choke his brother by the knot of his black kerchief.

"This time history writes a new page with a different conclusion. The Führer is not another Napoleon."

"I think that must certainly be true," Miroslav said.

Finally the all clear sounded through the black window.

"Only another false alarm then," Steinhardt said. "They say the British are flying over with empty planes just to provoke the warnings, to try to deprive the factory workers of their sleep. They haven't bombs in any case."

"One might think," Miroslav said in the hollow march up the cellar stairs, "that empty bombers would be as easy quarry for the antiaircraft as the others," but Steinhardt at the switch appeared not to hear. He put the cellar into darkness again, locked the door with the third key he tried.

Trn said, "Herr Steinhardt. You have not yet said what we are to do if some evening you are out and we have a warning."

The boys took the stairs at a sprint, the one trailing grabbing at the leader's leg to trip him.

"Yes, yes, I will see to that, Herr Trn. But we are so rarely going out evenings. Gute nacht."

Havlicek closed the door to his flat without a word to anyone. Miroslav went up with Alena and Aleks, who glanced back at Trn through the bulging eyes of his mask. Trn took Mrs. Asterova's arm while Dita went before them.

"It's so close there for eleven," Mrs. Steinhardt said to her husband. She repeated it more loudly on the landing and Steinhardt nodded.

"That bastard," Miroslav was saying as Trn came into the sitting room. "That ass."

"Auf Deutsch," Trn said.

"Ja ja ja," Miroslav said, waving his hand.

"Why does Mr. Havlicek have a broken foot?" Aleks said, his face his own again, his hair soaked black.

"Hitler is not another Napoleon. Scheisse. I should say not. Hitler was a goddamn corporal dragging dispatches through the mud from trench to trench. Arschlecker."

"Is it because he was a prisoner of the empire and they tortured him?"

"All those good men dead in Flanders and he survives. They gassed him and still he lived through it. Like a vermin."

"Why are you speaking German?" Aleks said.

"Yes," Trn said. "Mr. Havlicek was in the castle when he was a young man, when it was the emperor's prison, and they treated him very badly. Now let's get a towel for that wet head."

"If history doesn't repeat itself any longer," Miroslav said, "then why isn't the Führer on a stand in Whitehall tonight reviewing a Waffen-SS parade by torchlight? That's what I'd like to know. Ignorant bastard. Waste. Betrayer."

"Good day," the clerk said behind the counter. "May I help you?"

"Good day," Trn said, taking a basket. "I'm looking for toothpaste."

She indicated the far wall and as he passed the aisles he glimpsed a woman pulling her lip, pensive glasses overlooking the shelves. After he laid the toothpaste in the basket, he turned towards the packets of tissues to study her across the shelves, the lenses of her glasses so clean the bottles she examined shone in them. Her dark hair came out of her hat to whisper against her shoulders and as she bent to look more closely thin fingertips rose to catch the locket that swung on a silver chain. The shop smelled of new soap. She raised a bottle of lotion and the locket came to rest on her sweater, two fingers there to still it, one finger, the longest. She was slender and tall, taller than the man who stood beside her now glowering at Trn under thick brows.

"What are you looking at?"

"Nothing." Trn shook his head. "Only shopping." He showed his basket.

"You have no right." The man's black hair was oiled to his scalp, his jaw stubbled black. "You're a Jew, aren't you? You're not even allowed in the shops this time of day."

"I am allowed. I am shopping, like everyone else."

"He only shuffles like a Jew," the man said. "And ogles other men's wives."

The man would follow him to the counter, press against his shoulder. "You've no right to look at other men's wives." Trn handed his money to the clerk who watched him. The drawer shot open as the till sounded its bell and the eyes of the clerk shifted to the man behind him, Trn's hand ready to slide his change from the counter.

"Go home to your own wife and leave other men's alone."

"I'm leaving now."

But the man stood in the aisle and she was there too, eyes wincing behind her glasses.

"Mirek," she said.

"You don't understand," the man said. "I haven't heard you apologize."

"If I have somehow offended you, sir, I apologize."

He stepped to the right but the man blocked him again.

"To my wife, you filth. Apologize to my wife."

Trn looked over the man's shoulder through the lenses into the long-lashed eyes.

"I apologize, madam, for any offense."

"Mirek, he's said he's sorry."

"He's still looking at you," the man said. "Did you see? What are you, with that case on your shoulder? Some desk man?"

"I'm leaving," Trn said, stepping left. The man pivoted again and Trn dodged between him and the shelves, bringing to the floor a cascade of packages. The bell at the door tinged as another customer came through and Trn skirted her out onto the sidewalk but the man's hand caught his shoulder and reversed him, pushed him toward the blocks of the wall.

"Who do you think you are looking at my wife that way?"

Passing faces took them in and palely faced away. A man in a sandwich board came by, a new restaurant with a German name, over the board his blank stare gaping past. Trn looked down at the paving stones they stood on, the cracked one the man stood on.

"I think I should teach you a lesson," the man said. "How would you like that?" His cheeks shook when he spoke, his jowls, a froth of anger at the corners of his mouth.

"Mirko," the woman said. She shifted her bag, laid a hand on the man's shoulder. "People are looking."

"I'm going to provide you a lesson about looking," the man said. The hair at his temples grew to points that almost touched his eyebrows. He pressed Trn to the wall with a plump hand. "He can't look at another man's wife without something to remember."

"What if the police come?"

"He doesn't know what to do," the man said, "so I'm going to show him."

He stood so close the breath of his words came up Trn's nose, the sick lunch decaying in his belly, in his teeth.

"Maybe I should follow him home, let his wife see me teach him a bit. She might like that. If he has a wife. You got a wife?"

Trn looked down at a dark stain on the man's yellow tie.

"Mirko, come home," the woman whispered at his ear. "Come home and I'll give you something special."

A scoff gargled up from the man's throat as his hand dismissed Trn's lapel.

"He doesn't even know if he has a wife. He only looks."

"Come along home before the police come."

"I'll be watching for you," the man said over his shoulder. "I'll be watching."

Up the hill Trn took the first lane he didn't need to take, waited at a lamp post before correcting his way. He walked quickly, heelbeats sounding on the pavement, nothing behind but an old couple with a doddering dog. Further on he held to the iron stake of a fence and still nothing. At their gate he clinked through his keys, watching the empty street before and behind. In the dark well of the stairs he felt of his pockets, stopped and reached into his case, held it wide to squint and shift among the papers. Goddamnit. Six crowns and no tube of Chlorodont.

*
*

When the broadcast was over and the jazz began again Miroslav said, "It was the same as last night. What a waste of electricity." "What else could it be?" Alena said and left for the kitchen. Trn removed the Churchillka and replaced the back to the radio and tuned to Vienna so music waltzed into the room. The coil he wound three times in its linen and set in the sideboard drawer under the last tablecloth, the lace that had belonged to the mother-in-law he never knew. In Miroslav's room he found the boy sitting on his knees in his grandfather's chair, his figure huddled against the cone of light from the desk lamp.

"It'll soon be time for dinner."

The boy didn't turn. His geography book was open to the bulging form of a yellowed continent, the boy's finger tracing the names of colonies, rivers, settlements.

"Does the radio say there is fighting in Africa?"

"There is fighting in the desert here, along the coast."

"Will they explode the pyramids? And the Sphinx?"

"Do you have a test coming?"

"Next week."

"There is no fighting near the pyramids. So the Sphinx is safe. I'm proud of you for studying early."

The boy shrugged, turned back several pages.

"London looks a big city. You lived there."

"For a time. It was the biggest city in the world. I suppose it is still. I studied in a big library. For some reason it was called the British Library."

He waited for a smile to curve the boy's cheek but none appeared so he combed his fingers through the boy's hair twice.

"Is the British Library still there?"

"Yes."

"It hasn't caught fire?"

"No."

"And burned?"

"No, it's all still standing very safe and strong."

"How do you know?"

"I'm sure I would have heard."

"Daddy?" He unbent his legs. Out of their deep wells his eyes looked up.

"What is it, my boy?" Trn leaned and kissed almost the crown of his head but Aleks seemed not to feel.

"Is England going to save us?"

"Aleks. We must be very careful what we say. Remember?"

"But we're not outside the house."

"I know. But at times our tongues don't recall where we are and our words escape before we think."

"Like when Mother shouts."

"We all shout sometimes."

"I don't." His fingers traced the shores of Britain. "You don't."

"You remember what we said of politics?"

"It's complicated. It's what you hear on the radio."

"That's true. Politics is especially complex these days."

"Danko's parents listen to the politics too."

"How do you know?"

"He says they hold their ears very close to the radio like you do."

"Aleks, we must be very careful about politics and the radio now. We shouldn't speak about it. It's best if we don't even mention the radio."

Aleks looked down at the page, the map.

"Will we be rescued by Christmas? Can I ask that?"

"This Christmas will be like last Christmas, I think."

The boy laid his chin on his arm.

"Will we be rescued by my birthday?"

"We must all be patient. Even if it is very hard."

"I will be eight."

"We will plan a celebration no matter what politics says that day. Agreed?"

"It will still be permitted to have a cake then? A small one?"

"Of course Mama will bake a cake."

"Daddy?"

"Yes?"

"How is England going to rescue us if it's burning?"

He laid a hand over the boy's thin hand.

"I don't know, Aleks."

"Germany is burning too."

Trn nodded.

"But we're not."

"No, we're not."

"But I have my mask if necessary. When I put it on you used to say I looked like a mouse. You called me a little mouse."

The hand escaped and lifted the pages back until the old republic was before them, a plump salamander nosing into the green lands of the Teutons. Aryan lands.

"Daddy? Where are the scissors?"

"I suppose they must be in Grandfather's desk. Probably there in the kneehole drawer."

"Don't we have scissors? You and me and Mother? Our scissors?"

"I'm sure we brought them. Probably in a drawer in the kitchen. Why do you need scissors?"

"I'll show."

He pushed away from the desk, hopped from the chair, left the door open. Across the hall came the scrape of a drawer pulled out, another, Alena telling him to wash, clatter and rummage and then Aleks back with the long blades of Trn's old desk scissors in his fist.

"What are you going to do?"

"Mr. Fischer said to bring our geography books with us on Monday." He shifted the book on the desk, the yellow skin of the salamander pocked with local habitations, scars of dark roads. "Because he's going to cut this map out of all our books. He says it's no longer valid." His eyes looked up at Trn's. "He said those are his instructions."

"And so you're going to do it yourself first."

"No."

He fitted his slender fingers into the handles, turned some pages until Africa reappeared, lifted and snipped at the gutter.

"Aleks, what are you doing?"

The small teeth bit the lower lip as the scissors rasped and bit through the border of the page.

"Aleks, wait."

"It's my book," Aleks said. "It has my name in it."

The scissors opened and closed a final time and he brought away the whole continent, raised the jagged page with a small smile, his dark eyes beaming.

"If this is all we need," he said, "then I'll leave the book at home and take only Africa to school."

He hadn't put off his coat before she appeared from the kitchen and said, "A man came by today."

"What man?"

"He came about lessons."

Trn paused, hooked his coat.

"He said that?"

"He wants to learn German."

Her eyes never left him as he looped his scarf over the collar.

"He wants to learn German from me?"

"Yes."

"Why should he think I would tutor him for German?"

She looked at the floor.

"Who is he?"

"He left a paper."

She brought it from her apron pocket and he frowned at it in the dark hall.

"I don't know this name. Had you ever seen him before?"

"No."

"How did he get in?"

"I let him."

"Alena."

"He had graying hair. Father was here."

"And he came alone?"

"Yes."

"Don't let him in again."

"Why not?"

"Because he might want something besides lessons."

"He said he wanted lessons."

"I know. But that doesn't make it so."

"He's going to pay, Viktor. He said he would pay in Reichsmarks if that's what you preferred."

"I don't know him. And how did he learn of me?"

"But think of the money, Viktor." She held out a clutching fist. "You know they're going to cut rations again."

"They're always going to cut rations."

"And so we could always use the money." Her eyes scowled. "And yet you won't give lessons."

"No, I am not giving German lessons. If that is what he truly wants."

"And what about what your family wants? What about Aleks? Your salary means less every month."

He frowned at the ragged tassels of the rug, tried to toe one into place.

"I will find something."

"Something besides the library? Besides sitting at the dining table staring out the window?"

"Yes, Alena. Something besides that."

"Something with money in it. Something more than chess and the radio." She forced out all the breath she had. "When?"

"Soon."

"I don't believe it."

She went into the kitchen. He looked at the man's name again and balled it in his fist and left it in his pocket. Miroslav looked up from the newspaper in the sitting room.

"How was the library?"

"Quiet as the Capuchins in their crypt. That economist was there, Kovar, with Dolezal."

"He used to be a socialist, Kovar. I hear now he's a national socialist. Everybody's giving in. The longer it goes on the easier it becomes. Did you hear that Göring came to Prague yesterday and took our president to dinner? When they put the menu before him Hacha said, 'Now where do I sign?'"

The old man chuckled and Trn smiled.

"At least we can still laugh."

"As long as we've got that, Viktor, we've got something. What was Dolezal saying?"

"Dolezal wasn't speaking today."

"Just as well for you. I never liked Dolezal. Every time he came into the office to complain he would stroke that fat mustache and sit with his fat knees spread wide as if he had to accommodate titanic balls."

"Perhaps he does."

Miroslav frowned like a carp.

"I doubt it."

"Did you see this man who came?"

"No. I didn't."

"I wish you had."

"You think he's not what he says he is."

"Perhaps, but let's not say that. If he is more than that he seems only to be watching for now."

"Now that the whip hand is Heydrich's who knows where the crop will fall. All those dozens they've shot just to cow us since he came to the castle. The Reichsprotektor and his protection."

Trn nodded again and Miroslav handed him a newspaper.

"Nothing there you'll want to read. Looks like the Russians are truly kaput."

*

Vienna was playing Mozart. Miroslav slumped in his chair, trumpets and drums ebbing gently over his snores. Aleks considered the figurines on their shelf, brought one to Trn on the couch.

"What happened to her?"

"I'm afraid," Trn whispered, "an accident befell her long ago."

In his hand Aleks twisted the girl in her pink dress, examined the rough ceramic wound on her hand.

"You couldn't fix her?"

"No, I couldn't."

"What was here?"

"I believe a little butterfly. Pink like her dress. Let's put it back so we won't have another mishap. It's Mama's."

"It's already broken."

"Let's not make it worse," Trn whispered. Trumpets and drums. So Mozart was happy the day his heart brought his hand to these notes. As an ordinary man might hum on a sunny morning. Then the door rushed open.

"Dita doesn't feel well," Alena said, "and needs something from the shop. I'm going for her."

"I didn't hear her call. Do you want me to go?"

"It's female things."

"Oh."

"Please put all that away if you're done with it," she said, waving a hand at the board and scattered pieces.

Aleks said, "Daddy was showing me the Czech variation of the Slav defense."

"That must be the one where you lie on the floor while the others walk over you. I'll be back."

The door closed and the orchestra paused and then another movement began. Aleks put back the figurine and took down a squat pillar of wood browned at points with the oils of human hands. It filled his small palm. "This one is for chess." He looked up. "Is it all right?"

"Yes. This one's sturdier."

"A man in England gave it to you."

"That's right. A man in Oxford. A very nice man named Hugh Peterborough."

"Why did the man give it to you?"

"As a remembrance, so I would recall the times when we played chess together."

"Does it work?"

"Do I remember? Yes, I remember vividly. He had thirty-two pieces like this one. He and his friends carved them during the war so they could play when there was time."

"The last war."

"That's right."

Trn noticed Miroslav's open eyes. The old man reached for his pipe.

"Why I wonder do we never hear Liszt anymore? He's Hungarian and they're strong with the Axis."

"They play him sometimes. But you're right. You don't hear him so much. They're using a theme from Liszt in the fanfare for news from Russia. Next time there's an announcement you'll hear it."

"As soon as Leningrad falls, I suppose." Miroslav rang the bowl of the pipe against the rim of the ashtray.

Trn said, "You might think because Liszt worked with gypsy tunes they'd exclude him altogether. Since anything having to do with them is verboten now."

Miroslav nodded at the ceiling, spoke to it with a flourish of his pipe.

"Now we have the unending Deutsche. Beethoven, Sturm und Drang, Bruckner und Brahms. Both Strausses so the Wehrmacht can waltz across Europe from Finisterre to the Urals. All this patriotism, measure after measure of martial parading. It's all only organized farting."

Aleks laughed behind his fist.

"Every bar a thundering prelude so they can splutter on about the Almighty this and Providence that. God is there no end of Wagner? How much can one man write? He would be the Führer's favorite."

"They can hardly talk about Christ," Trn said, "since Christ was a Jew."

Miroslav nodded, packing his pipe.

"Did you hear about Heydrich attending his first concert at the Rudolfinum? It seems our Reichsprotektor refused to enter the building if Mendelssohn's bust was still in place on the roof so two soldiers were detailed to bring it down. The trouble was neither of them had the vaguest idea what the hell Mendelssohn looked like so they trooped three times round the perimeter without success. Then one of them snapped his fingers. Of course, it'll be the one with the biggest nose. So they began the round once more before they both said at the same time, 'There, that fellow over there, the one with the beret.' And they sprinted over the lead because the concert was due to start any moment and hauled down the bust of Wagner."

Trn smiled and Miroslav clapped his knee as the voice on the radio introduced an aria from *Parsifal*.

Aleks still turned the piece in his hand. He rubbed the rough bearded face with the pad of his thumb, the worn crown, the wooden eyes.

"It's the king, isn't it?"

"It is."

"Why did he give you the king?"

"I don't know why."

Aleks looked up into his father's face. His big eyes dark but open to the world, darker against the palest skin and the ghosts of veins at his temples.

"Why did he get to keep the pieces?"

"I don't understand."

"You said he carved them with his friends. But he kept all the pieces. Till he gave you one."

You cannot tell such a child all the truth. Such a child cannot hear it and remain a child. So you cannot say, "Because he was the last one left alive. He was the solitary survivor. The one who pulled his mask on first, the one who burrowed deepest in the slime, the one who didn't live just long enough after the concussion subsided to see the pair of his legs tangled on the far side of the trench before he whimpered and bled out all his blood." You must instead blink and stare across the emptiness of words between you and innocence and say finally, because after all something must finally be said, "I don't know why."

One evening at dinner Aleks had a story to tell.

"Three men came to my school today."

"Are you such ruffians," Miroslav smiled, "that it requires six extra hands to teach you?"

"They didn't teach us. One only watched. He watched the other two. One man had a notebook and he wrote down what the first man said."

"And what did the first man say?"

"Numbers."

"Only numbers?"

"Yes."

"Why was this?"

"The man had an instrument." Aleks chewed some potato. "In German, 'why' is 'warum.' Isn't that a funny word? Like an engine. Like the engine of a car."

"Aleks," Alena said. "You eat like a farmer. Chew with your mouth closed."

"You have one like it, Grandfather. With two legs, measuring legs. To tell the distance apart."

"Calipers?"

"Yes. I think. Calipers."

Trn and the old man glanced at one another.

"And what did the men measure?"

"Just one man did the measuring." Aleks took another bite, chewed. "Our heads."

Alena saw them before they could shift their eyes away again.

"How can I chew with a closed mouth?" Aleks asked. He swallowed. "They measured our eyes and noses. The metal was cold but not sharp. Not really. They measured us all, all over our heads. Franto said it hurt but I didn't think so."

Aleks's tines shrieked against the china and Trn winced.

"They moved up and down the rows. Warum did the men measure our heads?"

He looked into each face, stopped at Trn's. Alena looked at him too before she stared at her father.

"Daddy, why are you watching your food?"

Finally Miroslav said, "You know the Germans. They are great ones for numbers. For information. Data their scientists call it. They are great collectors of data. They travel the world, taking the measure of everything. For their sciences."

"Will the man come to measure your heads?"

Trn watched the cabbage congeal to his plate but it felt hung in his throat.

He coughed, said, "Have you finished your lessons for tomorrow?"

"I have one column of maths."

"Best to finish it now. The electricity may go out and you don't want to have to do your sums in the dark again."

The boy furrowed potatoes with his fork.

"Is this politics?"

"No," Trn said. "Only mathematics."

When the room was quiet, when they could hear Aleks telling over figures to himself at the kitchen table, Alena said, "I want to know why they are measuring his head."

Trn glared, leaned to close the door.

"You know very well why," her father hissed.

"Tell me then."

"To see what they are going to do with him. To see if he is Aryan. Or a Jew."

"He is no Jew, they know that. They can see he is no Jew."

"So you don't have to worry about that," Trn said.

"All the Jews already have their stars. The old quarter is the Milky Way, that's what everyone calls it. Nobody in his family has a J stamped in his identity card. So why then? Why this measuring?"

"Because they can read our blood," her father said. "If we aren't Aryan, if we are too much Slav to be made German, then we are to be sent to arctic Siberia when Russia is conquered. This land will become another gau of the Drittes Reich."

"How do you know this?"

"Everyone knows this." His thumb jerked toward the black curtain behind him. "Everyone. Haven't you listened? Those trucks that come to examine us for consumption, these mobile clinics, what do you suppose they're really doing? Think. They won't let Czechs marry Germans without their approval. They study pictures of them naked before they decide. So you tell me, what is the end of that? The end of registering our noses and indexing the color of our eyes to a patch on a board? Why does everyone suddenly need a new identity card since Heydrich came? We are being numbered. Can't you see? Weighed and divided. We are less than an inferior race. We are a foreign body, a vermin. A bacillus."

She rose and snatched the plates into a clatter. A knife rang against the tile of the floor as she pressed past Trn into the kitchen. In the sink water splashed and drowned Aleks's counting.

Trn leaned to retrieve the knife.

"Calipers on school children," Miroslav said. "My God. If that's not hell's own trigonometry."

Trn watched their dim light glint across the dull blade.

"There's nothing to be done," the old man said. "Nothing you can do."

"You know as well as I do," Trn said. "Siberia may very well be the best that can happen."

He shut the door against the wind with the little bell still ringing.

"Ahoj, Viktor. Where have you been?" Trn took off his gloves, blew into each hand. Ivan closed the newspaper over his paunch and pushed himself out of the chair, turned off the radio. "Take off your hat and let me see what I'm up against today."

"It's not so bad as you might think."

"True. Your hair grows faster in hot weather."

"It's not always the same?"

"You'd be surprised." Ivan swiveled the chair. "Have a seat. Shave today?"

"Just the hair, I think."

"Growing a beard this winter?"

"Perhaps. Alena says with a beard I look like a farmer."

Ivan rubbed his chin. "Perhaps I will myself. My face feels cold."

He snapped the cape, pulled it tight round Trn's neck and ran a quick comb through Trn's hair, exercised his scissors in the air before beginning.

"Where's Miroslav? Haven't seen him."

"He hasn't much hair left."

"But he used to stop in when he'd walk by."

"He doesn't walk much anymore. Especially in this season."

"I understand that. Family good?"

"As good as you could expect. Saint Mikulas left some candy last night so today Aleks's mouth is too full to talk. How's everyone at home?"

"My wife's been sick."

"I'm sorry."

"Oh, it's been going on a long while now."

"You didn't say anything last time."

"I guess it wasn't so bad then."

They frowned together into the mirror angled from the wall and then the scissors chirped to work again.

"See the paper today?"

"Not yet. I saw the headline though."

"It's bad," Ivan whispered. "It's worse every day."

Trn nodded and Ivan paused his comb to let him.

"They say the Russians don't have much left."

"It's hard to know how they could," Trn said. "The Wehrmacht encircles a quarter of a million men or half a million at a stroke in these cauldrons. If they stand and fight they lose. If they fall back they lose."

He looked into the mirror at Ivan's eyes already waiting there and when they met they glanced away. The hair tumbled into the lap of the cape, wisps of it on his shoulders vanishing against the cloth.

"They say they can see the spires on the domes of the Kremlin." The scissors drew back and the comb went a quiet rustle through Trn's hair. "But I don't believe it. If they were that close they could put a shell through the window of Stalin's study and if they could do that they would have done it already and told us."

"That's true," Trn said. "At least it seems the advance has slowed."

"But I don't know what's going to happen."

"The Russians and the Germans don't know either."

"The Germans sound like they do."

"They always sound like they do. Our hope is that they're lying again."

The chirping stopped with the bell and the pressure changed as a reef of hair scudded across the floor. Ivan glanced up and Trn in the mirror saw a man, his wide back, heavy overcoat, shutting the door on the wind.

"Good day, Mr. Nemecek. Take off that hat and let me see what I'm up against."

The man nodded at Trn. He tossed up his coat on the tottering stand and his hat.

"We're almost finished here. Just a moment. Have a seat."

In the mirror Trn could see him, a large man still rubbing his red hands, looking round at the shop, at the newspapers racked and hanging by their wooden rods on the wall.

"Well I'm sorry Miroslav doesn't come past anymore. Tell him I said he can't wait till spring though. I've got no machete or garden shears."

"Alena gives him a trim now and again but he'll need your attention. I'm sure you'll see him as soon as the thaw holds."

"I guess that will be June this year. Greet him from me. There, that should do."

He unclipped the cape and whipped it away, whisked the brush across Trn's nape, showed him the crown of his head in the hand mirror.

"Sorry I can't do anything about that." He tapped a patch large and bare as a coin.

"I will survive it."

"Want some powder?"

"It would just blow away."

Ivan laughed again and Trn stood and took the folded note out of his pocket while Ivan brushed down the chair.

"Thanks, Viktor."

From the drawer he began to finger up coins.

"No need, Ivan. Thanks. I'll tell Miroslav you asked for him. And next time I want to hear that your wife is well."

"Please do, Viktor. Thank you." Ivan held out his hand. "Goodbye, Viktor. Mr. Nemecek, I'll take you now."

Trn fisted on his coat, tugged at his gloves. Ivan took up the broom and swept hair to its pile in the corner, stooped to gather it into the dustpan. From the door Trn looked back as Ivan glanced over the man's head.

"It looks good, Viktor, the haircut."

"I'm sure of it, Ivan. Of course."

He put on his hat.

"Now you're fit for the world. But is the world fit for you? That's the question." He began to strop his razor. An eye winked over the man's head. "So. Mr. Nemecek." He frowned in study, reached for the radio switch.

"Goodbye, Ivan."

"Goodbye, Viktor."

"Happy Christmas."

1942

When they started out the eastern sky was a pale yellow blade prying up the dome of the night. Downhill even that glimmer disappeared and against the darkness they counted their steps by twos and when Aleks sighed, "Twenty," Trn said, "Good. Now let's count by threes," and Aleks said, "Do we have to? I'm tired."

"We just got up. How can you be tired?"

"Because it's so early in the morning."

Trn sighed too, a billow of wool out into the morning twilight.

"Come on. By threes and then we'll stop."

Aleks said three.

"Six."

"Nine."

"Twelve."

Aleks let go Trn's hand so one set of gloved fingers numbered the other. They passed the pole with the loudspeaker that would trumpet when day came how the Reich was victorious on all fronts.

"Fifteen."

"Good. Eighteen. Look out for the dog droppings there."

Aleks walked head down with slow steps.

"I can't do it. I don't know." He reared a foot and kicked at a loose stone. Missed. "I can't even kick. I'm tired and the day hasn't even started."

"It's all downhill from here."

"You always say that."

"And it always is."

"No. It never is."

They reached the corner and Trn looked up the black avenue. The single hooded lamp of a tram bore down the line lighting up from the dark the parallel curve of rails.

"Hurry. We need to make that one or you'll be late again."

They crossed trotting, Aleks leaping onto the far curb, his satchel tossing in Trn's hand as the tram came screeching past, a V for Victory whitewashed on the central window of each car. Aleks lifted his knees high for the steps, saying, "Come on, Daddy, we can sit this morning."

The tram clanged and eased into its glide, the passengers silent in the blue gloom, a girl across the aisle reading nevertheless, biting her lower lip, the book very close to her nose. Their breaths steamed out and Aleks said, "It looks like we're all smoking cigarettes." After the boy wiped the fogged window Trn could dimly see two dogs on leads tugging up the arms of two men talking in plumes.

Aleks took off his glove.

"It's wet."

Trn shrugged.

"I know," Aleks said. "Next time don't wipe the window." Then he said, "I didn't get a dog for Christmas."

The boy's eyes watched him before they went back to the passing street. The girl turned a page in her book and put her eyes close to the words again.

"I asked Baby Jesus."

Trn laid his hand on the boy's knee.

"Do you think I can have a dog for my birthday?"

"I don't know. I don't know how many dogs there are now, dogs for having."

"Franto's dog had pups."

"Really?"

"A lot." When the tram jerked to a stop on its rails they jerked on the bench. "Franto says his family can't keep them all."

"A dog means a number of responsibilities, you know. Feeding, cleaning. Walking every day, more than once. And you'd have to pick up his turds."

The boy shouldered Trn's elbow, a smile so secret he put his hand across his mouth.

"You said turd."

Trn whispered back, "So did you."

The track diverged from the road and ran north through a dead orchard into the valley. The snow retreated into blue shadows under the hill, crusted onto the saddles of tree branches at the next tram stop. A little bird there huddled so close it seemed without feet or legs.

"I know it's hard to have a dog," Aleks said.

"You're a good boy, Aleks. A very thoughtful boy."

"It's just that if I had a dog I would be less lonely. I'd have some-one to play with." He clasped his hands, one bare, one gloved in black. "But I know there isn't enough. There isn't enough to eat for a dog to have something too."

Trn reached an arm and the boy twisted away, his forehead pressed to the window, his breath blooming on the glass. Out of the morning a tram came blinking down the other line. The girl with the black beret and the black hair curled at her shoulders turned another page.

He would have settled for a shoulder. It need not be even a neck or lips. Just the skin of the shoulder rounded as an apple ripe for a kiss. That alone. His neck twisted and bent and his awkward lips pressed almost soundlessly against the skin of his own shoulder before the door opened and gusted the air and Trn slid into the cooling water.

"I'm in here."

"I can see that," she said. "And by the look of that water you should be."

"What do you need?"

The mirrored door of the cabinet flashed.

"Father has a headache."

"There are aspirin in the kitchen, with the vitamins on the shelf over the table."

"Here they are."

She closed the cabinet, went out with another gust.

Trn sank deeper, raising the pale islands of his knees stippled with a poor forest of standing hair. The tangled fen between them, its floating mat. The faucet dripped. Kop. Kop. Two notes. Kah-op. The entry of the sphere of water falling like a teardrop to break the tension of the surface and then the collapse of the water onto itself again in the concavity created by the impact. Kah-op. He reached into the murk of suds but what was the point and he let it all go again.

She slept deeply through the breath's descent, then the steady and profound exhaustion of the same breath as he lay and listened. After a stretch of three or four nights, a drought of sleep in the dark, she could always sleep so. "You can help me sleep." She used to say that. "No one can soothe me like you." She'd said it first in Luhačovice, on the honeymoon, in their meager room at the Hotel Alexandria, their monk's cell, laughing together after the narrowed silence when he opened the door. Laughing sometimes. He woke once in the afternoon and she was gone. The breeze shaped in the curtain, the light moving over the walls, the tubercular walls. He tried not to think of the coughs, the sputums of those the Alexandria once served as sanitorium, the town still a spa town for those seeking cure and for those young enough to stroll among its springs. Each with its name and medicinal qualities. Some among the evergreen hills at the end of meandering paths between rotting logs. Vincentka, Ottovka, Aloiska. But it all tasted like pipes to him. "You are not a true Czech," she said at his sneering nose. "Oh no. I am too much a Czech." She looked out at him from under that pale fallen hair but what did those eyes say? What did that dark in the center mean?

Brain, lungs, kidneys, bone, and bowel. The cures were universal. At one pipe issuing from a whitewashed building on the hillside a wizened woman in a headscarf drank a full measure toothlessly, massaged her stomach, then flashed her hands past her hips and laughed while Alena blushed.

The Alexandria was the best he could afford and that with Miroslav's help. Lavatories in the hall. Worried that smell was the remnant of formalin baths they'd given the rooms after the consumptives paid their bills and limped from town. It sat directly on the main street so the cars honked through the open window. You had to stretch your neck to glimpse the slow Stavnice gliding like glass under the wide pedestrian bridge. The clop of the horsedrawn ambulance making its way to the hospital. Seeking cure, all of them desperate to be well and whole again. To be unruined. Finally late in the afternoon she came back through the door and sighed, the breeze in the curtain. She tossed her purse on the table, sat in the one chair.

"Where did you go?"

"Out. If you were going to sleep."

"I'm sorry. I didn't mean to sleep. What time is it?"

While he pulled on his trousers she examined the figurine on the table, a little girl in pink, a thing he'd bought the day before because she touched it on some undusted shelf. He got his watch from the dresser. Somewhere an ensemble struck up its brass.

"Are you feeling better? Are you hungry?"

"I don't know."

"What would you like to do?"

She shrugged.

"What might you like for dinner?"

"I told you twice, I don't know."

"I want you to feel better and maybe keeping some dinner down would help. A soup maybe."

"I'm not sick. It was only this morning."

He tightened the strap of his watch, combed his hair in the mirror. She recrossed her knees and sighed.

"We had talked about going to the dam."

"Fine. Let's go to the dam then."

She set the little girl on the table with some force and swung up her purse and after the little girl went over no one stood her right.

"If you'd rather not."

"Why don't you decide something for once," she said. "Why don't you make a decision."

He centered his tie, glanced in the mirror at her profile. He took his coat from the hook, opened the door, looked at the carpet stained in the hall.

He was first down the wide stairs, held the heavy door at the entry, turned up the avenue that led them to the promenade where strollers took the cedared air, grave couples in stately clothes, husbands with silvered hair creased by homburgs, in wide-brimmed hats their ladies bound for the opera house, families with puling prams, young couples in arms temple to temple in the evening afterglow. The brass circled and swelled and he knew the music as he'd known it in the room from the first notes, the fanfare from Jánaček's *Sinfonietta*. It spiraled up into the September dusk, climbed round through the oak leaves that shook as if with the breath from the horns.

"We could have a drink. Would you like something to drink?"

"Hemlock."

He put his arm round her and they went into the wide square, the curving colonnade where walkers rested on benches before the fountain but the fountain was out of season. The water grew green as copper in its puddles and the wind sailed dead leaves across it like ghost boats.

"I don't see a bench but we could sit on the fountain."

He ran his hand across her back but not a bone unlocked. Her fists in her lap crimped the pleats of her skirt.

"Are you tired? We don't have to go the dam. We'll have time tomorrow before the bus."

"I said I'm not tired."

"What is it then? Would you like to have dinner?"

"When are you going to stop with all your questions? God can't you ever leave me alone."

"I'm only trying to find out what you want."

"I don't know what I want except I want you to quit interrogating me." Her breath profound and steady as she stood, the gravel cracking under her heels with each step she took away, Jánaček's fanfare mounting with each swirl of wind. He tried to still himself inside its ascent, listening, staring down at the gravel between his shoes, the dust of the stone graying the polish he'd applied before the ceremony, her breath interrupted in its passage by the first whimper, a distortion of the life inside her. The whimper rose to a moan in the dark while the little birds beyond the black curtain tried their songs against the cold. He set his feet on the rug between their beds and knelt beside her, four fingers on her shoulder. He called in whispers.

"Alena? I'm sorry. You're having a bad dream."

"What?"

"You're having a dream. Are you all right?"

"Yes. I'm all right."

"Can you go back to sleep?"

She swallowed in the night. "I think so."

"Do you want some water?"

"It was so dark."

"I'm sorry."

"My mother was calling to me."

His hand waited at her shoulder.

"Mother was calling and in the dark I couldn't see her but I could feel her reaching toward me."

"It's all right. You're all right now."

She sighed, stirred beneath the covers, rolled to the wall.

"Can you sleep? Do you want some water?"

"No. I can sleep."

He blinked in the dark, his hand on her pillow. They never had walked to the dam.

"There aren't any seats," Aleks said.

"There's one forward."

"Only one."

"You take it. I'll stand."

The boy knuckled the morning from his eye and yawned. The man already seated glanced up and glassed Trn over with his spectacles, pointed his yellow tramp's mustache back toward the frosted window. The girl was there again, reading. French. He could peer over her shoulder, past the black beret. Maupassant. So the running captions said. Contes. Perhaps not such an odd choice since the French were occupied too.

"Can you hold your satchel?"

"Would you hold it, Daddy?"

The girl beside her spoke and she nodded at the book. The girls in front peered over their bench and laughed and her cheek smiled.

"See it, Daddy?"

"What?"

Aleks pointed among the black and crooked limbs of the dead orchard as the tram went through and Trn bent to see.

"The cellar without a house."

"What do you mean?"

"I told you. The steps leading down? The cellar without a house?"

"I didn't see it."

The girl looked back over her shoulder at Aleks, up at him.

"You never see. Steps go down to a door under the hill."

"Like a troll's house?"

"No, like a real cellar under a real house except the house isn't there."

"I haven't seen it."

Aleks folded his arms, sat back with force.

"I'm sorry. I want you to show it to me again on the way home. Will you?"

She closed her book, opened her bag, brought out a tablet and put Maupassant away. She took a pencil from the girl beside her and made a notation, her slender fingers moving among the characters on the tablet's cover, beneath a larger script flowing into a name. Renata Florianova.

Renata Florianova's eyes cast up one glance and moved on and left him there gripping the bench, testing his lungs against the atmosphere as if all the air were slowly stuttering from the tram. She put her tablet away as the tram slowed and stood with her schoolmates. Trn made way for her and they did not touch in passing, the other girls all talking at once down the steps for the walk to the secondary school. She stood framed an instant there in the window as the tram lurched and started, Renata Florianova with her black hair slumbering on her shoulders, a curve of smile starting to her profile and Trn holding on for as long as longing lasted.

Trn put the ration tickets in his breast pocket and handed Miroslav the loaf wrapped in rough paper, took up the bag with potatoes and the package of ersatz coffee himself. Under a cold sun they looked up the long hill home and Trn trimmed his stride to Miroslav's. A man and woman paused before Kleindienst's bakery and solemnly gave the imperial salute to Hitler's bust among the loaves in the window.

"At least we don't have to do that," Miroslav whispered. "Did I tell you the joke?"

"Which joke?"

"The one I heard, last week? The week before? From Janek there in the shop."

Coming down the sidewalk toward them a lone figure bent and gathered something from the pavement, the gutter, came on and knelt with clutching fingers again.

"What the devil is that fellow doing?" Miroslav said.

He crossed the street as they approached, avoided their eyes, stooped again as they looked back.

"Cigarette ends," Trn said.

"Be glad you don't smoke."

"Or he's selling them. The shreds of them."

Miroslav paused, limped on. "How much can he get for shreds, I wonder."

"Less now than he'll get later."

After another pause to consider his watch Miroslav said, "Let's go by way of Janska-Street. I haven't seen the Deutschkron house since they finished the refurbishment."

"It's pale green now. With red banners."

"Of course."

"What's the joke you got by Jan?"

"Oh yes," Miroslav said. "Have I told you? A Pole and a Czech were yelling across the new frontier and the Pole said, 'You know what we did when the Germans marched in?' 'No,' said the Czech, 'what?' 'We slit their throats,' the Pole said in the most bloodthirsty voice. 'Well,' said the Czech. 'We couldn't do that. We thought it was against the rules.'"

"You can only tell that joke because you had one Polish grandmother and one Czech."

"True," the old man said. "And anyway, how many throats did the Poles actually cut?"

Within an hour every eye in the streets had changed. Guarded in the queues at tram stops, hooded on the scurry home before curfew, eyes that glimpsed the headlines blared from the newsstands. But few dared to stop and buy a paper. When you came out of the butcher with the stained packet stowed under your arm their gaze tilted at yours from under the brow or the hat brim, the graven faces drawn low into the chronicle of their tribe. Over the sunken cheeks the eyes of strangers darted a seeking glance and each pair spoke the same question: Is he dead? What will they do now?

But for all their searching the streets were sparsely peopled. Most shops were dark and locked and some had windows smashed, hate and hakenkreuzes scrawled on the walls. The trams ran on with fewer faces peering from the windows. Trn stopped at Mrs. Zigismundova's to get Aleks an apple but it was shuttered without notice. The Steinhardts' blood banner wrinkled in the late May breeze. The radio was on all day. When he came into the sitting room Alena and Miroslav looked up at him with the sagged expression of those in the street. Aleks came out of Miroslav's room.

"Daddy."

He put an arm around the boy, kissed the top of his head.

"I have a drawing I want to show you."

"And I want to see it."

"It's the one I told you about. The one I started at school. Do you remember?"

"The house you're going to build when you grow up."

"Yes."

"Why don't you go back to Grandfather's room and I'll be there in a moment."

"But I'm ready now. I have the elevation finished."

"Have you done the plan?"

"I've sketched it."

"Work on that a little more and I'll be there in a moment."

Aleks frowned at his mother and grandfather, at Trn. He shut the door behind him.

"The Germans say he's stable and recovering," Miroslav said. "They won't let a Czech doctor near him, you can be sure."

"What does Czech Radio say?"

Miroslav's hand dismissed the radio. "They can only give the list of executed."

"There's been shooting in the gymnazium all day," Alena said.

Miroslav said, "Did you see anyone who knew anything?"

"Whispers that they're already out of the country, in Switzerland. Nothing about Heydrich."

"I hope that bastard dies," Alena said.

The door opened.

"Daddy, I've finished the plan. Of the ground floor."

"That's excellent, Aleks. What about the cross section?"

"The cross section's hard. Will you help me?"

Alena and Miroslav were still looking at him.

"Yes, Aleks, I can help. But in a few minutes I want to come back."

The boy slumped into the chair at the desk, took up his pencil, pressed the point so it snapped on the paper.

"Now we'll have to sharpen it again."

"I have another." The boy sighed. "That's all you want to do, listen to the radio."

"So show me this house."

"There it is."

Trn angled the pages for the best light and said, "This is wonderful, Aleks. Look at this. These columns create such a classical effect. Why did you start with the elevation?"

"It's the way I saw the house first. In my mind. I want it to look like a museum."

"It's quite beautiful, Aleks. I admire all the windows. You'll always have plenty of sun." He lightly touched the shadings, the depths they created. "You're extraordinarily talented. Do you think you might like to be an architect someday?"

"I don't know. Maybe a scientist."

"You could certainly be both."

The boy sat up. "There's where the library is."

"I thought so. That was a very good idea to put it at the corner and have the benefit of light from two directions."

He gave the boy's shoulder a squeeze.

"Is he dead yet?" Trn watched the boy's eyes roam over his plans. "The Reichsprotektor. What everyone's waiting for. For Heydrich to die."

"We don't know."

"Do you hope he dies?"

Trn sat on the bed, leaned against the wall.

"I don't know, Aleks."

"He's a wicked man, isn't he?"

"Yes, he is."

"They call him the Butcher of Prague."

"Where did you learn that?"

"He's hurt many people."

"He has."

"Then why don't you want him to die?"

"If he does I'm afraid more people will be hurt. In reprisal. Do you know what that means?"

"It means shooting at the gymnazium. But won't they do that anyway?"

"Yes. They probably will now."

"So it's too late."

"It may very well be too late, Aleks."

"What about the men who shot him?"

"No one seems to know much about them."

"Do you think they were brave? To stop his car in the street like that, to try to kill him?"

"I think a person would have to be very brave to try that."

The boy picked up the blunted pencil.

"Do you think they'll shoot all night? At the gymnazium?"

"I'm sorry you have to hear that."

"I usually can't with the windows closed. But it's warm now."

The boy erased a line, brushed and blew the debris away, redrew the line with broken lead. Trn clasped his hands over his stomach.

"I wish you didn't have to listen to that."

"I know you do," the boy said.

"I'm afraid there must be some misunderstanding," Trn said into the phone. "I don't offer lessons."

"Yes, I see."

"I understand that this is what you have heard but I am afraid that is mistaken."

"I regret the confusion."

"Yes. Goodbye."

He went into the kitchen.

"I thought you were not going to speak to anyone else about German lessons."

"I thought you were going to think about taking on pupils," she said.

"I have and I have decided against it."

"Why, when we need the money so badly?"

"We're not so desperate yet."

"How do you know?" She turned to face him, a wooden spoon in her fist. "You spend all your time in that room or with the radio or at the library. You aren't seeing what other people see. You don't know where we stand. Staring at your precious chessboard how do you know what desperation is?"

"We have food and money for the rent."

"God," she said, prodding the roiling cabbage, "why are you so stubborn? Can't you understand we've had cabbage seven nights and this makes eight? Everything is falling apart while you're reading books. Mr. Havlicek says he'll build a hutch for us but I told him don't bother because I know you won't even wring a rabbit's neck."

Over the rising steam she wiped the hair from her brow with the back of her hand.

"I know the world is collapsing," he said. "But I don't see what I can do about it. Everyone is eating cabbage all the week. If they have cabbage."

"With more money we could have more than cabbage."

"So you want to risk the black market? Even if we're not caught we wouldn't be escaping the collapse. We must share in that."

"With you it's always only words. Fine words. You don't understand what you're talking about."

"I understand that even while the world is falling we must eat."

"They could decide to kill Aleks any day. Do you understand that?" She put down the spoon and chose a paring knife. "Give them the chance and they will come in here and shoot him or starve him or worse."

Their eyes met over the blade and she laid it across the palm of her left hand.

"You wish these men harm but you won't do them any harm yourself. What kind of sense does that make? What kind of man does that make you? If Adolf Hitler were in this room right now and you had this knife would you bother to stab him?"

"This is ridiculous." He rested his elbows on the top of the cupboard.

"Would you?"

"Of course I would but that doesn't make it any less absurd."

"There are men out in the world now fighting to kill Hitler. I'm sure to them it's not absurd. To Heydrich's assassins it's not absurd."

He heaved a chair from the kitchen table and carried it out to the balcony, shut the door, sat with elbows on the low wall, chin in his hands. The blood thudded in his ears. He could count each pulse in his skull.

Otherwise the street was almost silent. The blades of swallows' wings flitted, diving. When he was a child he sometimes thought them bats and slouched away through the village, ready to dodge if one swooped near. At night the other boys sat in a circle playing cards by the gas lamp, the ground beneath the grass still warm with summer. He watched and tried not to think of the strafing shadows as the bats darted through swarms of moths yellow and brown in the flaring light. For stakes they bet pebbles from the road and then bored of that tossed their winnings into the night. The challenge was to see who could lure a bat closest to the ground. He cringed down and they all scoffed, What are you scared of? You're so much bigger than they are.

"What are you doing, Daddy?"

Trn started as if asleep, reached a hand towards Aleks standing in the door.

"I was just thinking of a story I might tell you."

"What story?"

"Close the door and come here."

Aleks sat across his knees and he put his arms around the boy.

"Is it too warm to do this?"

"A story about what?"

"About when I was a boy younger than you are now. About swallows in the village where I lived. Look at them out there, flocks of them, see, swinging away from that larch. Can you count them?"

"They move too fast."

"And they're so graceful. The way they all change direction at once."

"Their tails are divided like the Czech lion."

"Very good, Aleks. I never thought of that."

"Is that a family of them, flying together?"

"I don't know. I suppose they must have families, in their nests."

"But some are alone. That one there."

A black shape with two curved blades on the wing looped and sailed over the street just before their eyes.

"Isn't that amazing?" Trn said. "What it must be like to fly."

"I think it must be very small."

"How do you mean?"

Trn chinned the boy's shoulder and Aleks settled to him, the thin face lifted.

"Everything must look small when you fly. From up there we must be very tiny. The buildings like boxes. The little people walking into them, we all so small. Planes look small from here but they are very great."

"I think you must be right."

Before them was the quiet of evening in the street, the pointed trees among the houses scaling the hill.

"Does Mother not love you anymore?"

"Mother's tired."

"She's always tired."

"These aren't easy days. They make everyone tired."

"I know." He snuffled in his nose. "She never hears what you say. You say something and she says, 'What?'"

"That's because I don't say interesting things like you."

He blew on the boy's neck and Aleks flinched.

"Daddy. You're tickling." But he was laughing.

Trn's arms locked round him. He could feel on his face the heat rising through the boy's hair. From the left a bright shape plummeted out of the sun into the shadow of their building, denser than the shadow, slowed and beat once and lifted back to the light in a climbing roll.

"Look," Trn said. The boy stood, Trn behind him, four hands waiting on the wall. "A hawk."

Wings braking, talons out, the bird dipped into the pinnacle of a spruce and the green spire obeyed, bent to receive him, the wings tucked shut, head with its sharp beak surveying the new world in one motion.

"He's big."

"He is, isn't he?"

"He's so much bigger than a swallow."

And Trn knew what he'd missed. "See how the swallows have all flown away."

"They disappeared," Aleks said. "Are they afraid?"

Before Trn could answer the air warped like a sheet of metal and fractured from the gymnazium to their balcony. The hawk uncoiled his wings and the tip of the spruce gave him up and swayed without him. The echo of another shot decayed and then two more in a close rank broke across the evening. One hand guided the boy back inside as the other lifted the chair, Aleks's dark eyes watching Trn lock the door. Over the stove Alena shifted her weight, wiped her brow with the back of her hand without turning.

"It's all right, Aleks," he said into the stare. "It's all right. Come and draw something for me."

"But I don't have any ideas."

"We'll think of something together."

"Aleks," she said without turning, "you need to set the table."

The boy leaned through the door into the dining room.

"I can't. There are books and papers covering it again."

She looked over her shoulder at Trn.

"You didn't tell me your story, Daddy," Aleks said.

"I'll tell it to you in the sitting room after I clear the table."

"I liked it outside."

"I know."

Aleks went into the hall, narrow back and slender waist, all so small. Trn hesitated at the door to the dining room. A pan scraped over the eye of the stove.

"I will find pupils," he said.

"When?"

"Tomorrow. I will begin to find lessons to take on tomorrow."

The somber music came mourning over the radio to interrupt an interview with a Czech horticulturalist speaking of the new exhibition at the botanical gardens and Miroslav unclenched the pipe from his teeth and said before the strains stopped, "Heydrich's dead."

The day after the funeral newspapers carried photographs of the draped casket on the gun carriage leaving the gates of the castle, the hands of Heydrich's little blond boys in Himmler's hands, his widow sagged under a black veil, the black banner of the SS with its lightning runes. Miroslav pointed to the foreground of a picture.

"Have they no sense of irony at all?" Under his finger a detachment of youths from the Reich Labor Service stood at respectful attention, each one shouldering a spade. "My God it's a funeral, and look at that congregation of shovels. Do the Germans not have eyes in their heads?"

"Perhaps the problem is deeper than the eyes," Trn said.

Miroslav meditated on the depth of his pipe, packed the bowl. "Everyone believes this is a great day because no one has ever struck a blow at a Nazi so close to the throne."

"It is a great day," Alena said. "Any day bad for Germans is a good day for Czechs."

Miroslav said, "Do you remember Poland?"

She recrossed her legs, adjusted her skirt over a knee.

"Is that what you want here? The country converted to Warsaw? You could bridge the red Vistula on the floes of bodies."

"I'm not going to sit here and listen to this anymore."

"You're going out?" Trn said.

The murmur of her coat muffling her shoulders came from the hall, the clack of the bolt thrown back.

"Be careful," he called. "The curfew. And they'll be marching." The door snapped shut. "In the streets."

Miroslav shook his head.

"Everyone who believes there are only two sides in this war are perfectly correct," he said. "But this is what Alena does not understand. There are those in front of the gun and those behind it and those in front must do and say what those behind say to do. These are the only two sides and the alternatives in front of the gun are to live or to die. These are the only alternatives."

"We're going to die anyway."

"Now you sound like you're defending your thesis again. This is not a thesis, Viktor. There is no degree at the end of this war. There is only life or death, that is all. Survival is no disgrace. Survival is your diploma."

"Or is survival another word for cowardice?"

"No, it's the antonym of death." Miroslav looked at him over his embering pipe. "You know that."

"But there are disgraceful ways of living." Trn lifted a rook and set it back in its corner. "Do you believe there is anything worth dying for?"

"Let's reverse the question and see the answer. What is worth living for?"

"I don't know." Trn shook his head. "Aleks. Beyond that I don't know now."

Miroslav gazed after the smoke he blew into the room. "Let's get to the heart of the moment's question. We are at war and Heydrich was a soldier in that war, so he must die. Otherwise there can be no victory. So runs the argument. But do you really think Heydrich's blood on the street will shorten the war?"

"Somebody's blood will shorten the war. One way or the other."

"Good. Let me tell you then. Heydrich's blood will shorten the war for all those the Germans will kill in reprisal, for the hostages they have already begun to execute up there on the hill and in a hundred other prisons. Let's be very clear about this. Of this vengeance we are certain. Whole villages. We will end up counting the dead at least in their thousands, for one man. For those people the war will be dramatically shorter. It will end now within the next few days or weeks or hours when the SS trucks halt in the squares and the gates crash down and the men in gray wool with the bolts on their collars thunder out with their black guns. For the men and women and children under those guns the war will be over very quickly. They will scream and beg for the war to continue, but their war will end in those few seconds."

Trn drew a hand down his face while Miroslav's voice went on.

"These patriotic assassins who killed Heydrich, who came down from exile in parachutes like angels from England, let's look at these men. Do they want to survive? Do they want more life? They manifestly do because they're in hiding. They've executed the bastard and now they want to escape with their lives. Exactly like everyone else. Otherwise they would have committed the deed and held up their hands on the spot or shot themselves on the street corner so not to reveal their secrets. They did neither. So is their survival cowardice or heroism? And the innocents who now are dying for that heroism, let's look into their eyes. How frightened they are now that the end has come, how they weep, the tears clotted on their lashes. The angels chose for them. Isn't that true? Which side of the war did they choose? They weren't permitted to select. They were selected. And one day their families with glowing pride will all be able to say the sacrifice was genuine and every drop of blood a glory to our sacred soil, the loved ones lost were bled upon the altar of national sacrifice so that we might live. But how easy it is for the living to speak of the sacrifice made by the dead. Will the war be one minute shorter because those innocents died in terror against the rough stone of a wall? Tell me this: what is the nation after all? Isn't the nation no more than its people and if we slaughter the people what remains of the nation?"

"Slaves," Trn said. "The ones who remain are slaves."

"Horseshit. How many dead innocents are the equivalent of one living slave then? Calculate that for me."

Trn blinked at the board, its scattered pieces, its empty squares.

"And so what do you say we should do?"

"We should survive. The fortunate among us will and will have some type of life in the aftermath. The life that the hour and our geography have bequeathed us. That's the life we have, the one chance at living we're allowed. For the first time I count my age a beneficence. I'm lucky to be an old dodderer and may live a while longer because of it. We're going to die anyway, just as you say, but let it not be today. Let us not die today."

He rang the pipe against the crystal of the ashtray and Trn looked up to see the dust rise from the ash.

"Hitler must be finished," Miroslav said. "We all understand that. And for Hitler to be finished children must die. But let's not let Aleks be one of those children. Let's get Aleks through this war. He deserves that and he needs us to do it for him. No war lasts forever. Let's outlive this one and then see how the ground lies on the other side.

"Do you see that, Viktor? You're right to think of Aleks. So let's think of him."

"I see very little else," Trn said, "but I see that."

He closed the door to the dining room and set out his books on the table and looked sleepily over the array. He opened one and found the place where he'd left off and before he'd finished a page rose and shifted a chair against the door and did something he had not done since long before the war. He turned to a new page in his notebook and wrote slowly, in English.

Dear Claire,

I often think of Oxford and the past. I think of it too often. When I hear the news from London I wonder where you are in it. The BBC says now that the raids are few there. I hope that it is so.

Here it is worse now than before. A few weeks ago the men who killed Heydrich were killed, in a crypt under a church in Prague. But you have heard this already. Will have heard it. I think what their last moments must have been like in that desperate dark. I suppose yet darker days are to come.

But Czechs are famous for saying, What can we do? We will survive it. I believe I told you this once.

I have a son now, Aleks. He is eight years old, nearly nine, a fine lad. I believe he will be tall. Taller than his father, I hope. The world is easier for tall people. Don't you think? They can see farther. They are looked up to. He does very well in school though just now education suffers here. Still he studies. Maybe he will go to university there one day. Maybe one day you will meet him.

The window panes were rounded with the mist of last night's rain. The sky dragged its nails over the roof of the gymnazium. From its brick chimneys smoke collected in the bodies of the clouds.

Sometimes, he wrote, *in the night I twist my pillow beside me and think that it is you.*

He ripped the page raggedly, tore a second time at the odd and clinging remnant in the gutter. He rose and removed the chair and in the kitchen listened to the silence of the flat. He took a match from the box in the drawer and downstairs went out into the garden where Havlicek's rabbits curled among the wet grass in their hutches, one pelt stretched and splayed into the four corners of a wooden frame. A breeze whispered a little of autumn already from somewhere to the north, rustling the leaves of the Steinhardts' apricot. He knelt and against the driest flagstone struck the match. The flame flared bright into the paper and he bore it quickly to the hedge trailing flutters of ash and dropped it in the soil under a bush and watched it burn out. After that he toed the flakes with his shoe until no sign was left except a slight sting in the eyes from the smoke.

The boy was not stupid but uninterested. He never did the lessons Trn wrote out and left on Tuesday for Thursday or on Thursday for Tuesday. He didn't care at all for declensions and even less for drill in lexicon or pronunciation. He slumped at the table in the family library, blinking under the globe of the lamp, the grain of the table shining through its varnish, the spines of books lining the wall, some titles in gold. He rumpled his cheek on his fist and mumbled once more that German was his father's idea. He was thirteen or so and had not bathed again and was as sleepy as the day outside that wept down the sky, as the clouds that lounged on the hills.

"Es regnet schon drei Tage," Trn said.

"I don't know," the boy said.

"Can you make out any of it? There's a hint out the window."

"Three days."

"Good. Very good. What about the beginning?"

"No."

"It has rained already three days," Trn said.

"Four," the boy said. "It's rained four days."

The mother knocked on the open door. "Your hour has ended, Ondraj."

Trn stood and began to stack his books. The boy rose in his reek of unwashed adolescence and stumbled toward the door.

"What do you say to Professor Trn?"

"Goodbye."

"Ondraj?"

"Danke."

He slouched from the room followed by his mother's frowning eyes.

"I must apologize for Ondraj." She came toward the table, looked down at his books. Trn glanced at her hand on the grammar, waited till it strayed before putting the book in his case. "He will behave in exactly the same manner tomorrow with his violin teacher." She smiled into his eyes. "So it has nothing to do with your instruction. It is entirely Ondraj."

"I appreciate your saying so but as I said last week, I wonder if it is worthwhile continuing."

"I very definitely believe so. Please don't let his attitude discourage you." Again her eyes smiled.

"Very well then. I will leave these pages and return on Thursday."

"But aren't you staying for coffee?" Her hand gestured toward the open door. "I'm sorry. I thought you said you would stay today for coffee to discuss Ondraj's progress."

"I suppose I thought we had discussed his progress just now. And I'm sure you have, you have matters to attend to."

"Hanka already has it prepared. It only needs pouring. I believe you said you don't take cream or sugar."

"Yes."

"It's in the sitting room." Her white hand opened the way. "Please."

Coal burned in the grate and the coffee was laid steaming on a silver service before two chairs facing the fire. A large portrait in oils hung over the mantel, she, younger, an impossible light falling over the high Slavic cheekbone of her averted face and onto the white hands folded in her lap.

"That was long ago," she said, pouring.

"It doesn't appear so."

She glanced at him, set the saucer and cup on the table near his knee. She stirred her own cup and lifted the saucer and settled into her cushions, sipping from the brim, sighing to disturb the vapor rising.

"I'm afraid it is. Commissioned just before I was married."

Trn nodded, took up his cup, paused.

"Is something wrong?"

"No. Not at all. This is very good coffee."

"My husband is well connected."

"It certainly tastes well connected." He drank again.

She laughed and stopped and then looked at him drinking, her face brightening to the light of the face in the portrait.

"Are you sure you won't take some cream and sugar then? They're also well connected."

"In that case," he said, reaching the cup toward her.

Clattering the dishes from the table, eating an end of bread left on Aleks's plate, he stopped when she pulled aside the black curtain from a corner of the window. He set the stack down and shut the door to the kitchen, licked his thumb and finger and hissed out the candleflame.

"What do you see, Alena?"

"Nothing."

In the silence he gathered the cutlery by touch.

"When I was little I had a friend in this neighborhood. Zuzka. Zuzka Sedlakova. A little girl my age. We used to play a game in this room. This time of night, stars coming out." The curtain moved further aside and the crescent of her profile shifted to a different portion of the sky.

"My mother had just died." She shook her head at the shadows. "All I wanted was to leave these rooms and now I never will."

Trn felt the table was empty, paused when she spoke again.

"We would stand in these chairs and rest our chins on this sill and try to guess which star God lived on."

"And what did you decide?"

She stared a long time, long enough for her body sagging against the white wall to come up in his eyes. She murmured something he couldn't hear in the dark. Then she said, "But now I'm sure he lives on none of them."

He balanced the stack ready for the sink. "I'll need to shut the door after me," he said.

She didn't say anything and he left her leaning on the sill in the empty room. He set the dishes in the sink and moved the candle away a bit and powdered the sponge a very little under the cold water. The next morning she went to early mass.

After his stamping up the carpeted stairs had faded she laid four fingers across the back of Trn's hand.

"Ondraj?" she called up the stairs. "Ondraj. I must go out for some things. I'll be back, soon. If you need anything Hanka is down in the cellar with the laundry."

"Ondraj? Did you hear?"

"Yes."

She slid back the door of the closet, took a coat from a hanger. He lifted it, molded it over her shoulders under his hands. A beautiful coat, long and tailored to her waist with a belt and sleekly black. She was taking up her purse from the marble-topped table in the hall, gazing into the mirror, glancing through it at him. She took the lipstick from her purse and studied her pout for a moment and capped the lipstick and put it in her purse without applying it, snapped the purse closed.

"Ondraj? I'm leaving now."

"All right."

She scarfed her hair in dark silk and Trn opened the front door. Outside she locked it doubly with separate keys. From the street she looked back at the house once and then without ever looking at him she fell against his shoulder and said, "Put your arm around me."

"Here?"

"Please. I don't care."

He pulled her to him and matched the stride of her heels and they tottered down the sidewalk awkwardly as if drunk with every step. The case in his far hand felt very heavy.

He said, "I'm sorry?"

"It's seemed an age has gone by in this last week."

"I feel the same."

"Do you?"

People passed, the march and murmur of their conversation. The sky was low and gray with early cold. A Wehrmacht truck roared beside him, its exhaust through his trousers hot against his leg for a moment, the heat dissolving with its black smoke. He raised a hand to pull his hat brim lower.

"Where can we go?" she said.

After a moment he said, "I don't know."

A tram clanged past, its iron wheels slurring on the wet rails, the face of an old woman scowling at him through the crux of the white V on the passing window. People hurried by to catch it except a short woman with her shorter daughter who stood against a utility pole in their yellow stars and watched it roll on. The man with his beard nearly all silver pushed the kino cart across the street toward them, its high mechanical tune piping like a calliope as the wheels went round. Some movie he didn't know.

He pivoted, taking her with him.

"Where are we going?"

"Come with me."

They crossed the street, he shepherding her more quickly now, their heads bowed a little against the wind. A block down he shifted her again to take the corner, across a second street as she looked up to his eyes under the hat. A few more steps brought them under the shelter before the ticket window. Trn reached into his pocket.

"Two, please."

"It started twenty minutes ago."

"It doesn't matter."

"First place or second place?"

"Second."

"Two times four and a half so nine crowns."

He paid with iron coins and took her by the elbow, pushed the glass door. The usher tore the tickets, handed them back with a whispered admonition for quiet. Trn blinked in the flickering dark as the flashlight showed them down a narrow aisle but he could make out already the empty row he wanted and steered her toward the corner, nodding to the puzzled usher.

They sat, the silhouettes of a few heads before them in the dark, one blowing up into the blue light a long trumpet of smoke. She leaned and he lifted the coat from her and in her two hands she caught his face and pulled it to hers before he had taken off his hat. When he opened his eyes hers were still closed. Lips lingered with his, on his jaw, a whisper into his ear and then her fingers wrestling with his belt, the buckle undone, a whispering kiss as the fingers moved down the buttons one by one. "Give me your handkerchief." He took it from his breast pocket and she took it from him so quickly it was as if she had never let him go. She kissed his lips again through her whispers. "That's it. There." Her lips kissed him. "Yes. I want you. I want you to be in my hand just like that. I want to feel you be."

When she said, "I must go home," he nodded and put on his hat and led the way through the dark. He kissed her a last time around the corner from her block, some steps down a side street against the monumental cornerstone of the faculty of law where the special people's courts now sat in judgment. She would not let him follow further than that. All his steps away were slow under the shadow of the castle on its crest, slower still when he came to the slope he had to climb. A tram stopped and he stood and watched it go and plodded on. The red placard with the black border announced from its pole the most recent traitors executed. He climbed beyond it, switched his case to the other hand. On the crown of the hill through the slats of St. Augustine's empty bell tower you could see the blank sky. Since they had craned down all the bells for cannon. A child was running a kite across the dying grass of the park toward another child and their strings twined and the kite looped and both came crashing down. On the far slope the way home descended but his steps were no faster, his slow eyes on the paving stones, conjuring the wilted handkerchief in the dark beneath the seat of the cinema where they'd left it.

With her fingers Alena began to pick at the leaves on the stone and Trn set down the pail within her reach. She took out the brush and swept the slab, scouring briskly in the angle where it met the headstone. Down the little lanes other mourners moved, other families bending over their stones.

"Is there anything I can do?" Trn said.

The brush swept the last brown leaf away.

"Why do we not visit the graves of Daddy's mother and father?"

"Because your father doesn't believe in such superstitions."

Trn said, "My parents are in the churchyard in the village where I grew up. It's a long way from here, more than a day even by train." He didn't say the churchyard was part of Hungary now and lay on the far side of Slovakia.

"Why are they there?"

"We still lived in that village when my father died and so he was buried there. My mother wished to be buried beside him and so when she died we brought her there too."

The bristles of the brush routed the leaf rust from the gray stone patch by patch.

"I need that cloth."

Trn took the damp rag from the bottom of the pail and handed it to her. It was cold in his hand, colder than the pail.

"And why do we do this?"

"To show respect," Trn told him.

"To show respect for the rock or for the people?"

"For the people."

"But they are dead."

Kneeling over the stone she looked up at Trn. "See what you've done," she said.

"Today is a special day," Trn said. "It's called All Souls' Day."

"I know."

"And on this day we show respect to those in our family who are no longer with us. We show our respect by this tradition, by this ritual of memory, by doing what your mother is doing now."

Aleks looked at the granite. "But they can't know. They're under the stone."

"They know it," Alena said. "They know it because they look down from heaven and see. They watch over us all the time."

"Are they mad if we don't clean their stones?"

"I don't know," Alena said. "Ask your father."

"Do you want your gloves?" Trn lifted them from the pail.

She took the gloves but didn't put them on. On her knees she worked the brush over the stains, scrubbed with the rag.

"Are your mother and father mad at you, Daddy? If they look down you are here."

"I think my parents understand that I am here now, with you and your mother, that I carried the pail for her today and that I carry my memories of them with me even though I do not live in their village now."

"How long has it been since you cleaned their graves?"

Alena stopped the brush to stare at Trn again.

"I haven't been there since my mother died."

"They're buried in leaves and weeds now," Alena said. "No one could read their names."

Aleks shielded his eyes against the sky. "And they're all watching now?"

"Certainly," Alena said. "They watch after us always."

"What are they thinking?"

"I don't know."

"They watch us when we sleep?"

"Especially then," she said.

"They watch when I take a bath?"

"I suppose."

"And when I go to the toilet?"

Her reddened hands dropped the brush rattling into the pail and she set her fists on her knees, glaring at Trn when she stood.

"I'm going for the flowers now."

"What's wrong?" Aleks said.

"It's hard for her, I think, coming here and thinking of her mother. Mama's mother died when she was a little girl, you know. Not much older than you."

Aleks looked over the stone, rubbed for a moment its chiselled corner.

"How did her mother die?"

"She had a disease."

"Do you have a disease?" Aleks said.

"No, I don't."

"Do I have a disease?"

"You had a cold but you are well now."

Another family came past, a white-haired woman leading three grown men with hands in their pockets and black armbands. Trn nodded and against the wind they murmured good day and walked on slowly to surround a plot down the lane.

Aleks was still looking at the stone. "What do the star and the cross mean?"

"The star is beside your grandmother's birth date and the cross is beside the date on which she died."

"I thought so. They put that on all the stones."

Trn bent and picked up the stained cloth, the gloves, dropped them in the pail.

"Yes."

With flowers clutched before her Alena came back slowly, her eyes on the white petals, her knuckles red.

"Would you like for us to wait for you by the gate?" Trn said.

She stood looking into the cluster of flowers, the stamens nodding in their throats till the wind gusted and closed the mouths of the blossoms altogether. Trn put on his hat and took up the handle of the pail and held out his other hand and Aleks took that. Families came slowly through the gate and they waited for a space to go out and then they stood before the window of the flower shop looking at the arrangements banked in display.

"Why do we put flowers on the stones?"

"Let's not touch the glass. Someone will have to come out and clean it."

"Won't they do that anyway?"

"Yes but it won't be because of us. They put flowers on gravestones as another sign of respect. We offer flowers to those we love."

"We love dead people?"

"Certainly we do. Think of it this way. They are absent from our lives but we still have feelings for those who are absent, possibly even stronger affection than when they were present. So when you go to school I miss you until I meet you at the school door again."

A slow tram braked with a muted squeal. The widows appeared as both doors folded open, heavily let themselves down to the pavement. One used for cane an upended broom, the handle tapping beside her as she toiled on thick ankles through the stone gate. Trn watched over Aleks's image mirrored in the window, nestled among roses and carnations. From a corner an illustrated poster made a plea for a soldier, a wooden arm strapped to his shoulder, a wooden leg strapped across his waist, an eye bandaged shut, a crutch under the sound arm. A gust made sails of the widows' skirts and Trn reached to hold his hat. Aleks winced and put his back to the east. The air stilled and Alena came through the gate, passed them and went on to where the tram stood open to the weather for mourners ready to depart.

Over the closing of the door he could hear her sigh. The hook received her coat. She called for Aleks.

"He's out," he whispered.

She came into the sitting room, the shopping bag still in her hand, scowled at the door that dulled her father's snores, sank into the large chair.

Trn switched off the radio.

"Is there any news?"

"London urges us to not lose hope. Benes says the war will be over next year."

"He said that last year."

"They're still fighting over the rubble of Stalingrad. Though the high command says they aren't. Greater German Radio tells in admiring tones the story of a distraught mother and her Luftwaffe son reported missing over England. Eight of her neighbors whispered she need not worry as they each heard on the BBC that he was safely in captivity. Now the Gestapo has added eight more to its sum of prisoners convicted for listening to foreign broadcasts."

"How could she do that?" Alena scowled again.

"So now a whole series of despairing mothers will be left to wonder what became of their sons because their neighbors dare not tell any news of them."

"I've got to put this away. Call Aleks in from the garden."

"He's at the Bergs'. I'll get him."

The sudden muscles changed every angle of her face.

"What is it?"

"He shouldn't be there. He shouldn't spend so much time with that boy."

"Why?"

"Peter is too old."

"But they are friends. He's only twelve, isn't he? He's like an older brother for Aleks, he's good for him. And it's not his age that worries you."

She sighed at the wall, the window.

"You know," Trn said, "Aleks has never once mentioned their stars."

"Only trouble can come of it. Going to his house."

Trn shrugged. "They can't go to the park anymore." He looked out where leaden clouds idled. "And for how much longer are they friends?"

She shifted the shopping in her lap.

"He won't be here much longer," Trn said.

Her neck was thinner, the line of the jaw sharper. Perhaps Havlicek would sell him a rabbit some evening. Or half a rabbit. The clouds remained unmoved.

"London says they're executing them, you know. Gassing them."

"That's only reports," she said. "It could be anything."

"If it could be anything then it could be worse than what London says. So for as long as Peter can have friends, for as long as friendship lasts now, let's allow Aleks to be his friend."

She folded her arms.

"Let's think of the day when he's fourteen and shipped off," Trn said. "How Mrs. Berg will feel when the notice arrives from their council appointing the day for Peter to heave up his suitcase and be sorted at the station and put in a car beside old men your father's age and men my age and boys of fourteen and trained to Terezin."

Her eyes traced over him as she stood and said, "You need to go get him, it's time he washed for dinner." From the kitchen he heard the cupboard doors, the echo of pans against the counter, a murmuring only to itself while he lifted his hat and coat.

"You had a letter."

"A letter?"

"From Mr. Herbst."

She walked into the bedroom and he followed, his overcoat still on. She took the envelope from the round silver tray where she kept her cosmetics.

"You opened it?"

"He said they won't be requiring your services any longer."

Trn folded out the page.

"Why would he dismiss you?"

"I'm not being dismissed. They may be moving. He spoke of taking his business to Prague." The page smelled of talc. "He works with Germans, you know. Business would be better there," he said.

"Had he paid you everything?"

"Yes."

"Good for that." Walking from the room she said, "I hope you'll find another pupil soon to make up the loss."

Trn shook his head over the note. "I'm sure they'll find a better tutor there. Though that boy was impossible."

"What?" she said from the kitchen.

The crucifix in the left aisle of St. Tomas was the one he thought the city's most realistic and this stretch of Thursday afternoon a good time to see it. Only a few still knelt over their hushed prayers along the empty benches, noon mass ended, no further confessions till Friday morning. He could stand on the frigid stone hidden by a colossal pier and admire the artifice.

An eagle at the head that clutched a banner in its beak heralding INRI was answered at the foot of the cross by a bristle of spears and another banner, SPQR. The eighteenth-century sculptor whose name he didn't know had left in relief three dice clustered to the beam beneath Christ's feet and above the suppedaneum the blue vessels stood out from Christ's stone legs with the strain of perching on his block of death. Heavy lids draped the eyes black and vision-ary, already nodding toward the next world. Only the nails were wrong, and the partisans, decorative nails without heads to hammer or fix the flesh, ax heads too golden for the rough hands of centu-rions striding Judea. But the man had captured suffering. Beneath its fret of thorns the pale face was a furrowed agony where every nerve branded muscle. The sinews strained and burned along their lengths. This stone suffered and Trn appreciated that he was not allowed to forget suffering.

Quietly when it was time he walked away past a pair of soldiers bowing heads at the end of a bench, coal scuttle helmets domed over their knees. An old couple wandered among the nativity scenes dis-played for the season, one the whole wooden city of Bethlehem and in its narrow corner the stable with real straw and a plaster child in the manger, golden paint for hair. The old man was saying, "How many years I've come to see these," and Trn went on and held the inner door for another slow couple entering. He put on his hat and pushed the outer door against the wind and the narrow ancient street was brilliant under the blue sky. A chatting pair of women preceded him and with them he turned toward the square.

The one in a gray coat had black hair and the one in a black coat blond. They were speaking something about shoes. Then a gust up the tunnel of the street furled their coat skirts and raised the trash in the gutter, put a speck in Trn's right eye that brought tears. He had to stop since blinking did no good. It demanded knuckles. From his wet eye the pair of black and gray was disappearing among the stalls going up in the square, the hammers pounding on naked boards. He sheltered at the tram stop, wiped a handkerchief at the sting. The clock on St. Jakub said nearly two, his blinking watch said a little past, and there was the girl sitting at the end of the bench in the shelter, reading. He took a step deeper inside so he could glance down but she would not look up. Beg how your eyes might. A tram clanged, a number four, clanged again and the girl glanced from her book. Reading French still.

She turned a page with thin fingertips, her thumbs holding the margins. Slender even in her thumbs. Where were her gloves?

He stepped to his left as if to make way for others and straining could read some words himself before her eyes rose.

Caught between a sigh and a breath he said, "I see you're still at your French."

With puzzled eyes she sorted his face. "Oh." She smiled a little.

"We don't see you on the tram in the mornings anymore."

"They changed our school schedule." She looked down at her book and then squinted at him again, the dark lashes swept over each eye.

"You read it very quickly. That's impressive."

"Not really. I've read it for so many years I should be faster now, I think."

Her thumbs kept the book pinned open, a refuge to return to, to hide her eyes in if he should look too long.

"A novel?"

"No. It's Descartes actually. *The Meditations.*"

"You like philosophy then."

"No. My father's making me read it. He says he read it when he was my age so now I must."

"But might you read it as well in Czech then if you're to read a translation? Descartes wrote it in Latin, not French."

"Oh. I didn't know." The wind swirled her skirt and she closed the book on a finger, reached to draw down her hem. "I don't read Latin."

"I'm sorry. I make no criticism." He bowed his head. "Reading *The Meditations* is admirable in any language."

"Perhaps I should tell my father."

"I'm sure he already knows."

"He's an engineer. What he doesn't know about other things is very interesting. Even though he travels a lot. Used to travel."

She breathed as if she had more to say but her lips closed. Then she said, "I suppose I should be reading German."

"Why?"

"When school is over for me I'll go there to work."

A bell clanged down the line and she looked through the shelter window and stood.

"My tram," she said.

"You don't take a number four?"

"No. No, I take this one."

The bookmark out of Descartes teetered and fell. Trn bent quickly, picked up the tarnished brass with a monogram, a flowering F.

She took it without touching his fingers. The tram rocked to a stop and the door jerked open and with a small smile at the center of her lips and the briefest nod she stepped past him.

"Goodbye, Renata."

On the first step she half turned and glanced over her shoulder, a large woman bumping up roundly behind her, a man on the pavement glowering for them all to move out of his way. And she did, climbed the last two steps, turning so that the door closed over her squint puzzling out this man who could name her. The door frame hid the face and then in their series the windows painted for Victory carried off the girl herself like a reflection lost in some moving waters. A bend of eddied thought where the current of his mind once ran.

1943

The light from the hall shot in and Trn winced to see Aleks leap and knee himself onto Alena's bed, his face scourged with crying.

"What's the matter?"

"Daddy said he would stay with me until I went to sleep."

Alena held out her arms to take him in and the boy clung to her. She pressed her lips to the top of his head. Trn switched on the lamp.

"When I close my eyes all I see is blackness but Daddy left me in the dark."

"Aleks, you were asleep when I left. That was hours ago."

"I never went to sleep." He snuffled at Alena's shoulder.

"What are you scared of, darling?"

She brushed the damp hair from his brow, kissed there. Trn sat on his bed looking at them, rubbing an eye.

"I don't want to see nothing but blackness for ever and ever."

Alena pulled him tighter.

"I don't want to die," he whispered.

She rocked with him in her arms, pressed her cheek to the crown of his head, glanced at Trn.

"I don't want to die," he almost wailed. "Please don't let me die."

"This is your fault," she said. "All the time nothing but the war news. Showing him the papers. You put death everywhere before him."

Trn looked down at the floor beneath his pale feet, the geometry of wood that patterned itself away into the shadows of the room.

"Mother's here, Aleks. I've got you. It's all right, darling."

The boy's hidden face sniffled in her gown and Trn pulled a drawer in the bureau, came back to hold out a handkerchief that she brought to Aleks's cheek. After a moment he took it and blew his nose.

"Would you like to sleep in my bed, Aleks? I'll go into the sitting room and that way you can stay close to Mama."

The boy nodded. "Can you push the beds together?"

"Yes," Trn said. "We can do that."

He moved the lamp, lifted the table away.

"Careful of the floor," Alena said.

"Can we leave the lamp on? Until I fall asleep?"

Alena nodded and smiled at him and he huddled down into the place Trn had made while she clutched the blanket up to his chin.

"Good night, everyone," Trn said.

Aleks closed his eyes and Trn closed the door behind him and put out the light in the hall. In the sitting room the little tree was gone and its little candles but the dark still smelled of resin and wax. On the couch he drew up over himself the covers already gone cold.

He and Miroslav swapped papers but the news was the same in either language. Donnerstag, 4 Februar 1943. Der Kampf von Stalingrad ist zu Ende. Sie sterben, damit Deutsch lebe.

Miroslav relit his pipe.

"So they died that Germany live. If that logic holds maybe Benes is right and the war will be over this year."

"Stalingrad's a long way from here," Trn said.

They studied the papers and Miroslav held up the picture of a tanker in his black tunic half out of a panzer on parade and said, "The other day Aleks pointed to such a photo and said they look like iron centaurs. That's pretty good."

Trn said, "I guess we'll have to be more careful about such things."

Miroslav nodded and shook his paper over to a new page and said, "If I had a face like Himmler's I don't believe I would speak of a master race. He could be Hirohito's brother. In fact," puffing once on his pipe, "you could compound them all into the perfect Aryan, couldn't you, the absolute Nazi. As prolific as Hitler with Goebbels's grace and Göring's svelte physique, Himmler's blond good looks and eyesight. And our dear departed Reichsprotektor Reinhard's deep and manly voice."

The knock rattled the door and they narrowed their stares at one another and Trn reached and switched off the radio, shifted the box.

Miroslav said, "You hide the Churchillka, I'll get the door."

"I'm coming," he called in the hall. Trn replaced the back to the radio, went to the wall and loosened a tile in the stove and Miroslav called again, "Coming," while Trn wrapped the coil in its linen and put that in a woolen sock in the recess and replaced the tile and the wedge of mortar that his fingers pressed into place.

The knocking came again and he heard Miroslav unbolt the door and the relief in the old man's voice. "Mrs. Asterova, good day. What is it? Are you all right?"

"Mr. Vesely? Is Alena here?"

Trn came into the hall dusting his hands on his trousers and Aleks came from Miroslav's room, his drawing pad hugged across his chest.

"She's out, Dita. What can we do?"

"My mother-in-law, Viktor. She's not well and I need to go out for the medicine Dr. Kobylka prescribed. But I've no one to watch her. I was hoping Alena." She looked into each of their eyes, even Aleks's at last, her hands tangled before her. "Will she be back soon?"

"She's gone for some shopping, Dita. But I'll come up. I'll sit with her until you come back."

"Viktor, oh thanks, thank you," and she was gone for the stairs.

The old woman was in the back bedroom propped on pillows, a blanket pulled to her breast. With lids half open she stared as if nothing were before her or as if everything were and none of it a surprise. Trn did not recognize her.

"She's burning with fever but the doctor says to keep her covered. I use this cloth to sponge her forehead. Will you do that please, Viktor?"

"Certainly, Dita. Of course."

"There's water in the kitchen. You know that, I'm sorry."

"It's all right, Dita. You go now."

She tied a blue scarf at her chin with quick fingers, sleepless eyes.

"Is there anything more I should do, Dita, anything I should know?"

Dita gazed a moment more, shook her head.

"She talks out of her head sometimes. Or she did until two days ago. It may be the fever but she did it before the fever. She's seventy-six now. Seventy-six last month. The war's hard on her. It puts us all out of our heads, I suppose."

"I didn't realize, Dita. You could have called on us before."

"I thought until last week she would get better."

She looked up.

"I'll hurry, Viktor. I'll be back as soon as I can."

He heard her boots quicken through the flat, the door whine open and closed. At first he leaned on the straight chair beside the bed, looking down, then he sat. The blanket labored, the vessels braided themselves with the sinews over the back of her hand. Her fingers twitched and were still. The room smelled of acid. Uric acid.

His father had lain so. His father's room had smelled the same. The sodden mattress, the pillows soaked with sweat. "But he doesn't drink anything, Doctor," his mother had said. The glass had stood on the decrepit bedside table, a skin of dust lying over the surface of the water. "That doesn't matter," the doctor said. "His bowel and stomach together will produce a liter and a half of excreta every day whether he drinks or not. But you must get him to drink if you can at all." Trn surveyed the familiar terrain, the old woman's face, the promontory of the nose sloping to the knob of wax that was her cheekbone, the vale from there descending to the withered abyss of the mouth. A rank air breathed forth from that underworld, the black caverns of the body.

"Won't you help me?" his father rasped. "What can I do, Father?" "Viktor's drowning." "No, Father. I'm here. I'm right here." "All I can do is lie here while Viktor drowns." "Father, I'm here holding your hand. Can't you feel that?" "I guess he'll just have to drown then."

A brain fever, a fever in the brain, that's all they knew to say, and his father suffered for it, thrashed under it, bleeding sweat from his scalp, his teeth clacked by some inner winter. The doctor whispered to his mother, "It's in the brain now, the infection." What did you know? I knew nothing. I did not even know that death was approaching there before me.

He took the glass to the kitchen and poured out the film of dust, tried to have her sip but she didn't know he was in the world, no longer knew there was a world beyond the glaze of her eye. Somewhere the Asterovi had a clock ticking but through all the time he sat there he never heard it chime. The doctor had whispered as their clock had ticked, "It's in the brain now. It's only a matter of time." As if it were ever a matter of anything else.

The light canted all the shadows of the room across the walls. He hoped for the door, turning his eyes from the woman on the bed to listen but no door opened so he watched the fading day fall across the casement. As he had done before, across the stark white walls, across the shelf of books. A six-volume encyclopedia his father bought for coins from a vagabond pushing a cart. A-Č, D-CH, I-L, M-Pol, Pom-S, Š-Ž. The atlas he could picture pages of as if the maps were painted inside his skull. The tome of translated Shakespeare in its red binding.

His father had built a crystal set and put it in the open window so the villagers walking past in the evening promenade could take up the earphone and hear the music. He was clever at such things and stood behind his machine to see the faces look up as they strolled by at dusk. To hear Strauss, Mozart, Beethoven, to learn that the frame of bedsprings on their roof acted as antenna. At least he remembered it so. After the war when the promise of infection was already there but latent. Dormant. Sleeping one day to quicken.

An old woman had stopped with her fists in the pockets of her long apron and asked up through the window what nature of machine was this, if this was one with an arm to spin and make the music trumpet from a horn she could not see, and his father explained that no, from this machine the music came because it captured waves from the air where they took a translated form and were translated again into electricity and then back into sound just as her ears were capturing the words in his voice. Inside the earphone a membrane vibrated like the drumskin of her ear and that vibration put forth the music and the voices and all else that came from the machine. The old woman removed a fist and scratched among the hairs along her chin and declined the earphone but smiled and said it was all God's work then and none of the devil's and she was glad to know it was indeed a miracle and not simply string launched from Hell to snare us in its pleasures or some scheme by the Hapsburgs to climb back onto the throne.

A strange burr opened his eyes. It caught in the old woman's throat and deeper still where two sheets of sandpaper dusted with iron filings met and crossed. With the cloth he wiped from her temples what might be tears. She murmured and he leaned to hear what might be words but it was only some sick breath coming up with the static from her lungs.

"Mrs. Asterova," he whispered, "would you take some water?"

He held the glass before her, tried to lift her from her pillow, but whatever her dazed eyes saw it had nothing to do with him. He touched away the rheum from the cheeks as softly as he could and then her brow began to cry too and instantly her scalp was soaked as if water ran through the wires of white hair that yellowed the pillow. He could not keep her forehead dry.

Her hands roamed the blanket in blind search and he put the cloth down, took up a hand cold as metal. Her throat cracked again all down its length, something broken behind the teeth.

"Mrs. Asterova? Mrs. Asterova?"

She closed her eyes to concentrate on the blanket, to fill and deflate it, raised the point of her chin to work the bellows, stretched open her mouth to let the heat out, gasp in the air for her fire. He held to her hand.

"Mrs. Asterova."

He dabbed at her cheeks, wiped her neck, the taut cords in a V that channeled the water to the well of her throat where he could not reach. It had been so with his father, a place no napkin could find. "Can't you give him something?" he asked his mother, for the doctor was gone, a neighbor on his horse was trying to find him. "Isn't there something?" Her eyes shot wide and a gargle jerked her rigid beneath the blanket as if a knife had stabbed between her ribs. Trn went still too, his hand empty.

"Mrs. Asterova?" he whispered.

The eyes stood open, glistening a shade of gray under the window light. He patted her brow again with the cloth and that was the last time. He sat and watched past his hands the carpet threads frayed and colorless with feet getting into bed, getting out of bed, and still the door did not open.

With his thumb and long finger he shut her eyes. One lid needed no help but the other would not settle and the gray iris drooped there as if exhausted with what it had witnessed. He drew the lace and the blackout curtain, came back to the bed and smoothed the blanket from its struggles. His mother had said, "Viktor. Pull the curtains," and he had. He had been fifteen and everything he saw before that darkness froze in his eye like rime crystalled across the panes when the first frost descended. That is what happens when our nerves begin to bleed, we close the eyes of the dead for our own comfort, that we might think them only asleep all the while. So that out of death their eyes will not stare us down and accuse us of living on.

He was still standing when the keys rang against the door and it rattled open and boots in the hall scurried toward him. Dita stopped at the threshold and the keys jangled to the floor. In a moment she became visibly smaller, shrunken under the lintel. Another moment and she was smaller still.

"Something told me. I couldn't see the windows but I knew."

"I'm sorry, Dita. I'm so very sorry."

With slow steps she came, knees buckling so that Trn thought she was falling but she dropped on the bed beside the old woman, the cold of February wisping out of her coat, and she took the old hand in both of hers. A sob started until her jaw clenched and caught and then she said, "Was it hard?"

She gazed at the withered face then back to Trn as her tears broke, her nose already red in the dim of that room and the vessels blurring in her eyes.

"Was it hard for her, Viktor?"

"No, Dita. It was like she slept. Like going to sleep."

"And I didn't even get the medicine. They didn't have any of it. He gave me a prescription for a medicine they don't have."

A point at the middle of his mind whispered, There was no prescription for this. It brought its own cure.

"What will I do, Viktor? What will I do now?" Her face pressed at Trn's chest, wet sobs buried there. A fist at his back beat slowly down as a heart dying in his arms. "She is all I had in the world. And she wasn't even mine."

Before he closed the door she thrust the page at him.

"I told you what would happen."

"What is this?"

"Just look. Look what I found in the box. I told you there would be consequences. But you never listen. Letting him play with that boy."

Trn squinted at the page in the hall.

You stinking jews!

He carried it to the kitchen for the light falling through the window of the balcony door.

You stinking jews!

You are coming to us and rob us of our meat, eggs, fruit, and chicken and we don't like it!

"What are you going to do now?" she said, glaring into his face, arms folded. "What?"

You live in a quarter where jews are not valid. Go.

Trn said, "This is deplorable Czech."

Go. Still yet all one of us has to is call a tour of the street and then throw in the Gestapo and they'll perform an inspection.

The last warning we send!

"They're obviously not Czech."

"And that's supposed to make it better? It makes it worse."

He went into the sitting room, still in coat and hat, and sat on the couch to read it again with Alena standing over him.

"You've seen this?" he said to Miroslav.

"Oh yes."

"It's obviously meant for someone else," Trn said, setting his hat on the table. "Meant to scare someone else."

"How can you be sure?"

"It's a mistake, Alena. There are so many mistakes in it. Probably someone trying to frighten a family out of a flat."

She snatched the page back. "Why did it end up here then?"

"Why did it end up anywhere? It's completely irrational from first to last and has nothing to do with us. Take a match from your father and burn it."

Miroslav shrugged at her. "What were you planning to do? Take it to the police?"

Reading it over she bit at her lip.

"What's for dinner?" Miroslav said.

"You can eat this," she said, glaring, holding the page toward him.

"It will have more flavor than turnips but might I have a little salt?"

"You're lucky to have turnips," she said and left them to consider one another under raised brows.

A woman's voice said, "Achtung, achtung. Enemy bomber formations approaching Carinthia, Styria." Aleks began a new drawing. Miroslav frowned into the newspaper and turned the page. The voice said, "Enemy bomber formations over Lake Balaton," and Miroslav said through his blue pipesmoke, "Do they have any idea where they are?" Trn marked a passage in his book and made a note in the margin and Aleks showed him his design for a desk with an adjustable writing surface. Suddenly the cuckoo's cry came four times over the radio and they all stood without looking at one another except Aleks whose eyes watched them all and the voice from Vienna said they had ten minutes.

They were in coats and shod and outside in less than three, Alena winding Aleks's scarf while Miroslav plugged down the boy's cap on his head. Trn held the flashlight, the night so dense with cold it felt like a solid they must walk against, not enough cyanotic light even to see the plume of his breath. The siren from the gymnazium spiraled up to its wail, met at that pitch in their ears the wail of other sirens through the clear air. At the end of the street they entered the woods Indian file, Trn first, the rustle of leaves and whispers.

"It's not a full moon," Aleks said. "I said it's not a full moon."

"You're right, Aleks," Trn said.

"Why is everyone whispering? It doesn't matter even if we whisper."

"Right you are, boy," Miroslav said.

The path curved downhill. Trn reminded them but they each tripped over the same root. When the path began to climb again among the black trees he saw the faint line escaping the door. He pulled at the iron handle, had to lean and haul again before it gave.

"Hurry," a voice hissed, "hurry with the door, they said ten minutes," and Trn swung it back into place.

Alena held Aleks in her lap in the last seat on the bench against the dirt wall, her face praying against Aleks's nape, and Trn and Miroslav stood. Most eyed the packed dirt floor. When the anti-aircraft began to pound their stares shifted to the timbered ceiling. The lamp began to smoke and a voice cursed and turned it down almost to nothing and Trn's eyes scaled the new gloom. So this is our salvation. They all went on scanning the beams, some squared, some still rounded with bark. This is how we are saved.

"You can't see the planes," Aleks said very loudly.

Trn touched his lips with a finger. "No but we might hear their engines."

"The high explosives whistle," Aleks said. "We will be able to hear those falling."

"Hold your thumbs, boy," Miroslav whispered, and Aleks folded his thumbs into his small fists. The old man did the same and smiled. The flak stopped suddenly and the wind whistled past the door. Then there was another burst and another and then the wind again.

Later a watch crystal flashed round and white beside the lamp.

"It's been nearly an hour," a voice said. Then the lamp dimmed and went out and the voice cursed again.

When the all clear finally wailed from the top of the hill Trn on numbed feet uncrouched from the angle of the wall and gave his hand to Miroslav rising. With another man he heaved stiffly against the door. All the stars stabbed very bright through the limbs. A horned moon risen above the trees gored all the silver clouds that rode the night wind west. They climbed the hill with the others, rattling the leaves across the path with shuffling feet, their panted breaths like mingled smokes among the trees.

"Another false alarm," Aleks said. "No raid tonight."

"If we have a thousand nights of false alarm," Miroslav said, "I'll take that."

The old man rubbed Aleks's cap and in the blue light the boy set his cap right again as they came up to the street.

"Does it work," Aleks said, "to hold your thumbs? Or is it like the bells, the sound of bells that keep the snow and hail away?"

No one answered. He exercised his thumbs again.

"I think it's just something we say," he said. "I don't think it brings luck."

Finally his grandfather said, "It did tonight."

Alena came out of the bedroom as he closed the door and looked up at him hanging his coat.

"Anamaria telephoned. She's had a telegram."

Trn stared at the hat in his hand. He stood very still on braced bones.

"Is Pavel dead?"

"No. He's being released. He's one of those the telegram said are being released to mark Hitler's birthday."

"I saw the Steinhardts' flag but I wasn't thinking why."

"Then what he did wasn't so bad," she said, "for them to release him."

"Bad enough for three years in Buchenwald. Three and a half. Did the telegram say when he will be home?"

"Anamaria said the telegram didn't say."

She went into the kitchen and he came beside her at the sink, began to take the dishes from the drain.

"I really can't believe it."

He clattered the plates into a stack, began to dry the cutlery. Alena said, "If you can't be any quieter than that give them to me," and gripped the forks out of his fist.

"I'm going to have a Becherovka."

"At this hour of the morning?"

"There's a little maybe."

He lifted down the emerald bottle, tilted it in the light.

"I think Father had the last of it."

"I think you may be right." He unscrewed the cap. "Oh well."

"Out of the bottle, Viktor? Out of the bottle? How very Deutsch of you."

"Only four or five drops. I know your father counted on that running to the bottom. Otherwise he would have thrown it away."

"You'll be a boor with a party pin next thing I know."

A small but pleasant patch burned at the back of his throat, trickled toward his heart.

"I'd forgotten how good that was."

"And now you'll have to forget all over again."

"It doesn't matter," he said, capping the bottle, setting it in the bin beneath the sink. "Pavel's alive."

The night fears continued for weeks of nights after the false alarm so that Trn stayed on in the chair when his story was done though he knew the vigil was useless. He left on the lamp but this too was no stay against the tears that fell every night.

"Do you want to sleep with Mama again?"

"I know I should stay here."

"Why?"

"Because I am big now. This is where I sleep."

"You can be big tomorrow. Tonight you can sleep with Mama."

"I will try to stay here."

He took Trn's hand lying there on the blanket.

"I'm sorry you're scared, Aleks. You're a good boy." He leaned and kissed the hot forehead and Aleks reached and clasped his neck and Trn felt the tears scalding through his shirt.

"You're going to be all right, Aleks. I promise. Do you have your handkerchief in your pocket?"

He felt a nod, the crying choked.

"I'm not going to be all right"—the voice ridden with tears in every word—"I'm going to be dead."

"Come here, sweet boy. Why don't we sit for a while. It will be easier to breathe."

Aleks clung, was taken up, and Trn sat rocking him within his circled arms.

"What can we do?" Trn said.

"I don't know. I used to have enough pictures in my mind to keep the black away. But now I don't. I don't know why. Now when I squeeze my eyes everything leaves me in the dark. I don't want to see only night forever."

"I know, Aleks. I know. I saw the same thing when I was a boy."

"What did you do?"

"I tried very hard to tell myself to think of other things."

"I try but I can't find a way." Another sob clotted in his throat. "I don't want to be under a stone."

"Sweet boy. Sweet boy. I love you so much."

Aleks stammered out something that hardened on his tongue.

"What is it, darling?"

"I'm scared of something more."

"What is it?"

"I don't want you to die."

"I won't die for a very long time."

"But when you die I won't see you anymore. And then I'll die."

They had stopped rocking. He sat Aleks up in his arms.

"Do you remember the time we talked about the parts of light? The time we held the crystal to the window? We didn't know the colors were there but they were held in the light all the time, present in the light even before it struck the glass. They spread across the wall, remember, and you put in your hand and turned it to the colors of the rainbow? And remember we said there are other colors in the spectrum beyond even those, more colors we can't see. Infrared and ultraviolet, remember? Some people believe in a world like that beyond the one we can see."

He took the handkerchief from the boy's pocket and dried the boy's eyes, his brow.

"In that world we'll be together and it won't be so dark as we fear. It's waiting for us now."

"That's what Mama says."

"Yes, that's right."

"Can it really be like that?"

"It could be that and more."

The boy collapsed against him, his thin arms tightening.

"I love you, sweet boy."

Trn kissed his brow and ears and nape and held him close and when Aleks looked up Trn could see by the dim lamp he was smiling under his tears. They held on and Trn rocked him and kissed his cheek where he felt the boy's smile still blooming.

"Do you think you can sleep now?"

"I will try. Will you stay here?"

"I will stay right here beside you."

He slumped in the chair, catching yawns in his hands, eyes tearing from weariness. The clock chimed the hour and ticked round and chimed again. He watched the boy's face soften under the solitary light, shadows cast past the eyes by long lashes. He reached and laid his hand on the boy's chest, on the ache of a heart in a heartless world. On the agony of being sane in the asylum. When the boy drew breaths deep with silent dreams Trn rose and washed his face, the door shut, the slow water in the sink the only sound. He raised his eyes over the towel and stared at the face masked in the mirror, the eyes of the swindler. He dried them too. Add that to your manifold sins. A liar along with the rest. Then he sighed and went back and sat with the boy in the dark another hour longer.

When Pavel stood to shake hands his wrist bone jutted sharply from his sleeve. The skin sank between the shafts of bone in his hand and Trn circled them gently in both his hands, leaned and held Pavel's shoulder too, also thinned to bone. But his voice was strong as always.

"There were a few times when I didn't think I'd see you again," Pavel said.

Anamaria clenched a fist at her lips and left the room.

"Close the door, will you, Viktor?"

They sat. He tried not to look at the hands, the ankle bones above the slippers, the hollowed face of shadows. But Pavel raised his eyes from their caves and Trn smiled again.

"What can I do for you, Pavel?"

"Do you cook a good soup? All I can have for now is broth or soup and Anamaria can't make either. She always scorches it." It was not a skeleton's hand grazing the face of a skull but it was nearly so. What stayed behind was a narrowed smile. "I'm not hungry anyway."

"Alena makes that wonderful chicken soup, you know. I'll try to bring you some."

"I remember it. And beef too."

"If only there were beef." Trn shrugged. "If only there were chicken."

"Just wave a chicken bone over the hot water," Pavel said. He closed his eyes, the smile going to sleep. Then he said, "I cannot remember the taste of beef. Can you? I try but my tongue doesn't water. I can't even recall the smell of it."

"One day not long ago I walked past the Grand Hotel just as an SS officer came out with the most wonderful warmth circling him and suddenly I could feel the meat on my teeth, my molars closing slowly through it and the juice on my tongue. But now it's gone again."

"You'll have to walk me past the Grand Hotel sometime. We'll mill about till the SS leave."

"I'd like nothing better."

"You must be running short of amusements," Pavel said.

"I'm afraid we all are."

"Except SS officers."

"Even the SS may well have fewer amusements than they once did."

"You can make an omelet of blood," Pavel said. "Did you know that? Cow's blood. It scrambles like eggs."

His eyes went shut again, blessed by long fingers of bone. After a few moments they opened with his weak smile and he said, "If only there were blood." The hands fell to stroke the cords in his neck and then pulled at the robe to cover the well behind the collarbone.

Trn said, "What was it like, Pavel?"

"Viktor, Dante could not have imagined these pits." He shook his head. "But in the end the Germans are the true poets of hell. When I used to go to Germany, to report from there, you know, they were a sober, friendly people. In Dresden in my cracked German I could ask for directions and the old men would smile and point the way. But these people." He shook his head again. "There's nothing human left. It's just animal hatred, that's all there is, a cruel joy in raising pain. I knew from the beginning that a special hell was waiting. On the judge's bench in the castle there sat a miniature wooden gallows like a toy that jumped each time he struck his gavel. Bang and the gallows jumped on the bench and the little noose swung and the man was led out and then it was my turn. Bang and I was taken out. Thirty seconds. My trial lasted thirty seconds."

"You're out of it, Pavel. You're home."

"For now. I know I'm being watched." From the depths of that brow he looked out. "That's why I told Anamaria to tell you not to come. They'll know. You'll go on the list."

"I suspect I'm already on some list. From the university."

"But you haven't had any problems."

"No more than anyone else."

Pavel nodded, his tight lips together.

"Anamaria thinks I'm responsible for your arrest."

The bird's chest rose inside the robe, subsided. "I know. I apologize for her. I think she will stop now." He shrugged. "But what can we do? The man is the head of the household but the wife is the neck. Sometimes the pain in the neck. Still we turn when the neck says turn."

"What will you do now?"

"Eventually I believe I can go back to the paper. Flower shows and Hitler Youth choruses. If they don't shut it down entirely. Which will come eventually."

The mantel clock struck suddenly one, two, three and Pavel jerked at each chime. He laughed and the clock ticked on towards another long minute.

"That goddamn thing. I'm going to pull the fucking pendulum."

The smile went away and his thin fingers brushed the robe over his square kneebone.

"Dear old Viktor. You always were one for companionable silences."

"They seem the best sort of silences to have."

"At any rate they're much better than the noises I'm accustomed to."

Trn let the clock run on and then clapped his hands on his knees and rose.

"You need your rest."

"Do you remember in the gymnazium when we dodged down into the cellar to escape class?"

"Especially geometry."

"Remember those rusted pipes? They're still there, the same dust and cobwebs, the same gray walls. But now they're spattered brown with blood. They shackle and hang you naked by the wrists from the pipes so you can't rest between the lashings. You get no peace there. They would gather us in the refectory before executions and we all knew this so they used it to their advantage. They make leverage of everything. So they would file a group of us in just to scare us. The first time I shat my pants. There where we used to eat, remember those benches and tables? Sausage and cabbage soup on cold noons. I shat right there and it flowed down my pants legs to the floor."

"You're out, Pavel. You're right here now, in your old robe, sitting on your own couch."

"Do you know what station the trains come to that carry prisoners to Buchenwald?"

Trn shook his head.

"Weimar. Of course when I saw that sign at the platform how could I not think of Goethe. And then of something he said, something like, 'There is no crime of which I cannot conceive myself guilty.' That's right, isn't it?"

"That's right."

"The Goethe oak is there, right by a barracks. Where he wrote *Walpurgisnacht*."

"Maybe you can sleep, Pavel."

"One man was already dead in the wagon when the train bumped and stopped. They beat him so he bled to death."

He suddenly looked up at Trn.

"And Viktor. You can put that hundred crown note back into your pocket."

Trn frowned. "I'm afraid I don't understand."

"Yes you do. The hundred crown note you put between the cushions as you sat."

Trn held out open hands.

"I saw. Anamaria told me about the stuffed chair in the sitting room that spawns money by the hundred. Czech furniture is well made but it's not capable of immaculate conception. So. You need to take your money with you, Viktor. Anamaria's family helps us and will go on helping us. The journalists have a fund I can draw from too, until I go back to the paper."

"Let's tell Jakub to find a book on engineering. How is he?"

"He's gone out." The hand of bones dismissed the window. "I told him to go. He's been against my ribs since I got home. We're both suffocating, and Anamaria on top of us."

"He's a good boy."

"He is. But he's changed."

"He's grown."

"He's been affected. He'll never be the same. The time was too long and his age too important for it not to have damaged him." The deep eyes stared into a corner. "I know none of us will ever be the same but when it's yours it makes a bigger difference."

"It makes all the difference in the world." He leaned to touch Pavel's shoulder. "You rest. I'll come again."

"See that you do. Now don't change the subject and take your money."

"I have no idea what you're talking about," and he shut the door behind him before Pavel could wince and rise.

The tram stood on the rails on the short street outside the city hall, a bouquet of browning flowers tied over the blinkered headlamp, swags of something green tacked at intervals round its roof over the white V replicated down the windows. The crowd like a cork stoppered the Gothic portal to the magistrate's office so they could behold the couple and their witnesses coming down the passage, the shying couple caught fast inside the phosphor flash of the camera, the chatter of celebration, a cheer from the party as they kiss. The bride smiles at the groom and pecks him again, at the jaw. Another flash, another cheer. A handsome pair, shielding their eyes, posing once more. They pause on the tram steps to wave, the driver clangs and off they ride toward the honeymoon, smiling now to wave through the rear window, two boys in short pants giving chase, their black ties flying over their shoulders in the wake of the tram. The last festivity, the last festoon, the crowd dropping their hands almost as a body, almost sagging as one. The party dispersed, couples and families and solitaries taking their separate ways down different lanes.

He didn't know when the hiring of trams had become popular but it was the fashion now, the wedding party singing among the benches from church to city hall, speeches perhaps, toasts along the way. Once they were gone he went into the street himself, past the ancient portal, the passage dark as the Middle Ages from which brides and grooms for six hundred years had emerged into their coupled life, as he had done. The same white petals curled on the pavement, strewn and bruised. A printed invitation with a footprint. On the stone bench chiselled from a block of the building a book lay closed, dark blue, a golden sword standing on the cover. The slap of soles came running and he looked up at a voice calling back two boys with a caution about the state of their shoes and they went sprinting away down the cobbles, ties over their shoulders. He sat beside the book, opened it. Presented on the occasion of the celebration of your union. A personal gift for each joyous couple in the Dritte Reich. His tinted portrait gazed there as the frontispiece, imperious, protected behind a tissue of onionskin paper, the indomitable blue eyes with black centers, the tramp's mustache. Steps came echoing down the passage and Trn opened his case and thrust the book inside, striding on as if he'd never stopped.

"How is Jakub?"

Pavel shrugged. "I think he may be better."

On the couch beside him the newspaper lay open under his hand to the death columns.

"And Anamaria looks well."

"She's becoming accustomed to my presence. At first it wasn't so easy. My things on the floor again. My hair clinging to the soap. At least the lice have departed." Pavel lifted a brief smile. "But I'm becoming familiar to her."

"And are you becoming accustomed to the world?"

"I am stronger. As you can see. I must have added three or four kilos. But it feels very strange to be starting at the paper again. We watch one another. I know I can tell you these things in confidence. They watch me and I watch them and the Germans watch us all. They wonder how I came to be released, I wonder what they're thinking when they won't look me in the eye. So I'm making new friends, away from the paper."

"I'm sorry."

"We live in a time that makes cowards by the millions. I was thinking the other day, of a line you told me once. An American you'd read. 'Man is a god in ruins.'"

"Emerson."

"And I was wondering. If man is a god in ruins what is a man in ruins?"

"Just a man."

Pavel shrugged. Trn stared down at the carpet.

"But things change. This too won't go on forever. Even the war," Pavel said. "Look." He lifted the page with its columns. "This is just the names of those who enlisted from the Protectorate. If we had a paper from Frankfurt or Berlin imagine how much more ink it would take to enshrine all the blood. And this doesn't include the casualties from air raids. Those they won't release unless Goebbels thinks he can lever some spiritual advantage out of the rubble, like he did with Stalingrad."

Trn settled back, hands clasped.

"And when the war gets close," Pavel said, "when it arrives, there will be an uprising. The people will rise up." He looked at Trn. "You don't believe it?"

"As I've said before, I do believe. To what depths will they rise though? That concerns me."

"You're being a cynic again."

"The cynics were looking for wisdom. So I'm not really a cynic. I'm a historian looking at human nature and its past. When the war approaches it will bring with it greater chaos than any of us here has witnessed. And in that convulsion what savagery will erupt? History gives me reason to worry."

Pavel waved his hand. "Don't speak to me of history. We are becoming history. We ourselves are history. You won't help the Germans but you won't hinder them either. Is there nobility in that? Is that an honorable course?"

Trn sighed. "It is neither honorable nor noble."

"What is it then?"

"It is my course. The one I have chosen."

"Because you think it the safest way."

"For now, yes."

"So you're choosing your own safety over your country's future."

"Not solely my own." Trn opened his hands. "That I live in this time or place is historical accident. Had an ancestor moved west instead of east."

"I know all of that." Pavel's fist came down on the paper beside him and the paper rattled and crumpled. "Had a diplomat's pencil shifted slightly on the map, then you'd be someone else living somewhere else with another mind entirely."

"Yes," Trn said. "And you would be another speaking to me there of my allegiance to a different flag, a different set of strangers. We might well be speaking German in that conversation, have Gott mit uns on our belt buckles. Our names might well be in one of those columns in that newspaper. So given the contingencies how logical is the patriot's position?"

"Since we don't live in contingencies but in a world of right and wrong it's a position clearly more logical than yours. There are plenty of patriots out there with guns and belt buckles ready to slaughter everyone you know. Without hesitation. The only logic that exists now is to kill Germans before they kill us. I hope you're not going to say that their reasoning is sounder than mine."

"It sounds bloodthirsty. Like the most murderous universe imaginable."

"It's not imaginable, Viktor. It exists. It's here. And I say then let's murder the murderers before they come to the door."

"I understand."

"You understand everything so well but can you take that understanding comfortably to the grave?"

"I'll take a great many things to the grave, I suppose. A great many regrets." He glanced at Pavel's face drawn into deep lines, dropped his eyes again. "I don't always feel this way."

"But you think it was bloodthirsty to kill Heydrich."

"I think it took tremendous courage. I try to feel the muscles of those men on that bend in the road waiting for the car to slow, their hands tensed but trembling all the same."

"They did no more than their duty. The butcher was going to go on slaughtering till he himself was slaughtered."

"And then the assistant butchers took up his blades and went on slaughtering with a vengeance."

"Then we'll have to slaughter them too."

"They're the only ones with knives," Trn said.

"Not the only ones." Pavel looked out the window as if expecting more than light to pass through the curtains. "You have an answer for everything except the only question that matters. What are we going to do about the horror we find ourselves in?"

Trn sat forward. He pressed his palms together, watched his joined hands. The clock began to chime and Pavel set his stare to Trn, the wrinkles radiating from the eyes till Trn breathed deeply and looked back into his hands.

"I am thinking," Trn said slowly, "of another horror. The slave ships that sailed with their cargo in irons from the coasts of Africa to the new world. The ships were always surrounded by sharks drawn to the filth thrown overboard but mostly by the bodies of the dead put over the side, captives and crew, so these sharks would follow all the way across the Atlantic where they would be joined by sharks from the other shore. New world sharks. The captains of these slavers cultivated sharks, they wanted them in their wakes because they became a force of terror, as you can imagine, the boiling of the red water the moment a body broke the surface. So captains deliberately baited these sharks, not just with the dead but the living. There are accounts of live Africans being roped and lowered into the water as examples to the remainder, the bodies hauled aboard only torsos, blood and bowels still streaming below the ribcage. To enforce discipline, to curb any impulse toward insurrection."

"And yet," Pavel said, "there were insurrections still."

"True. With great bloodshed and almost none with success."

"That was always your talent," Pavel said.

"What talent?"

"The talent of the historian. To drag up the past from its forgotten and stinking grave and put the gore on display so it paralyzes the future. I think that's why you're paralyzed. Your mind is stocked with so many dead yesterdays your eyes aren't able to see the day after tomorrow. For you, to accept slavery would be better. To let the sharks win."

"There's another way. Not to cooperate, not to be consolidated. To keep the mind out of bondage."

Under a heavy breath Pavel muttered, "Goddamnit, Viktor," and shook his head.

"The war is coming here, Pavel, just as you say. And when it passes over us there will be peace again. Some kind of peace in the aftermath. It's a matter of time."

Pavel flung up his gray and bony hands and said, "I've heard this counselor of patience before, longing for peace but unwilling to go to war for it. We're to let others do our fighting for us. Let someone else die to liberate us. I won't accept that. We ourselves must make sure that the conquest isn't worth it to the conqueror."

"I'm not choosing for anyone else, Pavel. I'm choosing only for myself."

"And I'm choosing too, Viktor. Have already chosen."

Trn's eyes passed over him, gazed at the newspaper lying with a tear across the print.

"What about Jakub, Pavel, and what about Anamaria? What will they do if the worst happens?"

"What is the worst, Viktor? As the only person in the room who's been among the sharks, I ask you, what is the worst? I have been down to those depths and I have been given another chance that no one should ever see that dark again. It is a great gift and I will not waste it."

Trn looked back into the face hewn to its bones.

"I hope you will be careful, Pavel. For yourself and for Jakub."

"There's no such thing as care anymore, Viktor. We must act or not act. That is the only choice that exists now."

Trn raised his cuff though the clock ticked there on the mantel. "I should go, Pavel. Let you rest. Please keep well."

Pavel stood to take his hand, one quick wrench of the wrist as hard as his fixed eyes.

From his case he took the book and squared it on the table, traced out with his finger the sword embossed on the cover in the cold morning light falling through the window.

At the Front a man may die, but the deserter must die.

I was then a soldier and did not wish to meddle in politics.

He didn't begin at the beginning. His eyes fell where they would, caught on snags of words.

This motley of Czechs, Poles, Hungarians, Ruthenians, Serbs and Croats, etc., and always that bacillus which is the solvent of human society here and there and everywhere—the whole spectacle was repugnant to me.

Even if we cannot conquer we shall drag the rest of the world into destruction with us.

Toward the end he found a passage he read over twice. He looked out the window before he read it again.

The lives of a million German soldiers lost at the Front would have been saved if twelve to fifteen thousand of these Hebrew corrupters of the people had been held under poison gas.

He went back to the portrait, lifted the onionskin. What dust was so malign it could distort the eye, alter its tension so that every alien thing focused on the retina loomed up a monster? But the eyes were only the nerves the brain reached out to figure the world.

However he began he became a maker of widows. Fathered a million orphans. It wasn't gassing at the front that poisoned those eyes.

The door swung open and Alena came in saying, "Hadn't you better leave now?"

He closed the book.

"I have a few minutes."

"What is that?"

"I found it."

"Where?"

She lifted it to look at the spine.

"You're not, Viktor. *Mein Kampf?*"

"I just began looking it over."

"Why? Why in the world would you read this? I can't believe you would bring it into the house."

"To know one's enemy is a positive good."

"That may sound very wise but it's just reading all the same."

"Yes, it's just reading." He stood, looked at his watch. "So nothing to worry about." He opened a hand toward the book.

"Where did you get it?"

"I found it on a bench at the city hall. Apparently a couple left it behind after signing the registry."

"We don't have money for books."

"You can look at the frontispiece and read the stamp."

She scowled, dropped it on the table. "We can always burn it when the coal runs out. Which won't be long without pupils." She turned back to the kitchen. "And don't let Aleks see that. I don't want him to know there are such things here in this house."

Through the dim evening he heard the tapping ahead and nearing it made out on the sidewalk the blind man of the neighborhood all in black caning his way along. The taps halted as Trn came close and the man hooked the cane over his arm and felt at his wrist, fingered the face of a crystalless watch as Trn passed, then took up the cane and tapped his way more hurriedly. Trn consulted his own watch and smiled to think that the blind too kept their appointment with the BBC, smiled to think of the blind foot keeping rhythm with the jazz interspersed among the reports.

As he let the black curtain fall back across the door several men looked up, among them Pavel sitting at the table in the corner just where the note had said, the note he had destroyed with a match in Miroslav's ashtray. The man in the workman's cap beside Pavel he didn't know nor the man across the table who pointed a black beard toward him as he approached through the cirrus of smoke layered out in the room.

"Speak of Viktor and here he is. Sit down. This is Silvestr. Radek."

"Good evening."

They shook hands among the glasses rimed with foam and Pavel raised four fingers toward the barman. They looked at the varnished planks of the table till the beer arrived and they centered their glasses to salute together.

"Na zdraví."

Pavel tipped his well back and leaned on his elbows after.

Trn said, "You're looking fit."

"What?"

"You look well."

"Nothing better than Czech beer to heal the sick or raise the dead."

The man in the cap said, "I'll drink to that," and did.

The other man grinned in his beard and said, "It is a gift from God. It gives us strength and courage."

Pavel said, "We'll need both."

The din went round them through the smoke. Not one table untaken, men in coats leaning on the wall, lifting glasses of Friday beer, wiping away the foam and the fatigue of another week with the backs of their hands. The man in the cap said, "So. What a pity they won't let that third district team play the Germans. They could teach them how to play hockey."

"Never happen," the bearded man said. "The supermen won't risk it."

A waiter in a filthy apron set a tray of empty glasses among them and leaned to murmur. The bearded one glared at the paper tacked to the wall.

POLITISCHE GESPRACHE VERBOTEN.
POLITICKÉ ROZHOVORY ZAKÁZANÝ.

"How is Jakub?"

"He's well, Viktor. Thank you."

"And Anamaria?"

The cinder at the end of Pavel's cigarette brightened to orange and the smoke he blew bounded off the table and rose among them.

"She's well too."

"How is the newspaper?"

Pavel's shoulder shrugged up his mouth into a mold between a frown and a sneer.

Trn nodded, drank. The one with the beard said, "He certainly asks enough questions." Under his cap the one called Silvestr watched his beer. The man in the apron came and adjusted the blanket over their window. Even the bow of strings at his back was stained.

"We're minding the sign," Radek said. "But when did hockey become politics?"

The man in the apron looked around the room and said, "Shut up," and Radek's hands twisted his empty glass round and round.

Silvestr tipped back his cap and said, "Since we can't speak of hockey I wonder if it is permitted to speak of football."

"So long as you give the fucking Hitler salute," Radek said.

"Quiet, Radko."

"So what is this business?" Trn said.

The empty glass stopped twisting.

"Viktor," Pavel said as they met at the eyes. "Come with me for a moment."

The other two also stood but Pavel said, "Silvestr, you watch," and Silvestr sat again.

At the back they passed through a curtained arch and Radek pushed heavily against a door that seemed at first nailed in its frame. Pavel entered, Trn followed, then Radek who kicked open the stalls to glare at the empty toilets. Pavel spread his legs at the wall and let his water ring in the lead trough. Radek propped himself against the door.

"You sure he can be trusted?"

"I've known Viktor since I could walk," Pavel said over his shoulder. "And I walked early." He buttoned his trousers, turned. "He's one of us. We come from the same village in Podkarpatská Rus, I told you. And then when he moved to the city I found him again at the gymnazium. We're almost brothers. Isn't that right, Viktor?"

Radek folded his arms, his brows gathered dark as his beard.

"Brothers don't mean much these days. Look at the Slovaks."

"His father was a hero in the war, Radek."

"Wrong war," Radek said, "wrong side."

"So what's this about, Pavel?"

"It's about winning the war, Viktor. Czechs helping to win this war we're in."

Pavel's lips went thin when a thud came at the door. Radek shifted and another heave brought in nearly falling a man with grizzled jaw, a creased brown jacket so large that only his fingertips emerged from the sleeves. He looked round and nodded up at each of them and apologized as he backed away.

"Sir," Pavel said and glanced at Radek, who caught the man by the shoulder. "We were just leaving, sir." The man entered a stall, coughed.

Radek shoved at the rear wall until a door without a handle gave onto the night. Pavel looked back at Trn and the three of them went into a black alley, into a cold mist. Radek walked several steps down the alley and Pavel said, "That's one reason we like this place so much," and Radek scanned the other direction.

Crates began to take their cubic shape from the dark and their three breaths assumed a density of mist different from the night. Radek sat on a stack of crates that cracked beneath him and his breath smoked out and cursed the crates in particular and the world generally as he scrambled to stand again.

Pavel laughed into his own breath steaming down his nose. "See, Viktor. We're not such a bad lot."

"I never said you were."

"But I see the distance in your eyes. The worry. The reluctance."

Trn shook his head.

"We need an observer, Viktor. Someone with a sharp mind who can distinguish the significant from the inconsequential. It's more difficult than it may sound."

"Observe what?"

"Movements. Trains. Which units barrack where, transports of munitions. You can imagine the type of information. We would give you the details."

"And where are these observations to be made?"

"You travel north of the city five days a week. The east-west rail passes within three kilometers of your son's school. So you know the place. You'd have to cross a ridge to get where we need you to go. From a second ridge with field glasses you could command the line."

"And you'd supply the glasses."

"Of course. And a bicycle."

"These trains run mostly at night."

"And this would be a duty you'd assume only occasionally, in rotation. It would be infrequent. There are also a number of buildings near your son's school where troops are quartered, sometimes on leave, sometimes as temporary billets. You could walk past some of those buildings naturally enough or go into a shop, for instance, or a restaurant, and note the designation of those soldiers, any unit markings. We will teach you what to look for. It would be the work of a few seconds for someone with your memory."

The alley smelled of stale urine, old beer, a vegetable rotting to dirt again.

"You said he was a patriot," Radek said, "a complete Czech."

"He is. I'm certain of it."

The alley seemed to grow darker as if a light had been put out somewhere.

"I will have to think about this, Pavel."

Behind his knuckles Radek whispered at Pavel's shoulder. Pavel nodded and went on.

"I knew you would, Viktor. But Viktor, don't think too long. The whole time we are thinking the war is going on all the same without us. And the war is killing people. Your people."

"These observations will stop that?"

"They will serve to stop it eventually. Don't you believe in hastening the end of the war?"

"I'm going to leave now, Pavel."

"Let me ask you this, Viktor. If you were to walk by a house on fire and spy a man, a woman in the house, a child crying for help, wouldn't you try to rescue them?"

"I believe that I would wish to try to rescue them."

"So do I, Viktor. So do I. And now your whole country is aflame and all your countrymen cry out for you to save them. I believe you will listen to their cries."

The other man was also staring him down.

"I know conscience is important to you, Viktor. This is the path for you to become part of the conscience of the country. Your country."

"I must go home now, Pavel. Thank you for the beer."

A hand when he passed took Trn's arm with fingers sharp as bone. "Then when will I hear from you?"

"I don't know. I don't know that either." He looked from Pavel's eyes to his hand and the fingers released him.

"Sir? Sir."

Trn stopped.

"We will be watching you, sir. Don't speak to anyone of what has been said here. We have been watching already."

Trn walked on across the cobbles rounding his worn soles. He looked back into the alley and said, "Give my love to Anamaria and Jakub," but no one responded. He took a crooked course home, head down, hands in pockets. He paused under the dark of a streetlamp and waited and went a long way out before coming right again. The puddles in the gutters were pricked with starlight now, one blotted with the shadow of a man's head and shoulders. He spat at the dark face reflected there and walked on.

T he man behind him in line propped on the wall, raised his shoe to examine the sole. The two women before him mumbled through close lips. "I heard it must be over in the spring—it was supposed to end this spring—or the year before—that's what Benes always says—but they have these Wunderwaffe." They glanced over their shoulders and Trn took out the paperwork from his breast pocket again. It seemed in order. Teetering on one foot the man checked his other sole, then doffed his hat and wiped a handkerchief over his bald head.

Two order police sauntered past, the long coat of one swaying over the tops of his tall boots, the other so well fed he stretched the buttons of his tunic. The women became quiet. The fat policeman stopped, rocked on his boots, eyed the crowd in line. The black gun slanted across his belly.

They walked on and a city policeman in black met them, ex-changed nods and came on down the length of the line. He told a woman to move her baby carriage to clear the sidewalk. She looked at him, his domed black hat, his round black eyes, complied. A truck wheezed past, the charcoal tank on top belching black smoke high through a pipe, all of which Aleks would have liked and which Trn would have to remember to tell him.

In the sky he could see no sun. Sudden cries came from the car-riage and the woman, she looked not much more than a girl, bent and lifted aside the veil, knelt low toward the child, and as suddenly another wail bore up from the siren on the pole at the corner and overcame the baby's cries. Some broke immediately, hands on their hats, coats flying open in the dash across the street, vaulting the island where those in the tram queue joined the race. A tram halted in the middle of the street and its passengers came tripping out the folding doors followed by the driver in his cap. Then came the second wave, understanding the cry more slowly, and then the stragglers, women tottering on high heels, the old in couples or alone, stooped on crooked knees, children by the hand, the scurrying woman with the carriage bumping over the curbstone. The line reformed under the glaring windows of the girls' school, brick and half a block long and three stories tall.

But a policeman with the armband of the Luftschutzraum warden came up the steps and waved them away. Trn scanned the white sky for planes but saw none, no throb he could hear over the sirens. A little girl had a finger in each ear, eyes shut tight, her mother tugging at her elbow as the policeman made a megaphone of his hands. "It's full. Go to Viktoriastrasse, the shelter on Viktoriastrasse," and they broke again, two long blocks the other way, the stamp of feet under the wail, the slap of Trn's own rotten soles on the road, the ache thrumming along his foot bones.

Down the stairwell the steps divided left and right. Luftschutzraum and Nichtarien Luftschutzraum. A warden eyed him. How many non-Aryans are left? he wanted to ask. Which way for Slavs? He heard a cry from behind and looked back. The woman gripped two fists on the bar of the carriage and the Ordnungspolizei in his long coat had a fist between hers. She was saying, "But someone will steal it," and the policeman was shaking his head nein.

Trn went back, spoke to the policeman. "Ja ja, verstehe," the policeman said loudly. "Verboten."

"It's not permitted," Trn said to the woman, "but there are a dozen others here, you can see. I'm sure it will be safe."

"It belongs to my sister-in-law."

For the first time he looked at her face, smoothed with light freckles, red hair curling from her black hat.

"I'm sure your sister-in-law would want you to leave it," and then the thudding began. "That's the antiaircraft," Trn said. "I know you want to get your baby below." The woman gathered the white bundle onto her shoulder and went ahead of Trn down the steps. When she stumbled once he took her elbow, gently, a guide down, and she glanced up at him over the blanket.

A tremor different in kind and degree tunneled under the concrete and Trn knew he'd felt his first detonations. He sensed it was south but burrowed here he might have lost direction. They would have had the radio on. Miroslav would have. They would have heard the sirens. By his watch he tried to time the intervals but another tremor and another rolled beneath their feet and finally there were no intervals. He closed his eyes in the dim light to feel the explosions. South would make sense, the station, seven or eight kilometers from the flat. Alena would march them to the shelter. Eight kilometers on a straight line probably. The naked bulbs strung along the ceiling with braided wire swayed each at a different point in its arc. He was between the station and the flat so he'd know if they passed over. The woman looked up at the ceiling, at him.

"What's that hollow sound there?"

"That's the flak again. Firing at the bombers. It sounds different down here."

"My first raid," she said. "Warnings but never a raid."

"Mine too." Trn smiled a little. "Quite an exercise, isn't it?"

"I hope no one takes that carriage."

"I think everyone is too distressed to worry over a carriage now. Even the thieves are underground."

"But they could sell it on the black market. It would get a good price."

Trn nodded at her eyes and she whispered, "My sister-in-law bought it on the black market. It's very hard to find carriages now." Then she stared wider. "You don't think it will be blown up, do you?"

One string of bulbs along the far wall pulsed and faded to orange coils and went dead.

"Wouldn't you like to sit? This may last some time."

"There aren't any benches?"

"No. I'm afraid you'd have to take the floor."

Then to a general gasp all the bulbs failed. Through his coat sleeve he felt a sudden clutch at his arm.

"It's all right." He lowered his head, his voice. "It's all right."

A narrow ray lanced the dark, swept the low ceiling and over them and on, the warden's flashlight, making a crescent profile of her face. The hand left him.

"How can you be sure it will be all right?"

"It's perfectly natural for the power to fail in a raid. They cut it, you know, to forestall fires. It's a good sign."

"But what about the ventilation?"

"That's a good question." He surveyed the concrete beams shifting their shadows in the glancing light. "It must be run by generator."

"Do you really know this or are you only saying these things to me?"

He could smell her hair, breathe again from the wisps of it, its copper haloed in the fugitive light, sweet with soap and tinged with smoke.

"It always comes back, doesn't it? I'm sure you've lost your lights at home but they always come back. It doesn't stay off forever."

The baby gurgled and she whispered into the blanket. The solid floor shook again in waves matched to a series of concussions. He counted six but there might have been more. Maybe in the shelter Aleks wouldn't feel them on the other side of their hill.

"That's another one," she said.

"Yes but it's far and moving away. Did you notice how slight that was compared to the one before?"

A match sparked against the wall and the warden's light leaped toward it. "Nicht rauchen, nicht rauchen!" The man's haggard face behind the flame explained that he was only looking for his papers, he was worried he'd lost them, and the warden said to put out the match immediately, there might be gas.

"What are you thinking?" Trn whispered.

"What?"

"Your eyes are elsewhere."

"I hope my family is well."

"I'm sure they're well. I worry about mine too but I'm sure they're fine."

"My brother had to take my sister-in-law to the doctor. And my mother is at home. She is supposed to be at home." The baby gurgled toward a whimper and she shifted the bundle higher on her shoulder, began to bounce the baby on her bobbing arm. "Can you tell where the bombing is?"

"There seems to be a lull," he said, head tilted. "The first wave must have passed. I would say south of here, from the concussions. The rifle and pistol works probably, or the rail lines. The marshalling yards south of the station. That may be it."

She cast her eyes over the dark ceiling again.

"My mother is alone."

"I'm sure your mother is in her cellar right now wondering about you and look, here you are perfectly safe, just like her."

"The cellar in our building is flooded. But she goes to the next building. The Sochorovi are her cousins. They've been her neighbors a long time."

"Then she's sitting with the Sochorovi right now in a cellar far away from any bombers. Perhaps she won't even be able to hear them. What district does she live in?"

"In Nove Sady."

Trn nodded.

"But that's near the station."

"That's true."

"But you said the rail lines. We can almost see the station from our flat."

"But the explosions seem to be far south of here. Don't you think? Well beyond Wilson Station. The marshalling yard's still some distance south from there."

She didn't say anything but she was looking up at him.

"I'm sure she's fine."

"We're not supposed to say Wilson Station anymore."

"I guess it was awfully shortsighted of us to name so many places after an American president. I always forget. Will you forgive me?"

"But if a German should hear."

"Then I'll keep my voice down." The lights pulsed feebly and came up and he saw she was smiling in the orange light.

"There," he said. "Right on schedule."

"You're very positive."

"It runs in the family. I inherited it from my father."

"I don't see how you can be so certain. I don't know anyone who's an optimist anymore."

"Sometimes I'm not but today the company makes a difference."

"You don't even know my name."

"True. But as an optimist I look forward to that changing. I'm Viktor."

She heaved the baby higher on her shoulder, held out her hand. The freckles moved to smile when she spoke, when her eyes smiled.

"Magda."

"The circumstances are most regrettable," Trn said, "but I'm pleased nevertheless."

She twisted to look into the blanket, her lip jutted, with smoothing hand settled the blanket. Her lower lip was slightly fuller than the other.

"He looks like a stout boy."

"He takes after my brother. He was also a fat baby."

She sighed and heaved him higher.

"You've been holding him a long time now. Why don't you let me take him for a moment? I know your muscles must be ready to cry."

Her eyes looked up into his. Not dark but gray, the color of some waters.

"I promise I'll be very careful."

"I cannot ask such a thing."

"But your back. He looks so heavy."

"You're certain?"

"I've held much heavier."

"You're certain you don't mind?"

He reached out his hands.

"I can be very gentle. Really."

She offered her shoulder and Trn carefully lifted the baby onto his chest, cradled him there. He pulled back the blanket from the bald head.

"Poor fellow. He's wet with sweat."

He looked down at the lipstick kiss light on the brow, the little lashes closed, the ripe cheeks. One hand came up and balled at the puckering lips. The first time he'd held him Aleks had had thirteen lashes on one lid and twelve on the other. Because he came early. They'll be on the bench now, Alena on one side and Miroslav the other, holding their thumbs, Aleks saying that does no good and impatient because of the American planes he's missing.

"What is this boy's name?"

"Viktor."

"Truly?"

"No. Jaroslav."

"So. I see you're an optimist too. Only optimists surrender to joking in air raid shelters. But he's really warm. Let's take the blanket down a little from his shoulders."

"I don't want him to get too cool."

"I think he'll be fine. It's close in here."

"And the smell."

She scowled around the orange dark, her nose wrinkled.

"What can you expect in a country of rationed soap?" he said.

She tugged up the blanket.

"When will this end?"

"Soon I'm sure. Wouldn't you like to find a place to sit? I'll follow you with Jaroslav."

"I've just cleaned my coat."

Her hair tossed copper lights. The smooth jaw traced its way to a gentle chin that lifted toward him again. He wouldn't look away.

"Thank you for your help."

"There's no need of thanks. This is what we all must do now. In dark times."

She pressed a palm to the baby's sleeping back, the mysterious hand, its finger without a ring. But she did not wear mourning.

"Do you have children?"

"I have a son. He's getting big now, he's nine, but I remember the days when he was like this. Not so big as this but he gained quickly, heavy as a sack of stones asleep against my chest. But he didn't sleep much and he was much more difficult than Mr. Jaroslav here. How old is he? Six months?"

"Five. Five months next week." She smiled. "He is a good boy. Very good."

"Soon it will be done and you can take him home out of all this."

"I'm afraid they'll be frantic for him. Do you think the doctor will have a shelter?"

She glanced back at his eyes.

"Oh." She shook her head. "No. My sister-in-law. Hana. He's not mine. He's my nephew. I'm only watching him while Jirka takes her to the doctor. Hana's not been feeling well really since the baby. I took half a day from work." She looked at him with a little smile that became a little laugh.

He laughed too.

"I'm sorry. Please excuse me. You are, so sweetly careful with him. I saw how you must love him."

She reached for the baby and Trn opened his arms as the bundle went back to her.

"I never put him down when Hana brings him." She pulled the blanket higher. "She and Mother say I'm spoiling him. They say he'll never learn to walk so long as I'm about."

The thunder fell again from a far horizon and trembled a long while. Her face disappeared to the eyes inside the blanket.

"They're all precious," Trn said, "and one day you'll have one of your own equally precious."

She didn't raise her eyes, didn't speak.

"Are you well, Magda? I'm sure it will be over soon. It can't last much longer."

When she nodded a tear tipped over to run toward the corner of her mouth. Another when she blinked. The blanket caught them and the strap of her bag fell to her elbow and she had to lift it back to her shoulder.

"I'm sorry," Trn said. "I say the most inappropriate things. I didn't intend to upset you."

He brought out his handkerchief, folded the best corner toward her.

"Excuse me," she whispered. The point of her chin rose when she swallowed. She put the handkerchief to the angle of one eye and examined it when she brought it away. "They say I'll not have children. Even one." She blinked. "Three doctors have said the same. But he's so dear."

All the lights went out again and no one gasped. A child cried, a little boy who wanted to go home please.

"Magda, I'm often very stupid in what I say. I apologize."

"I think that's why they let me take him so much, for a whole day at the time. So sometimes I can almost pretend he's mine."

The storm rumbled in from the horizon and collapsed overhead. A great weight exploded directly above and the dark they stood in shook and buckled their knees and the concrete groaned. When the warden flashed his light through the falling dust her hat was crumpled against his chest, the baby between them, Trn's arm round her shoulders, one hand on the baby's head. Six, seven, eight, he counted and then another series of eight.

"Hold me," she was saying and still saying when the explosions died and the dust kept raining, "hold me hold me," and he did.

Finally the bulbs glowed sickly pale swinging on their wires. She remained in his arms when they stopped swinging and the filaments glowed yellow. The people uncrouched and brought their arms down from their bent heads. Standing or sitting they all gazed at their portion of the ceiling. Babies were crying and one woman hobbled to the door and beat against the metal with both fists until the warden and a hushing man pulled her to the wall. Muffled between them Jaroslav was crying too through closed eyes. She cooed to him and hummed and sang at his cheek a lullaby Trn had never heard. The baby was quiet again when the all clear began to rise, faintly at first in the shelter where bodies uncrooked themselves, hands pressed low against the ache in the back. The lights came up a little more but their eyes were completely overwhelmed when the outer door grated open to a solid shaft of daylight. They climbed through motes that were carried up with them into the smell of burning smoke and ruptured sewers. He and she shuffled with them amid scattered voices, his hand cupping her elbow step by step, the sparse and sudden laughter from a few throats. A man clapped the back of the policeman so his round helmet jogged and the policeman smiled and then his brown teeth looked grim again. On the street you heard the sirens of the fire trucks and Trn stood still to sort them by quarter. Smoke spiraled to the north, a high and ascending column, but it was only a few blocks away, under the castle district. Magda found the carriage with the others, dusted the ash from its hood. Jaroslav arched and whimpered, stretched and began to kick when laid inside.

"He'll be very hungry now, I suspect," Trn said.

She looked around as if lost.

"What's wrong?"

"I don't know where to go. I wish I could call my mother."

"The telephones will probably be out now." Trn walked beside her as she began to push the carriage. "How will you get home?"

"I need to get him to Hana first. It's nearer. Jirka has a telephone, if it's working."

"Can you walk there? I doubt there will be trams or buses for a while."

"It's not far."

He looked north and she hesitated beside him.

"So. I will leave you. Be well, Magda. Jaroslav is very lucky in his choice of aunts."

Her eyes were still gleaming but it may have been the smoke.

"Thank you. For all your kindness." She rocked the handle of the carriage and Jaroslav was quiet again. "Ah. I almost forgot." The handkerchief was clutched between two fingers. "It has my mascara. I can wash it."

"You don't even have to say thanks, Magda. It's a small thing. Keep it, for the smoke on the way home."

She did not look away.

"Where do you work?"

"Where do I work? At the bandage factory. Not far from where we live. My mother and I."

"I think I know where that is. Perhaps someday I'll be in the neighborhood when your shift ends."

She squinted, her head tilting to one side. "Half past five," she said. "Most days at half past five."

He nodded. "Goodbye then, Magda."

"Goodbye."

"I'll do it soon," he called. "Otherwise you'll forget this day."

She shook her bright hair.

"I don't think I'll forget this day."

He lifted his hat when she looked back from the corner and then the carriage disappeared and then the girl with her copper hair.

The hot air burned. To the south smoke stirred with clouds on the move. He went on quickly and passed a small half-circle standing at the requisitions office. He made sure with a touch of his coat pocket of the application for a child's shoe voucher as one man pulled at the handle despite a paper scrawled in Czech and German that said the office was closed until further notice.

Two trams were stalled in different directions, both empty, ash layered on the roofs. Two automobiles raised clouds of dust from the road into the smoke and then an ambulance with its siren wailed by. The smell of running sewage grew stronger here. A clutch of people waited at a tram shelter and looked up the tracks and he hurried on. Not copper, no. Needles fallen from pines and dried in the sun after rain. That was nearer. Water streamed in the gutter to meet him before he could see the pumping trucks blocking the street. Policemen were motioning a crowd away but it didn't move, all their faces lifted to the burning façade of the girls' school. There was no smoke at all to the north toward home and Trn watched the two jets of water shoot into the shattered windows of the second floor overcome by the flames that seethed out. Something behind the brick wall collapsed in two stages, the second very loud, and the crowd backed away a few steps. Great sparks flew up inside the shaft of smoke. The jets moved on to other windows where the brick was blackened above the frames and the fire in the windows left behind leaped higher. Through the top story you could see smoke rising into the sky for the roof was gone.

A man beside him shifted his hands in his pockets.

"It's bad," the man said. "Even though they say the firemen came before the all clear."

"Now that the Americans are in Italy," Trn said, "I suppose we can expect much more of this."

"They say a bomb landed at the end of the building. They say it angled in and pierced the wall and hit the gas and started the fire."

Trn shook his head, looking on.

"I'm glad my daughters don't go to that school." The man took off his hat and fanned it before his face.

"Do you know how many were inside?"

"It came in at such an angle it hit the boilers," the man said. "Flooded the shelter in the basement." The man coughed into the tunnel of his hand. "They say it killed everyone inside. But they may have scalded to death before they burned."

When the Siberian highs descended from the east they freed the sky of all but blue and dropped the blood in the glass to minus fifteen or twenty or minus twenty-five. Seeing Aleks to school these mornings Trn felt the hairs in his nose stiffen with frost before he could cross the street, Aleks beside him wrapped like a bedouin. Twenty steps from the house a weird white patch blossomed on the dark scarf where his little mouth should breathe. At the top of the first hill he could see Aleks's hand in his but for all he could feel it might as well have been in another man's hand. By the time they reached the tram stop small tacks of ice through the backs of his gloves needled his fingers and hands. Thumbs suffered most, exiled from the others. Sharp iron spiked down the marrow into the last joint.

The tram rattled on its rails beside the river arrested in its course. Little concs of ice fell from the pines along the bank and lay white on the water frozen black. After the swaying carriage the trudge between the houses to the school and in the shoe room he helped Aleks with his wraps, boots, books. The boy whispered a goodbye and ran to the classroom. There was a stove in the classroom.

Coming away alone, flexing his fingers against the frigid sting, Trn skated through an alley of chestnuts, boggy ground where the ice lay in swells and troughs like a frozen sea. No satchel to carry, nothing live to grip. His shoes slipped and his arms wheeled for a balance he barely found and he wondered how Aleks would have laughed at such a sight. Walking uphill home he listened to the creak of snow compacted under his soles, his dead fists too thick and awkward for the pockets of his old coat. In a naked and solitary tree four doves perched. Gray backs and white breasts, cooing their short mourning, each on a different limb. He couldn't remember the last time he'd heard a dove's hollow moan. They seemed asleep and he stopped to watch. Gaunt-necked doves no longer plump. The winter's work or the war?

He wanted something for his hands to do besides hold up his gloves in a world so far below zero.

Beyond the mist snow blotted the gymnazium, the roof where all the pigeons were gone. A rumble approached through the muffled world and a truck churned and smoked over the ice, slid past him and bounded two tires over the curb. Two men from the cab clanged shovels from the bed and began to splash sand over the pavement. Trn saw the driver in the cab as he passed, newspaper propped on the steering wheel, the great nose thrust over the walrus mustache. Trn walked quickly on but he could hear the truck door groan, slam.

"Viktor. Viktor, that is you, isn't it?"

Trn stopped to look back.

"Viktor." His gloved hands out, Dolezal called like their offices were down the hall from one another again. "I haven't been to the library in a while."

"I haven't been in a long time myself."

"I don't suppose it matters. Do you really think they'll let us open again?"

"No. I don't."

"So. What are you doing with yourself?"

"I begin teaching in the new year. At the school in the valley. Latin. Only temporarily." He thrust his hands in his pockets. "Their teacher died suddenly."

"Where there's death there's hope." The walrus mustache smiled, lifting the glasses. Dolezal looked over his shoulder toward the truck.

"You can see what I'm doing. What the municipality tells me to do. Today it's drive these fellows about with the sand. Tomorrow it might be repair workers to the train station, show a new officer his quarters. Next week something else again. Find a billet for a whole battalion on furlough, I don't know. Mindless chores."

Across from the truck a woman stooped to set a basket on the sidewalk. A small dog leaped out on short legs, padded quick and brown over the hard ice to yellow the snow drifted against an unswept gatepost.

"You're wise enough," Trn said, "to be the one with the newspaper and not the shovel."

Dolezal's laugh smoked the air between them. "You always knew what to say, Viktor. My mother is sick, I had to take what there was." He shrugged, removed his glasses and circled a fold of his sweater over the lenses. The dog trotted across the street, hoisted and pissed the nearest tire of the truck. "You know what these times are."

"I'm sorry to hear it."

"But everyone's old mother gets sick, don't they. And we all have to take what there is. You and your Latin."

"It won't last. There's little enough call for dead languages these days."

Ice lengthened along the gray hairs under Dolezal's nostrils. The dog leaped back into the basket, the woman stooped for it, covered the dog with a cloth and set off slouching over the ice.

Dolezal sighed, pulled at his running nose, looked out over it and over the rims of his glasses.

"I know they could use a translator."

"Who?"

"You know who."

"Why not you?"

"My German's nowhere near as quick as yours. I couldn't reach their standards."

Trn looked down at his shoes flecked with dirty snow, shook his head at Dolezal's wet boots.

"I don't think I have standards anymore."

"You're sure? But what about Alena, and your boy? The money would be better than Latin lessons I'm sure. Miroslav still with you?"

"We're still with him. All home together. Same flat."

"Eventually they'll call up all males to dig snow. You know this?"

"I've heard."

"It's backbreaking work. Look at those two fellows there. A translator wouldn't have to do that. Or be called out to hammer on the railroad beds between here and Prague every time the line's sabotaged. Or haul stone block for that new trestle over the gorge. They may not exempt teachers."

"I know."

"And pay. More marks than schoolboy Latin."

"I'm sure anything would be better."

"So why don't you take it on? Come to the German House in the Zentrum and ask for the municipal office. Ask for me. They'll know where I am. And then they'd know I had something more than hair under my hat, if I brought in a translator with your—" Behind the glasses the black eyes consulted the wind edging round the cornices and blowing crystals of snow from the roofs. "With your precision. I'll introduce you." He tapped at Trn's shoulder. "These Germans know nothing about putting their proclamations into our old Czech."

"I'm afraid I have very little of everything these days, Dolezal. Especially precision. But I appreciate your thought."

"You'll think about it?"

"No but I appreciate it nevertheless."

"Ever the diplomat, Viktor. No wonder you were so popular in the department."

"And all this while I thought it was because I was married to the chair's daughter."

"Viktor. Viktor." Dolezal shook his head. "Tell Miroslav I said hello. He's well?"

"He's getting on."

"And your boy. How old is he now?"

"Aleks is above his mother's shoulder."

"So? That's good. You take home what I've said and reconsider." Dolezal offered his hand and Trn took it. "Just think now."

Again neither took off his gloves to shake bare hands.

1944

One morning late while Alena was out and Miroslav slept and Aleks yawned in school he took a blade from a packet of razors, wrapped a slip of paper over one end and taped it and in the hall fixed the blade between the wall and the lintel of the door to the sitting room. He stood at various points with the light on and the light off and saw that the paper blended with the wall. He'd need a second method if he couldn't reach this in time and since one from the kitchen would be missed he took the key from its nail in the larder and went down the stairs to the storage closet. He lifted and rejected what came to hand until almost in the dark he found a small knife rusted at the back of a shelf and tested the broken point against the skin of his palm. The short blade notched the shelf well enough when he ran its edge over the wood. The rust might even be an advantage.

He knew he'd already decided where to keep it and when he was upstairs again he took a length of sellotape and went to the bedroom and crouching at his headboard he stood the broken tip on the floor and bound the blade inside the wooden leg. He shifted the bedside table a little and lay supine on the mattress and rolled to reach and it was there. He lay prone and on each side and each time he sprung the haft met his fingers. If the knock came in the night, if his name were called through the door, he might count on seconds enough, perhaps a full minute, to do as much damage as the short blade allowed. He practiced from all four positions again, imagined himself groggy in the process. Start at the left wrist, preserve the right. Save the tendons there in the stronger arm for at least one more draw. He lay back, rested an arm across his eyes. A wrist was not wreckage enough. A wrist could be bound up but not a throat. He lifted his chin and felt with his fingers the cords go taut. To leave the strength for that you rely on the better hand. If they come for you. If he were dead already they might leave the house alone. That much he could hope for.

He lurched to jerk the knife from its cache, broke the tape and pressed the blade to the lump in his throat. Betrayed and found out he would at least betray no others. He got another length of tape and laid the trap again and in the mirror as he raised his chin to shave saw the rough trail of rust he'd left behind.

Frost ferns burgeoned across the panes and they bundled behind crystal windows until the blackout, the police hour, when all the curtains came down. Outside the different snows went on falling as he watched through their winter days. Grit like white sand that pelted down and ricocheted off the ledge of the balcony. The slender curls that tumbled end over end onto the palms of his gloves, curling like an eyelash, like the rods of a bacillus. Finally the great plump flakes that chuted down the cold air, broad enough to cover the whole width of Aleks's tongue. The boy caught another and Trn watched it fade from the border till the vivid tongue lapped it away.

"Now you, Daddy."

Trn looked up into the gray swirling sky, tilting among the flakes to fix his target, sidestepping and nearly tripping to gather one that caught across his nose.

"You missed."

"I missed."

The boy captured two more, the second before the first had disappeared.

"You're very good," Trn said.

They turned down the lane and across the bricks in the deepest shadows someone had painted in broad white letters DEATH TO

FASCISM and Trn tried to hurry their steps beyond it. Aleks said, "I can read that."

"I know you can."

"It says, SMRT FASISMUS." They walked on toward the square and Aleks said, "Will someone get into trouble for that?"

"Probably."

But in the square the boy's attention was drawn immediately to the active corner, the clang of shovel and pick.

"Daddy, what are they doing? It's the biggest hole I've ever seen."

He clung to the timber barrier, leaned to look into the pit, and Trn clutched at the shoulder of his coat. On the other side were two piles, the heap of cobbles taller than a man, the heap of mud taken from below taller still, all fleeced with snow.

"I wish I could dig a hole like that. What is it for?"

"It's a cistern. To store water."

"Water for drinking?"

"No," Trn said into the pit.

"To put fires out?"

"Yes."

A worn barrow came up drizzling mud. Three men in stripes strained at the rope and the pulley creaked on the tripod of poles and a fourth man dumped the mud on its heap while the guard fingered the works of his rifle. Another soldier came out of the sentry box in the center of the square to join him and they watched together.

"Will the cistern take the whole square?"

"No. Just this corner, I think."

"Will we have the Christmas market here then?"

"It's a long time till Christmas but I think they will have some kind of market."

Aleks turned back with his hand in his father's, looking over his shoulder.

"You can't see the man all the way at the bottom," he said.

"No," Trn said. "You can't."

A man who smelled of drink under his fur cap squinted at the factory gate and muttered that the workers might leave by this gate. He looked back at Trn. How the hell would he know. Maybe it was a different gate. His beery breath steamed out and he rubbed together hands black with grease.

"I'm supposed to meet a friend here."

The man went his muttering way down the street rubbing his hands together and Trn waited with his back to the wall. A couple came past and stopped their talk to look at him and then talked on. Traffic slushed past. Trn frowned at his watch again. Finally the first of them began to come out in their dark coats, hands in pockets, heads tilted against the cold. No one looked at him, none of the pairs or trios veering left or right, walking home, walking to the autobus. Then the gray coat appeared behind a chatter of voices. The copper hair under the hat, a different hat.

He waited to see which way she would go, relieved the cluster before her stopped at the gate to huddle round a packet of cigarettes so that she turned right alone, and he angled across the street and measured his steps to come beside her. She slowed at the sluice of his shoes in the gutter, glanced as he drew near on the paving. He took off his hat and held the brim in both hands.

"Oh," she said. She had stopped walking.

He tried to smile and there they stood.

"May I see you home?"

She kept looking but he saw no more expression behind the gray irises than in the gray sky. Her eyes narrowed in such a way to stretch the freckles across her cheeks and then she said, "I suppose."

He put on his hat.

"Was it hard work today?"

"Not hard. Long but not hard. Mostly it's watching the looms."

"You seem weary."

"They're so loud all day. The looms. The snow's so quiet."

She would look only at the pavement before her feet and he tried not looking at her.

"We cross here," she said.

They waited for a truck to splash by, men with shovels in the back staring. She kept her head bowed as the truck chugged on.

"They're digging a cistern at the end of the street," she said.

They crossed slowly. Her profile watched her steps again, the little black boots that displaced the snow.

"The guards always whistle and call after the girls."

"At least this evening they left you alone," he said.

"It's mostly girls alone they shout things to."

"I'm sorry. Of course they should not do that."

"Men are men, they do as they please. My mother says men are dogs." She hesitated a step. "I should not have said that."

"It's hard to look round these days and think your mother isn't right."

They crossed into a narrow street with blocks of flats shoulder to shoulder, their doors at the sidewalk, the sky darker for the crowded space, the space darker with the blank faces of the blocks.

"Number twenty-one," she said.

He looked down the street receding in its dreariness as she removed one glove and retrieved from her bag a ring with two keys, put one in the lock and left her naked hand there.

"I didn't know you would come."

"I hope you'll forgive me. I've tried before. Today I was fortunate."

"I can't ask you in."

"Of course. I only had my good deed left to do for the day and now it's done I should go."

"My mother's in."

"Of course. I hope your mother's well."

A gust of crystalled wind closed her eyes, the coppered lashes. It stung half his face, his ear. He noticed in the failing light for the first time the lint of cotton batting that clung in the fringes of her hair, whitened it.

"I did wonder," he said, "how many of your suitors would I have to duel if I asked to see you home again one day."

Her gray eyes glanced and she shook her head. "No suitors," she said.

"Maybe I can walk with you another time then."

"My days are the same, every day. Except Saturday. Only half day on Saturdays. For now. Everyone says it will be full days again in the spring."

She looked at her bare fingers on the key.

"So. Good bye, Magda."

He smiled and turned away with his hands nested in his pockets and looked back only once at the closed door of number twenty-one.

The second group was always better prepared than the first. With the exception of two or three among them they filed in and sat with the book open, their translations out. They read out the Latin when he bade them and then their own Czech versions, their faces down, eyes lifting by increments at the end to see if he approved. Was Aleks so in class? No, he filled his margins with whorls and creatures, the geometry of daydreams that overran his eyes. School was an interruption of Aleks's imagination. As it had been for him. Trn read out a passage himself, blew his nose, stuffed the handkerchief into his trouser pocket.

"Excuse me. Now notice that this Latin is not so good as Caesar's, nothing as eloquent as Cicero's. The language has fallen off, it seems, decayed. Which may explain the Roman defeat we're reading of, or at least be another symptom of Rome's decline and eventual fall. In two generations the tribes will be at the gates, the barbarians will swarm the capital, the sacking will begin and civilization will never be the same."

A few eyes blink but most of them have dulled even in this group. History is not his responsibility. Mr. Schmidek takes history for himself and they know this. His responsibility is little more than hic and ille, amo, amas, amat.

"Pavlina, could you take the next passage please."

She has red hair, like her mother. Once at the door in the beginning of the term he had passed them. She squints at the page, closer. Glasses so hard to come by. War monopolizes optics. Toward the end her voice stumbles, halts.

"I didn't know what to do with those words, sir."

He leans both hands on the desk, scans, lowers a finger to where he believes they are.

"That's fine, Pavlina. Does anyone have a solution for this difficulty?" He retrieves the handkerchief. "Excuse me."

None looks up, no hands rise. He stretches so that his watch rides free of his cuff.

"In that case let's all go on to the next page for tomorrow and sleep on the difficulties of this passage tonight. I'm always surprised how often the mind can solve its problems while we sleep."

The light applause of closing books. They lean to whisper across the aisles, to gather up their things with lightsome arms, bone ends like marbles in their wrists, skin paler than the paled blood pulsing there. Round noses in profile. The hope of us all. He stands beside the desk as always to see if any approach with questions but lunch waits for them, the cauldron of soup. Their nostrils tell them it's cabbage again. Pavlina smiles goodbye, Barbora her friend dodges down her dark head. "Goodbye, ladies." They giggle behind their hands through the door. He packs his own books away, the corridor droning with the queue. Under his contract lunch is provided, he too could have soup, at the faculty table, but he takes under his arm the case with the broken handle, the latch broken too so his arm also serves to keep it closed. On the shelf by the door one of them has left open a book for the illustrated teaching of German. He puts down the case. You can tell the Jew by his nose, the page reads. It looks like the number six. His lips are puffy. His eyes are deceitful. If you have a good nose you can smell the Jew.

The figure is round and buttoned up in a fat coat. The head is round with grizzled curls, thick lips. The nose is indeed the number six.

With his time before Aleks is dismissed he walks into the woods, hurries to the nearest point of the lake. Ice still spikes from the mud along the shore. He wipes his nose and takes the book from his case and slings it far over the water. It skips, the wings of pages fly apart, swimming. He waits for the saturation point, looking at his watch. On the path back he checks over his shoulder and there it floats still, suspended, barely beneath the surface.

"Have they finished with their cistern?"

"Yes. I think so."

"I hadn't thought to notice until now that we missed them today."

Her hand left the key in the lock and Trn saw that the skin was chafed red across the knuckles. She took a step and hands at his lapels leaned in to him, her cheek against his chest, but before his arms could complete their circle her hand was at the key again and she was inside, closing the door between them without once raising her eyes.

He saw the sparks thrown from the funnel before he heard the locomotive. It rattled west with a rhythm that sounded as if it passed directly over the ties and without slowing took the narrow bend between the hills, its plume of orange stars lighting a tunnel through the trees. He squinted into the field glasses, adjusted the wheel.

Eighteen, twenty, twenty-four, twenty-seven. Pavel would say he should get closer. Three tanker cars. Six flat cars, shrouded. Maybe scrap but why cover scrap? Certainly he didn't know. Couldn't know. He peeled off his right glove and searched for the stub of pencil from his trouser pocket, took out a fresh scrap of paper from his coat pocket and scrawled in the dark third class, twenty-seven quizzes, six translations, three exercises, nine absent. Perhaps field guns bound for overhaul. That was for another mind to decide.

He folded the paper into his trouser pocket with the pencil and the other papers, put the glove on again. The third tonight, all going west. If another came his relief on another stretch of the line could mark that and pass it on. If his relief were there. And that man would think the same of him. Who knew what got through unseen. He crushed down through the path he'd made when the moon's sickle lazed in the needles of the highest pines, in the hour when he could still feel his feet. As he descended the rounded hills became blacker than the sky above, the village below resolving out of the gloom into its dimensions, smoke he could smell but not see. At the bottom of the slope a branch cracked beneath the snow.

He waited. The white walls of houses, the darker roofs of tile, squat chimneys of brick began to quicken. From the treeline he watched the gray and empty road running toward dawn. Never any patrols here, Pavel said, this far from town. But Pavel never came here. He stayed in the city and worked over his map. This village strictly speaking isn't even on the line, Pavel said, so it should be perfectly safe. Then he folded his map. Trn took off his gloves and blew his fingers, dried them on his coat and removed the pin so the cylinders of the field glasses came apart in his hands. He put one in each pocket and gripped them in his fists.

Nothing came along the road and he crossed quickly to the shed, opened the door on its squealing hinges. A shard of day fell through the dirty window and the wind whistled at the cracked pane. He felt for the sacks in their corner and scuffed away the dirt over the boards, pried them out with his nails, wrapped the cylinders in rags and replaced the boards and swept up dirt with both hands. He stirred the sacks back into place, dusted his palms and began to put his gloves on again.

"It's well you're so careful about that."

Trn dropped a glove.

"Christ." He looked at the silhouette framed in the door, breathed before he bent for the glove. "Is it necessary for you to do that?"

"Only keeping you alert." The old man's shadow shut a nostril with a thumb and blew a gob of snot to the dirt floor. "You ought to shut the door though."

"You ought to oil those hinges. The whole village can hear them scream."

"Ah, that's just the way. If I oil them they'll know I'm about something."

Trn lifted the bicycle, reversed it.

"All the same I'd prefer you oil them. Since I'm the one who opens the door in the night."

"We shall see."

The old man pressed the opposite nostril and swelled behind closed eyes without effect.

"I'm going." Trn put his case in the basket.

"Here." From his coat pockets the old man took four rolls. "Wrap them in your basket. Your excuse today will be a friend had some extra bread for your family. You've got a family, don't you?"

"Thank you but I've already got an explanation."

"Not a sick friend, I hope. They know what horseshit that is. Well. Take the rolls anyway."

"And be thought to have bought them on the black market?"

"Four rohlik doesn't make a market and if they do, better pieces of black bread than spying on the railroad."

"Thank you."

"Ah." The old man waved him away with both hands. "The sun will be over the hill before you can climb on that contraption."

Trn knelt and dusted his trousers, folded his cuff into his sock and wheeled the bicycle out.

"Till next week," the old man said.

"We shall see."

Trn stepped down on the slow first pedal, waved without looking back and glided away. He smelled a roll still warm in its pith and took a long bite despite the old man's nose. Pedaling the empty road he let the bread cool on his tongue. For an old man he talked too much and he would talk too much again next week if they still had breath for words.

Aleks closed his notebook on his grandfather's desk and stared when Trn opened the door.

"Dinner."

"I'm coming now."

"Are you writing a story?"

Aleks looked at the notebook, laid a hand on its cover.

"Only a card."

"To Peter?"

"Yes. To Peter."

"That's good. I'm sure Peter will like to have word from you."

"He told me I can only write thirty words. That's the limit they allow. You can't send picture cards."

"Did you count them?"

"Yes. Thirty exactly."

"If you want to give it to me I'll post it tomorrow."

The boy nodded.

"I can take it now if you're finished."

"Now?"

"If you're finished. I might forget tomorrow."

With round eyes he handed up the card and in the queue the next day Trn read it.

Dear Peter,

Remember the day we threw rocks at the ravens in your apricot tree and walked along the road and you taught me marbles? Remember.

Your friend.
Aleks.

He licked the stamp, affixed the Führer's blue face and dropped the card through the slot into the box for Terezin.

After she had unlocked it she stood in the open door and only slowly raised her face to him from the stairwell still dark with the long winter.

"Would you like to come in?"

He nodded and stepped inside, took off his hat.

"We live on the third floor."

She went the first flight never looking back. He watched her inside her slender coat, looked up for her face at every landing but it was never there. She used a brass key to let them into a hall as dark as the stairwell.

"Mama's visiting her sisters."

She wadded the scarf in one pocket of her coat, her gloves in the other. The hall was narrow with two doors shut and a third open to the only light. She turned to look at him, the crown of his hat cupped in one hand.

"I'm sorry. Please. Hang your coat. I think we have some tea."

"Thank you. But I'm fine."

He followed her into the sitting room. Two chairs at a table, two beds pushed into a corner. Lace curtains brighter than the clouds beyond the windows.

"It's nice to be so high," Trn said. "The light is very nice."

"I don't know." She gazed at the window. "The stairs are hard for

Mama. We were waiting for a flat on the ground floor. A smaller flat. The climb is hard for her knees, she has sharp pains and they swell. But then the war. Or actually before. A couple from the Sudetenland took it. They knew the owner a long time. From outside Karlovy Vary."

Her hand rose toward the chair and she said, "I'm sorry," and perched on the edge of a bed made up with cushions against the wall.

Her gray eyes glanced round the room. A dark chest with a bit of lace and on the table a porcelain shepherdess dressed mostly in blue, no doubt from Meissen in better days. One pale arm missing at the shoulder.

"I'm sorry we have no coffee. But I think there is a little tea."

"Thank you. I really couldn't take anything. But please, you've had a long day."

The eyes roamed and came to his and fled and she said, "You don't talk much."

"I prefer to listen to others speak."

"Why?"

"I learn more that way."

"What are you? I don't even know."

"A teacher."

"You seem like a teacher."

"Is that good or bad?"

She shrugged. "It depends on what type of teacher you are."

"Perhaps the best answer to that is that my students come each day hoping for the sirens so we'll have a drill instead of class."

She smiled a little.

"What do you teach?"

"Latin."

"Latin? I never studied it."

He smiled, nodded.

"Where do you teach?"

"In the valley, north of town."

"Oh, near the lake? It's nice there."

"I never see the lake because it's one stop farther on but yes, that's it."

"I like how the tram runs beside the river for a time and then goes on to the lake. We used to go for picnics there in the hot weather. When my father was alive. There was a hill on the far side of the dam and he would spread the blanket there."

"I know that hill."

"You don't need to look sad. Mama's actually quite happy he's gone."

"And you?"

Her hand smoothed out a wrinkle in the counterpane.

"He wanted a son. I never spent much time with him. After my brother came he never spent much time with me."

"I'm sorry," Trn said. "I've seen that before."

She shrugged, pulled the skirt over her knee, the shin narrow in her hose. The room grew shadows. On the table beside the shepherdess were a lamp and three kino revues. On the cover of the topmost he could see a German actress beneath a coating of dust. The sky barely summoned itself through the windows but he could see the dust lying white on the table, the magazine.

"I don't know why I keep those." Her eyes shied again. "I never read them."

"You're wise," Trn said. "They never say anything."

"You say odd things."

"It's only fitting, I suppose. I may be an odd person."

"Are you?"

"Do you think so?"

Her smile was going now and she said, "I don't know."

Her fingers played a game of joining and unjoining while her eyes looked on.

"How is our Mr. Jaroslav doing now?"

"Oh he's very well. Hana says he can stand alone now." Her hands put away their game. "He may take his first steps any day. I do hope I can see that." She looked away, the dim window shining in her eyes. "I suppose I should put up the papers now."

"Would you like me to help?"

"I will do it."

From behind the chest she took a frame of black paper, lifted the curtain aside with the back of her hand and fitted the frame into the casement, twisted bent nails to hold the screen in place.

"I hate doing this every evening."

"I think everyone hates it. But that's no consolation, is it?"

She took up the second frame but set it on the floor again, leaned her elbows into the deep sill. A few steps and he was near enough to touch her, to see her brow pressed against the glass, see how her hair cast coppered sparks into that one zone of the evening, white lint still in her hair.

"I can help," Trn said.

"I suppose if we don't put on a light we can let it be a while longer. Don't you think? Maybe the trustee won't notice when he goes by. There are so many windows."

And she turned to him. Knowing he was there she turned even so and he raised his arms and she fell against him.

"Hold me," she whispered, "like you did before."

Eyes closed, her face lifted as if in search while the light failed. He stooped and raised her, his arms a cradle, and she opened her eyes as from a dream.

"Not that one. The other."

He laid her on the counterpane as she pulled at his lapels, at the knot of his tie, at the button behind it, her eyes there, not on his eyes. He watched as she shifted her fingers to her blouse.

"Here," she said, and pushed him away, stood and threw back the covers. The sheets were frigid at first, her nipples the color of her lips, and he kissed them all naked beneath the blankets and she said again, "Hold me like before. In the shelter."

"It is necessary that you teach history," Schmidek said. "Another chance with history. You should be delighted."

Trn stood before the desk, waiting for the eyes to move from the papers, for the bearded mouth to speak. A picture of President Hacha hung on the wall behind the desk. Schmidek adjusted the history text on its stack of papers, tugged at his armband.

"This carries with it the responsibility of your teaching German too, I should say. Come the fall." Schmidek's eyes appeared suddenly over the glasses pinched on his nose. "Since history by this directive is a subject to be taught in German with immediate effect." Schmidek's fingers drummed the calendar on his desk. "I suppose we will have to recalculate your salary. This will mean a new set of classes per week. With history, that is."

On a cabinet beneath President Hacha a small bronze figure sat, youthful, head at rest on one bent knee as if exhausted from a naked foot race. Beside it a potted plant without flowers. In a cabinet drawer perhaps there was a picture of the Führer biding his time to join Hacha, to replace him.

"I will consider it, Mr. Schmidek. Thank you."

"You will consider it?"

"Yes."

"I don't think you understand, Trn." Schmidek sighed as he would over a slow pupil, leaned his eyes over his glasses. "Come the fall you will teach German here or not teach here at all. That is the choice. And history since history is a subject to be taught in German with immediate effect. There will be no more Latin, Latin is to be discontinued."

From the wall President Hacha jutted a lip toward him too, white hair a thin halo round the plump and lined face. Schmidek joined his hands into one great fist.

"So what do you choose to do, Trn?"

"When do you need my response?"

"Why, today. No moment is superior to this one. If you decline then I shall find another candidate. I've received a dossier here"—he moved the history text, shuffled some papers from a folder and unpinned them—"a young man, he was at the university when it was closed. Like you. He's just twenty-four, I believe. I have not interviewed him but I'm sure he'd make a most enthusiastic teacher at that age. Don't you think?" To the desk Schmidek fixed the pages with all ten fingers, lenses darting among the lines. "I'm sure the students would admire that in him." He paused. "Aged twenty-five." Schmidek shuffled the papers about. "Impeccable German it says here in a letter. The very highest references. No presence before a class more inspiring than a vigorous presence, don't you agree?" His fingers moved down the lines. "A vigorous youthful presence." He licked his right thumb and lifted a page. "Superior marks through school, including university. His mother's German, it seems."

"One wonders why he's not already volunteered for the front," Trn said.

Schmidek glared up from the word his index finger seemed most to want.

"Have you other offers, Trn? I certainly will not stand between you and a more advantageous position." The eyes over the glasses blinked once, twice.

"No, Mr. Schmidek."

"No?" Schmidek creaked in his chair. "No?"

"I have no other offers."

"And so?"

"There will be no Latin? None at all?"

"I have already explained this, Trn. Now if you'll excuse me I must attend to these. Administrative work can never be delayed."

Schmidek grunted, began rustling papers.

Trn said, "I will teach German. In the fall I will teach German, and I will begin teaching history now."

"Very well. I will have the new contract drawn up. You may come by to sign it, on next, shall we say." Schmidek set the calendar down, traced the lines intersecting his days. "Shall we say Friday. That should be sufficient time for Mrs. Vodova. You will then begin history the following Monday."

Schmidek bent with his pen to make a brief notation.

"Of course all new contracts contain the clause stipulating that given the exigencies of the war all agreements may be invalidated and rescinded without notice."

He made a second notation, looked out over his glasses again.

"Is there something more, Trn?"

"No." Trn shook his head. "Nothing more."

"So you are away again tonight then?"

He lifted another plate from the rack, wrapped it in the kitchen towel.

"And won't be back till tomorrow afternoon."

"Yes."

He added the plate to the stack, took another.

"That's the second night this week."

"It's better not to count."

"Do you enjoy these excursions? You said when you were young you didn't like sleeping out, didn't like army life."

"I wouldn't call it camping."

"What would you call it?"

"I don't refer to it at all. You shouldn't either."

"I wonder sometimes."

"Try not to."

"What you're doing."

He lifted the four plates and set them in the cupboard, shut the glassed door.

"But of course you can't speak of this. I've learned that. No names, no places."

"Yes, that's best."

"All this silence and secrecy. Sprung up so suddenly."

"Not so suddenly," he said.

Trn took the silverware to dry piece by piece, bedded them one by one in the drawer. Alena leaned back against the counter.

"Your lips are thin," she said. "You're angry again."

The last fork rang against the others, the last knife. He shut the drawer and it all rang together.

"It's very frustrating. You know I can't speak of these things."

"Yes, your unspeakable nights."

Aleks stopped in the door, looked at each face.

"Will I have to go to school by myself again tomorrow?"

"I'm afraid you will, Aleks. Your father has other business."

"I thought you liked it, on your own," Trn said.

"I did for a while. Now I'd like to go with you again."

"I'll meet you after school and we'll come home together."

"Mornings are hardest. After school the hard part is over."

"I'll take you the morning after next."

"And the one after that?"

"Yes. The one after that too."

The boy pivoted on one foot in going.

"Brush your teeth," Alena called. "And get ready for bed."

Trn looked at his watch. As he went into the hall Alena called, "Have a good time."

The all clear brought them out into the cracking cold. It had been midday when the metal door was shut against the woods and the sky but as they broke it open the sun was setting or would have been could they see it. Smoke coiled thinly among the trees but beyond the forest the world blurred and the path ahead dimmed like some warped gray glass retreating. A little bird trilled its notes in the aftermath and then somewhere went silent again.

"I count seven," Miroslav said and put his handkerchief back to his nose.

Trn said, "At least."

From the crest of the hill they could see to the south and southeast black pillars of smoke propping up the furious sky. Aleks's hot hand squeezed his and Trn looked down.

"Is this the worst yet?"

"I'm afraid it looks to be."

Alena stood with her fists in her coat pockets, shaking her head.

"And on Sunday."

"They're thinking the workers may not be at the factories on a Sunday."

"How do you know what they're thinking?"

Trn shrugged still looking south.

"The last raid wasn't on a Sunday," she said. "I know it wasn't. We just came up on the calendar today, that's all. And where do they think the workers' flats are, in the country?"

The Steinhardts' red banner loomed up through the smoke. Where the sidewalk began Trn's loose left heel clacked against the paving stones and Aleks said, "I'll get the glue," and leaped the curb and ran to the gate. In the entry they met the others creeping from the cellar stairs. Havlicek nodded and went in at his door. Dita was going up and came back two steps as they came in.

"There's room enough now," she whispered. "With the boys gone."

"I'd be perfectly content with that," Alena said, "but he refuses. He prefers that we tramp through the woods with the bombs falling."

"The Steinhardts made it clear their shelter wasn't for us," Trn said. "They made their feelings perfectly comprehensible."

Miroslav said, "Damn right," and took Aleks by the shoulder.

"Come along, boy. There's an odor beginning to rise here."

A ring of keys jingled and the Steinhardts passed, Frau Steinhardt's Mother's Cross pinned at her breast, shadows for eyes, lips stitched with wrinkles into a face more skull than skin. Herr Steinhardt nodded once for them all and slowly climbed the stairs behind her.

"They don't say a word in the cellar," Dita whispered. "They just sit there staring at the stones in the wall. You know one of them's missing. In France."

Alena said, "No."

"It was in the paper," Trn said.

"You didn't say so."

"When you step forward for the Waffen-SS," Trn said, "when you raise your arm for flag and fatherland, certain consequences follow. I'm going up."

Slowly Sunday returned. Miroslav sneezed and checked Aleks's lessons, practiced him for a test in history. Alena brought some potatoes from the larder and Trn put away his grammar and took out their eyes with the tip of a knife and peeled them. When the bowl was filled with their pale bodies he set it on the counter and stepped out on the balcony. Alena said, "Hurry and close the door." After a time Miroslav joined him in the smoke and they watched the underbelly of the storm swollen orange in that quarter of the sky. In the wind you could hear faint sirens.

"Looks like the rail yard again," Miroslav said.

"And the pistol and rifle works."

"Maybe they'll see not much is left and not come back."

Trn shook his head. "No. They'll come back."

Miroslav coughed and they went in and Alena said, "Close that door." But there was no room where they could not smell the city on fire, no bite of food that didn't taste of burning.

On the streets, in the trams, they hunched their shoulders more deeply as the fires embered into the week and smoked the glass of every eye. The men pulled tighter at their hat brims, women with a hand always on the strap of their bags. Maybe he only imagined.

Maybe the world had crouched to ward off the next blow for a long while now. Children with both hands pocketed, chins hidden in their collars.

"Why has everyone's nose grown so large?"

"It's not their noses," Trn said. "It's rationing. We've all lost weight in our faces."

"Even me?"

"No. Your nose is still perfect."

"When will they put out the fires?"

"As soon as they can, I'm sure."

"I hope it's soon."

"I agree," Trn said.

"Because that smoke is like a signal the bombers can follow straight here."

It hung in every tree, clung under the eaves. Their clothes were threaded with it, their hair. Trn rested a hand on the boy's nape and they passed the post office, had to leave the sidewalk for the queue moving one by one through the door to mail the special postcards saying the sender had survived another raid.

Aleks coughed, said with his fist over his mouth, "May I draw before homework?"

"Certainly."

Alena was resting, Miroslav sat with the paper across his lap. "I don't need a pipe any longer," he said. "All I need to do is breathe." He closed the paper and handed it to Trn.

"Nothing there you'd want to learn."

"Where are the Russians today?" Aleks said.

"All over the Russian front," Miroslav said, "but you'd never know it because they don't put maps in the papers anymore."

Aleks smirked and with his drawing pad under his arm shut the door.

"Is there any news?"

"The usual organized horseshit. With the invaluable assistance of German personnel and equipment all fires have been extinguished.

Natürlich. And some woman at the bottom of the hill threw herself under a number eight tram."

"Did it kill her?"

"Yes. But why do it now when the tide's turned? When they give the Sieg Heil these days you can see just how much they're sweating."

"Maybe it wasn't the war."

Miroslav frowned and nodded. Trn looked over the pages. Another long train of volunteer labor departed for the Reich. A flower show would open tomorrow at the botanical garden. The day's war dead were rolled out in bold print.

"They've found the Steinhardt boy," Trn said.

"Found?"

"Dead."

"The one in France? I didn't see that."

"It's not in the paper. I heard it from Mrs. Zigismundova."

"Isn't the other somewhere in the east?" Miroslav chewed his pipe. "What should we do?"

"I don't know. That's the question."

"Flowers, I suppose."

"I'll get them tomorrow." ř

"I wouldn't be extravagant," Miroslav said.

"I won't be."

The center pages were bordered in black and his eyes scanned the columns inside. The dead identified to date. The victims of the latest American terror raids, the missing unaccounted for. The wounded recovered, in that column Kristek, Jiri. A former student. Not very bright. A few lines below, Prokolev, Josip, probably the owner of the shop he and his mother had frequented years ago. Back in the village as soon as the kitchen was cleared of breakfast his grandmother would shuffle to the undertaker's window on the widest lane to see the notices framed in mourning behind the glass. Black stars, black crosses, the names of the survivors and the time of the service to be held the next day or the next. That was her news and so in his generation he had his. Tomas Zeleny, a casualty, perhaps a class ahead at the gymnazium. Dead was Volf, Vlastamil. The name he knew but Trn had lost the memory for faces he once had. Once he could look over an old roster and conjure features for each name, put them in their chairs. But those days were gone.

"Are you all right, Viktor?"

He blinked again and stared at the old man's bleary eyes. He tried to swallow but his throat seized as the bile rose and scalded his tongue.

"Yes."

"Someone there you know? Your face is gone red."

"A former student."

"Too bad. Did I know him too? Doubtless I did."

Trn blinked back at the page but the black ink lay unmoved. Kalistova, Magda. From the column of the confirmed dead. His brow crept with sweat and something crawled the surface of his brain from the top of the spine beneath the skull, something hot then cold beneath the scalp. Directly above was Kalistova, Katerina.

"I found several I knew," Miroslav said, his lower lip sympathetic. "Decades ago now. Two of my oldest students. They should have moved away long ago. But perhaps they didn't have a choice." He shook his head, folded his hands.

So they had her body. Hauled from rubble. The crumbled block and mortar, rods of steel pointing at the sky. Her face asleep, her clothes torn in the dust. The flesh that gave under the fingers and kept the glow of the hand.

With his finger he tested the list and they were there, Sochor and Sochorova. So they got the whole building. But no other Kalistovi, no infant christened Jaroslav.

"And two old classmates from university," Miroslav was saying. "They're closing on us from both ends."

Trn coughed, caught his breath. Her hair powdered with plaster, cement dust, aged in seconds. Less than seconds. The old man was leaning to look into his face.

"This smoke is getting to us all."

"I'll take a walk. While she's resting."

"A good idea. The air will cool the shock."

Trn pushed himself from the chair. He tried to hurry his coat but his arms felt limp, his legs not stern enough for the next step.

Aleks came to him at the door.

"Daddy, where are you going?"

"A walk."

"I can come with you." He reached up for his coat.

"Not today."

From his feet all the feeling had gone as if he were walking on the stumps of his ankles.

"It's not too cold."

"Not today, Aleks. I'll be back."

She had wanted to dance with him, without music, her head on his shoulder, and he'd said, "I'll only step on your toes." "That's why I have ten," she said. Then men with bandages over their noses had shifted the last timber, the last jagged stone, and limped with her in a blanket toward a range of street cleared from the ruins. He bent his steps towards the woods but didn't enter. The next moment he did, tripping downhill in a rush through the dead leaves. At the door to the shelter he reached for the handle, his mind unscrolling the scene as they straightened her down in the row among the lost, a bare mangled foot escaping from the canvas, a tress of copper hair.

The door shrieked and a young man's broad eyes appeared out of the shadow and finally in his trailing hand the hand of a girl with a mass of black curls and eyes cast down. With her free hand she was failing to button her coat. The young man bit his underlip and the pair of them broke through the brush and disappeared among the trees, not taking any path.

Trn slid to a crouch against the plate metal, sat in the dirt. She might have burned in that cellar, beneath those bombs he heard falling. Bandages. His joined fingers could not stop their trembling. That was her contribution to the war. Slaughter the stanchers and win the war. His teeth clacked upon themselves and he clenched his jaw. None of it worked. She might well have ascended into those black thunderclouds while he stooped on this hill and watched her, just so much human smoke. In the end he clasped his face and behind his palms, as if he wore a mask, all he heard was the slow coming and going of his own muffled life.

"Why don't you cook tonight then, Father?" Alena said and Miroslav said, "Perhaps I should. How does coq au vin sound to everyone? We have wine, I'm sure."

Alena rolled her eyes and three quick raps came at the door. Miroslav's stare engraved his whole brow and he said, "Who could that be at this hour?" The raps quickened and Alena stood and looked down at him. Trn scanned the room and she stepped to the coal bin while the door shook. Miroslav said how did they get in and Alena had the Churchillka in its wrappings dusted with coal in her hand and Aleks came in saying why don't you answer the door. Trn said what are you going to do with that and she said they won't search me and Miroslav said whatever we do we've got to open it now. In the hall Trn reached down the razor from its lintel and stood it in the right pocket of his trousers.

Two of them loomed on the landing in long coats and the larger one frowned in at Trn.

"Herr Trn? Viktor Trn?"

At the end of a chain from his pocket the man held in his palm the burnished oval of his warrant disk. The eagle flung its wings and roosted in the center. The man reversed it quickly to show Trn the four digits stamped unevenly in the brass.

"My name is Rademacher and this is my colleague, Herr Buben. We should like to speak with you."

They came into the hall and kept their hats on, the shorter taking his fists out of his coat pockets. Trn loosened his tie. Rademacher coiled the chain back into his pocket.

"What is this concerning?"

Rademacher pointed with his chin and Buben went into Miroslav's room.

"You are a teacher, are you not."

"Yes."

"Under the supervision of a Herr Schmidek."

"That's correct."

Rademacher reached into an inner pocket and brought out a notebook that he opened but did not look into. He reached again for a silver pen from which he removed the cap with his teeth and looked at Trn while he held it there for a moment like a cigarette before taking it in his fingers. His hands were large, thick in the fingers and palms so that the notebook looked very small.

"And what do you teach?"

"History. And German."

"Why do you teach? You continue to draw your university salary."

"Inflation has made it necessary."

"And your father-in-law lost his pension from the state. Isn't that so?"

"Is this about history and old age pensions?"

The man made no expression. He did not appear to have shaved today.

"Your family is here?"

"In the sitting room."

"All of them?"

Trn nodded and unbuttoned his left cuff and folded the sleeve twice and then unbuttoned and folded the right cuff.

"Is there anyone else here in the flat?"

"No."

"You are friends with a man named Pavel Novotny."

"Yes."

Rademacher looked into his notebook.

"And when was the last time you saw Herr Novotny?"

His eyes left the notebook and moved over Trn, stopping at his hands before rising to his face.

Trn scratched below one eye. "I think it was about two weeks ago."

"Where?"

"We went to a restaurant. Hudek's."

The smaller man came out of the sitting room into the hall and shut the door. "The papers are in order for those three," he said and Rademacher nodded. The man pushed open the door to the toilet and looked in, then went into the lavatory.

"Inflation hasn't yet reached restaurants?"

Trn shrugged, slid his right hand into his pocket.

"Unfortunately it has but I allow myself a beer as an indulgence about once a month."

"With Pavel Novotny."

"Often."

"Isn't Hudek's rather working class for a journalist and a professor?"

"I am no longer a professor."

"And what do you and Herr Novotny discuss?"

"Our children for the most part. I am godfather to his son Jakub."

"So you discuss your children."

"It may sound very tedious to others but that is what Czech fathers do."

"And when you don't discuss your children?"

"We speak of our work, my teaching, his newspaper."

"You resent the closing of your university?"

"I look forward to the day when they will all reopen."

"I was not aware the Reichsprotektor had declared they would." The planes of the man's face tilted down over Trn as if by cogs, his eyes sleepless and blue. "The Czech universities, at any rate."

"I hope that they will reopen. The Reich benefits from an educated citizenry within its borders."

The smaller man came out of the bedroom and left the door open and went into the kitchen. Trn could see the sheets pulled from the mattresses, the doors of the wardrobe standing open, a slip pooled on the floor. He could hear cupboard doors squealing, dishes rattle. He would have walked into the hall with the knife in his hand if he had found it. He would have come through the door brandishing it for Rademacher's eyes.

"Your son's name is Aleksandr. A Russian name." The man shook out a cigarette and put the packet away, thumbed the rasping wheel and drew in the fire. Nostrils flaring smoke, he clicked his lighter closed. "Why did you name him so?"

"I am from the far eastern part of the country where that name is more commonplace. Podkarpatská Rus. It was my father's name. That will be recorded in my registration. I have always liked the name."

"Or what once was the eastern portion of the country. Since now the Hungarians have it back."

"Yes," Trn said.

Out of the shadow of his brow, his hat brim, the man's blue eyes would not let go.

"And no one but your family is here? No one else stays here?"

"No. No one else."

"Do you resent what happened to your country, Herr Trn? The partition? The Protektorate? That Ruthenia is Hungarian again?"

"History is what happens to countries and to the people in them. As a teacher of history I understand this."

"But as a man. How do you understand it as a man?"

"As a man I understand it too."

"I will examine your papers now, Herr Trn."

The man's eyes roamed over the hall as if they knew the texture of everything, the coats hooked on the wall and the worn shoes below, the shabby carpet onto which his ashes fell. He lifted the phone from its cradle and listened to its tone and replaced it. He consulted a page in his notebook, slowly though it was a short page, and then his eyes came back to Trn.

"Why do you burn documents in the garden, Herr Trn?"

"Documents?"

"Yes. You put a match to the pages and watch them burn. In the back garden. Beneath the hedge."

"They are not documents. They're old papers, old notes from research I did long ago. On a project long finished. I no longer have need of them."

"Then why not burn them in your stove? You have a stove, do you not?"

Trn tried to settle his eyes on the man's face, to keep them from the wall, the carpet, the shadowed angles of the room, tried to bring them back to Rademacher's eyes.

"Occasionally I discover pages from a private correspondence. They concern only me and another person. A person with whom I no longer correspond."

"A person who resided," Rademacher's slow eyes examined the page again, "at Komarovska twenty-one."

Trn looked up into the malarial face, the sagged skin.

"Yes. Twenty-one."

Rademacher's lower lip shifted as if behind it his teeth were slowly biting thin strips of skin.

The voice of the other man called out in Czech and Rademacher glanced at Trn with narrowed eyes and in his heavy shoes followed the voice through the kitchen, Trn behind him, hand in his pocket, the slip of the razor between two fingers. The smaller man stood over the table in the dining room shifting Trn's things, leafing through the book open there.

In Czech he said, "Look at this."

Rademacher lifted the book, examined it carefully, set it back and shuffled among the notes on the table. The room was crowded with the three of them standing there. Trn kept the doorknob in his left hand while Rademacher took up the book again, examined Trn's words in the margin. Shut the door behind you, hold the knob with your left hand and cut that wrist. You won't be able to hold the door after that but maybe it will be long enough.

"These are your notes?"

"Yes."

"Why are you reading *Mein Kampf*, Herr Trn?"

"I am studying it, Herr Rademacher, because of my interest in history. I thought it would prove useful in teaching to make my own study of it, to make extracts."

"And has it?"

"It is a complex document, a complicated testament, but I believe I am beginning to gain some understanding. I intend to continue. As you can see I am making a thorough attempt. I have made some progress."

The men looked down at the papers again and then at one another and Rademacher pressed the book to Trn's chest. His squint took in Trn's face a long instant till Trn took the book in his left hand.

"Then for the moment we will leave you to your meditations, Herr Trn. Guten Abend. Heil Hitler."

In the hall he was still holding the book when he closed the door. Aleks and Alena and Miroslav were peering out from the door to the sitting room.

"Who were those men, Daddy?"

"They were officials, Aleks."

"Will they come again?"

"What have you done?" Alena said. "What have you been doing?"

He went through the kitchen to the dining room, began to gather his papers, Alena behind him.

"I want to know what you have been doing."

"No. You don't."

"Do you want to see us all in a camp? Or dead?"

Trn made a stepped pyramid of his books.

"Is that what you want?"

"What do you think, Alena?"

"I wish you would just leave. I wish you would just get out. Go one evening and never come back."

"If I do what will you eat?"

She stared at him, at one of his eyes, the other.

"I will manage. Believe me. Just as I have always done."

Trn sat, laid his hands over the books to still them.

"I cannot believe that you would risk Aleks's life. You don't give a damn about me, or Father for that matter, I know that, I've known that for years. But I can't believe you would be so stupid that you would actually bring those men here where Aleks is."

"No matter what I do," he said slowly, "I risk Aleks's life. I put his life in danger the moment I consented to give you a child."

"To give me a child?" Leaning over the table she shot a laugh at him.

"Even before we married you begged me, Alena. I know you'll remember. You pleaded with me every day for a child. And I gave you Aleks."

"You give me a child? I never heard that before." She slapped the table with her flat hand. "I gave the child." He looked at the books, the veins standing under the skin of his hands. Drops of blood made an odd pattern across the cover of the one on top, four drops, and he found the cut at the end of his long finger. He sucked the blood away and watched the slice well again.

"Let there be no mistake about the child," she said and slapped the table so the papers lifted. Then she switched off the light and switched off the kitchen light and he sat like that alone until he thought he heard Aleks murmur through the dark, "Daddy? Daddy? I'm ready for something to eat."

Hunched against the wind he walked quickly through the square, the heap of cobbles mounted now with trophies from the sky, a silver and riddled Soviet plane, half the green wing of a B-17. He boarded a number nine tram on a side street and rode six stops and got off and walked a crooked path through three streets among the apartment blocks and took a number five autobus two stops and walked past the long wall of a cemetery. The wind tore at the last leaves curing like leather on the trees. The rubbled buildings across the road stood like a set of molars rotted down to their roots and at the end of the cratered street big trees lay toppled this way and that as if they had fallen trying to outrun one another. Now men were sawing at their failed limbs. He passed the flower vendors and turned in at the gate and wound through the gravelled paths and waited under a yew fretted with snow where he had a long view of the avenue. No one entered. He went on toward a bench where an outsized monument of a man rested a sledgehammer on his shoulder, a barefoot woman looking up at him in her stone skirt, a barefoot child holding her hand and also gazing up. The bench was stone and would never warm no matter how long he sat watching the man with his hammer. On the hillside tombstones rose from the mist like postcards to the dead. Or rising from them. The gravel broke along the path and an old man with a cane and a black armband passed, watching his feet stir the stones. Through the laurels bowered round the bend the wind hissed and Trn listened to the gravel churn. Pavel came from the bend and laid a clutch of flowers at the man's booted feet, then sat on the bench. He leaned to strike a match and put it to the cigarette in his mouth without ever looking at Trn. Trn spoke his report into the wind.

"What else?" Pavel said.

"The collar insignia was red."

"Anti-aircraft battery?"

Trn nodded.

"Then they haven't pulled all their flak out yet. But we're going to need to find a new observation post."

"Why?"

Pavel mumbled around his cigarette. "The old man was picked up."

"When?"

"Days ago."

"Is that why I received a visit?"

Pavel looked at the tip of his cigarette glowing in the wind, put it out in sparks on the stone of the bench, cupped the end into his pocket.

"If he'd talked you and I would be buried by now but it wouldn't be here."

"Has anyone seen him since?"

"His wife. In the morgue. But she couldn't recognize him."

A woman came past with the wheels of a carriage plowing the gravel. She skirted wide and pushed on. A single oak leaf went scratching down the path before the wind, clawing at the stones as if to escape being blown into winter. Pavel brought out the cigarette end and examined the black stub of it and put it away again.

"So is there anything else?"

"Do you remember that hospital train I told you about some weeks ago? It came through just as evening was falling."

"What about it?"

"The windows in some of the cars were shuttered, I suppose the most severely wounded were there, but in the other cars the windows stood open and the men inside were singing. Their heads wrapped, their arms in slings. Bodies slung in bunks against the walls. Standing on crutches they gathered and sang. I couldn't hear their words but they were singing with full throats."

"The Reich's most gallant," Pavel said, "joyful to have escaped Russia with their lives."

"Have you noticed their pockets?" Trn said.

"What about their pockets?"

"If you get close enough look at the breast pockets on their tunics. When they marched on us five years ago their pockets had pleats, the cloth of the flaps was sewn in scalloped edges. Now the pockets are flat, without scallops. I would wager even the buttons are fragile. And the Allies have more men and material and generals every day."

Pavel sighed long through tight lips.

"I'm done with this, Pavel. I've finished."

"Because of pockets. Because of one Opel sedan and a knock at the door."

"Because my observations have proven to me that the end can't be far off. The Germans are nearly at the last bullet. You don't need me to finish this war with them."

"This is precisely the time when we need you most. The resistance is going to tie down fifty-thousand German soldiers."

Trn looked off at the wind in the naked trees.

"If everyone believed as you do, Viktor, what would be the end of the war then?"

"If everyone believed as I do then you and I wouldn't be freezing our asses off at opposite ends of a stone bench beside a senator's grave. There would never have been a war or any cause for one."

"You won't answer the question then."

"I've been answering your questions for the better part of a year. You have my answer. Now I'm going home. I'm done with the war."

"But is the war done with you?"

"No. Absolutely not. But I'll hazard it on my own terms."

"Those terms sound like surrender to me. I thought that was the reason you despised and left the church, because it compelled everyone to surrender themselves to God's will. They abdicated all responsibility, you said." Pavel's red hands pressed flat against the stone. "Aren't you doing just that, resigning yourself to fate? To the will of others?"

"Not at all. I'm electing my fate the only way I know how. I may not like it any better than any other possible fate but at least it will be mine, drafted by me."

The wind lifted Pavel's black hair and his dark eyes looked away.

"You're free to think what you like," Trn said. "That's the way I would prefer, and for me to have the freedom to do the same."

"Very well then," Pavel said. "Not everyone is forged to do what we must do." He leaned and pulled up a sprig of grass from the path, tossed it to the wind before the tomb. "So. There's no point in our seeing one another again."

He pushed himself to stand and stepped aside to avoid two halting widows and Trn watched him resume his course kicking stones from the path until it bent out of sight.

Trn said, "Eighty-two."

"Seventy-nine."

"Good. Seventy-six."

Aleks put his head down and Trn heard the murmur inside the scarf.

"Seventy-three. But I don't see why we have to practice if there's going to be no more school."

"That's exactly why we have to practice all the harder. Seventy."

"But today's the last day."

"I know. Now, seventy."

Aleks huffed and the breath bloomed through and widened the round white patch on the black scarf.

"Why do you go so fast?"

"To give you plenty of time to think."

"I'm thinking, I'm thinking. I'm walking and I'm thinking."

Through the dawn placards on the walls said CONSERVE GAS! CONSERVE WATER! CONSERVE COAL! A red poster on a pole warned of saboteurs. The loudspeaker on the pole said nothing yet but it was early. The bin in the larder was down to the last layer of potatoes, Alena told him again, and what would he do for work now that the announcements on all the school doors said CLOSED FOR THE DURATION OF THE WAR?

"Forty-nine."

"Right. Forty-six."

There wouldn't really be a Christmas this year. Out of the gloom across the street two men with bow saws were already at work on the limbs of a weeping cherry. A third tossed the lengths into the back of a truck. An ax wedged in the next trunk waited to deal the coming blow. Aleks tugged at this hand.

"Thirty-one."

"Thirty-one? Twenty-eight."

They would be late again today, would have to wait for the tram again. Longer every morning. But it was the last day. A shop door said SOAP WITH COUPON ONLY. The shoe store had one pair behind the glass. Men's shoes. Small men's shoes. The boy's fingers, he could feel, were too long inside his gloves.

"Eight."

"Wait. When did we start subtracting by twos?"

"I don't know. Eight."

"Six then."

"Five."

Alek's eyes squinted up through the slit between the scarf and his sock cap. The cap was truly too small now, stretched over the dome of his head, down to the secret eyes.

"You trickster."

"Five, I said."

"Very well then. Four."

The screech of the tram came down the hill with its nearly dead lamp and Trn pulled Aleks into running. They'd make it. They said the cold was so severe this winter the iron of the rails was cracking but they'd make it.

"Three."

"Two."

Aleks leaped from the curb.

"One."

"Zero."

1945

The world collapsed to sky and mud. From the trench that was all you could see, mud to the eyes and sky above that and the major's stalking boots, his saurian eye. "This is your homeland," he bellowed over their heads. "You are working for the protection of your own hearth." The boots carried on. A shovelful of mud was thrown onto the parapet as he passed. "Dies ist Ihre Heimat. Our watchword must now be stand and fight." His right sleeve was empty and pinned at the shoulder and when a superior approached he raised his left arm for the salute.

"Sweat and dig, that's what he means," the man beside Trn muttered.

They shoveled up the mud they stood in, received the mud from the tier below and heaved up that.

"I shouldn't be here in this shit," the man said. He lifted his hat, drew a wrist over his brow, spat at the mud. His hair was white at the temples, over his ears.

They heard the major shout, "We must hold this ground if Germany is to save the future of Europe."

"I'd like to see him come down here and dig a little with that stump he's got," the man said.

The boy on the other side of Trn looked up and said, "Don't you think they'll let us go home today? They'll bring up another detail today and let us go home won't they?"

"They said day before yesterday they'd let us go yesterday," the man said. "So don't believe a goddamn word they say. Understand?"

A sergeant came glaring along the line and all their eyes went back to the mud.

"Noha," the sergeant said, "the Jews dig better than you."

The boy squinted up as if the sun were out.

"But Sergeant, we aren't Jews."

"Shut up and dig," the sergeant said. But he was laughing, the mud sucking at his bootsoles as he strolled down the line.

"Is he gone yet?" the boy whispered.

"I can still see his Grosses Deutsches ass waddling away," the man said, "but he's gone. Maybe a shell will land on his helmet and send him to his fucking mother."

"I'm tired," the boy said. He propped his elbow on the knob of his shovel and his chin on his elbow and slowly his head descended as the shovel sank in the mud.

"Goddamnit. These shovels aren't even good for sleeping."

His cheeks were red and streaked with mud. Then the back of his hand streaked his brow.

"And I'm goddamn hungry too. When's the soup coming?"

A shout came from the ridge behind and a whistle shrilled. An explosion followed where they were dynamiting the ground before the shovels went in. In the silence afterward the man said, "You idiot. What do you want, soup or home? They aren't going to give you both, you know."

The boy cursed and Trn whispered, "He's coming back," and the boy jerked his shovel from the mud.

"I don't see the good of this," the boy muttered. "As soon as I fling it up there it just rolls back like a turd of shit and I fling it up again."

"The major showed me your labor form, Noha," the sergeant said. "I saw where you put down Guitarspeilen and Kurzschrift as your skills. I'm surprised you didn't put down comedy. Beer hall dancing."

"That's right, Feldwebel. I'm a man of many talents, including smoking. Got any cigarettes today?"

"You're a boy full of shit, Noha, that's you, and you're lucky you're not shot already."

"What are you two going to do?" the man said when the sergeant passed on. "Is he going to leap down here and start kissing you? You want us all to look away when the two of you go to your knees like hogs in the mud?"

"Shut up."

"I just see how fond our superman is of you and wonder what form your collaboration will take."

"Shut up, you old assfucker. You talk so much about it you must be the one who wants to collaborate with the sergeant like pigs in shit."

"I'm only forty-four," the man said. "That's not so old."

"I'm sure that's old enough for the sergeant," Noha said.

The man stared contemplatively into the mud. "I hadn't thought about it before but if my parents had only fucked a few months earlier I'd be forty-five now and they couldn't call me up for this shit."

Trn said, "He's coming back."

"So. Look at that."

The sergeant stood fists on hips glaring over their heads. Noha squinted up at him.

"Is it the soup, Sergeant?"

"Better than that, you lucky bastard. It's your relief."

Coming down the ridge behind were two soldiers, bayonets higher than their helmets, guiding a winding line of men on a track through the trees. They came in ranks of two, some in coats and ties, sliding, slipping, catching their hats, stalling their canted weight with arms out, with muddied hands fixing trilbys or workman's caps, some boys in tams.

"Alles raus," the sergeant called. "Leave the shovels in your places."

Climbing the slope Trn fell and slathered his whole left side with mud.

"Let me give you a push," Noha said, and he fell too, mud to his chin.

"Wait. Your glasses." Trn pulled them from the muck, the frames slimed. They had no lenses.

"I don't know why I bother to carry them," the boy said. "They've been broken six months, I guess." He put them back inside the pocket of his coat, patted the mud there, laughed. "My mother won't let me in the house, I'm sure. You won't get in the front door either, will you?"

"I guess I'll hose off in the garden."

"That will be cold."

Trn nodded, examined his shoes, took up a stick in his red hands to pry the mud balled round the soles, work it from the seams. The boy watched and when Trn began walking the boy kept at his side. They crossed the wilted grass, leaves and snow dead and wet upon it, in company with the ragged range of men heading generally south and home, all with their hands in their pockets, their breaths blooming before them.

"How far do you have to go?" the boy asked.

"About ten kilometers. It's in the north of the city so it's not far. I could catch a tram at the end of the line."

"If they let you on."

"If they let me on. How far away do you live?"

"I don't know. How far is the Masarykova quarter?"

"Nearer. Maybe six kilometers."

"I know the way but I don't know how far it is."

They came down out of a gap between two hills to a level road, crossed a bridge over the river sliding by as smooth as a solid in its channel with darker ice slow in the current.

"I guess they'll be mining this bridge soon," the boy said. "I saw them drilling holes in the pilings of the bridge near the lake when we were digging there."

"I suppose they can be counted on to have a plan for everything. To blow everything."

"I wish the plan for today had included soup."

"I'll tell you the truth," Trn said. "I would have liked a little soup myself."

"The potato's not bad, if it has potatoes and you get a ladle from the bottom. I got that once. The cabbage is only green water. What do you see?" He squinted. "Is it a plane?"

"No. I was looking at the trees. It's too early for any buds but I go on looking."

"This is a long winter. My mother said she never saw a harder winter."

"I agree with your mother."

The boy said finally, "Do you think that hole we're digging will stop a tank?"

"Should we hope that it won't?"

"I guess so."

"Or should we hope that it won't have to."

"You think the war will end before the Russians get here?"

"No. It will go on long after the Russians have passed us." Trn stopped, put out his hand.

"I go this way now. Good luck."

With his next step the boy kicked something along the road, sent it scattering the leaves. He bent to rustle it out of the ice, squinted at a mass of fur in his hand.

"It's still cold," he said. "Firm. Must have been hit by a truck."

The shocked head was flattened, one black eyeball bulged in a dead stare at Trn. The fur bristled with spikes of frozen blood. After weighing it in his hand, the boy spread the muddy pocket of his coat, maneuvered the carcass head first.

"Now Mother will be glad to see me."

He grinned so the mud cracked across his cheek and he walked on, the orange brush of the squirrel's tail bobbing beside him.

Trn came up the stairs in bare feet, damp prints of the ball and heel of each foot vanishing on the step left behind. His limp socks in his hand, his wet trouser cuffs rolled up his calves, an ache like a bad tooth in the bones of both shoulders. His absurdly white ankles shone in the dark, feet pale as fishbellies leaping in the dim stairway. He spread the socks on the banister and unlocked the door and listened out into the silence of the flat.

Miroslav called from the sitting room, "Who's that?"

"It's me. Where are Alena and Aleks?"

The old man sat in the chair before the window, blinking at the sun.

"I'm sorry. I was having a dream."

"Are they all right?"

"Oh yes. I think so."

"Where are they?"

"Well." Miroslav tapped three fingers to his lips. "They're at chapel, I think."

"Chapel? You mean the little one?"

"Yes. They went down the hill about, about ten? Eleven maybe."

"It's nearly three now."

"They should be back soon then."

He was still blinking.

"Why are they at the chapel?"

The old man looked at him, rubbed an eye.

"Since the schools closed Alena has been taking him there to be taught. On days when you're not here."

"To be taught catechism?"

"No, I don't think so. I think it's the usual subjects. Maths and geography, grammar."

The fingertips of one hand padded against the fingertips of the other.

"Who is teaching?"

"The priest. Father—I can't remember. Can you? The young one. And some others too, I guess."

"No. I don't know him."

"Would it bother you if it were the catechism?"

"Is it catechism?"

"I suppose some of it must be."

"I can't teach him catechism. But the other things I could teach him."

"I know. But your work details, no one knows when you'll be home. When you'll be called up."

Trn nodded.

"I don't believe we expected you today."

"I never know what to expect myself."

"How did the Übermenschen treat you this week?"

"It's not so bad now that it's a little warmer."

"You must be hungry."

"A little."

"We must have something."

"I'll look after I have a wash."

"There may not be any hot water. The gas went off again, day before yesterday? Maybe the day before that." He sighed and looked out the window. "One day is much like another."

"That's true," Trn said.

"But it's like that. For an old man. It's been that way for a long while."

"I'm going to wash."

"Come back when you're done. The Russians have moved into East Prussia."

"That will give the East Prussians a lot to think about."

"I heard it on the radio. Come back and we'll look at the map. After you've eaten."

They formed the line for the issuing of coupons they received now for their blisters. Trn looked over the thin sheets of poor paper, left a thumb print in mud on the corner of each page.

"You're not like the others."

He looked up at the captain two paces away, folded the coupons away inside his breast pocket.

"Excuse me, Hauptmann?"

"You're not like them."

"I don't understand, Hauptmann. I am exactly as they are."

The captain took a step forward, one hand behind him.

"No. I don't believe it. I've seen you here three days. You do your duty. Without complaint." The captain's bright eyes radiated. "But you are wondering what is one's duty these days." He took another step and now his shoulder patched with its V for victory was close to Trn's muddy shoulder. "I see that in your eyes."

Earth smeared the captain's high boots, stippled with mud the tunic and the Iron Cross at the captain's throat.

The captain made a scoffing noise in his nose.

"That cross. Everyone looks at it. Let me tell you it means nothing. They disperse them these days like syphilis. In the name of morale."

Behind the unblinking lids his irises were iced steel piercing out the world. Arctic eyes.

"Listen this once," the captain said. "I know you hate us. How could you not? But if you hate to be occupied you will hate liberation more." He leaned to whisper. "These Russians are animals. Primitives. I say this to you. I served on the eastern front. Too long I served there. Two years."

"Thank you for telling me, Hauptmann."

The captain lit a cigarette between his teeth, looked at Trn.

"You have a family, I think."

Trn nodded.

"Hide them. Hide them all. Hide your women."

"I'm sorry?"

"Have you daughters?"

"No, Hauptmann."

"But a wife."

Trn nodded.

"Don't let the Russians see her. Keep her out of sight. We retook a village in Romania and the Russians had pillaged all the women in the two days they were there. That's how they spent their time, that and thieving and drinking. I suppose that's how we were able to retake the village." His cold eyes glared out as if the lids had been sliced away. "Old grannies, hairless girls. Any pair of legs they could part. So hide them all. Verstehst?"

"Yes, Hauptmann. I understand."

"First they'll sing, then they'll drink, then they'll grow morose and start smashing all the wares that break. And human beings break. This have I seen." The captain shook a cigarette from the packet as Trn watched. "Here. Take it."

"Thank you."

"Aren't you going to smoke?"

"Later I'll need it more."

"Then have another for later."

"Thank you, Hauptmann."

"Jager! Herkommen."

The captain turned stiffly as they called and called back, "Tell the Sturmbannführer I am coming." His lips pressed the cigarette end flat. Twin plumes of smoke billowed from his nose. He nodded tersely over his Iron Cross and limped away.

Trn made his way through the slow landscape, through the outskirts to the city, the windowsills stuffed with bedding to air, past a long apartment block gutted with stray bombs. Convoys geared up along the roads and a woman hurried a little girl by the hand away from a howitzer being rolled into a lane. At a tram stop on a sandbagged corner a man leaned his back to the wall, fingers shelled around a match. Trn watched him, brought up the cigarette from his pocket. The man lifted his chin, held the match forward in his hand.

"No. Do you want to buy it?"

The man shook out the match.

"How much?"

"It's Russian," Trn said. "How much will you give?"

The man looked at the cigarette, pocketed the matchbox, produced some coins and separated three into his palm. Trn laid the cigarette there and took the coins one by one and then brought out the second cigarette and the man paid for that too.

Through the long windows in the wooden doors Trn could see the benches were empty, the altar cleared of all but the crucifix fretted with gold. The rusted handle when he tried it gave nothing and he stepped back, looked up and down the street. A woman with a bag hanging from her shoulder slowed, dodged his eyes, walked on toward the corner. He tried again, pushed until the weathered doors clattered and the woman with her bag stood there, his hand on the iron.

"It's closed," she said, her eyes stopping at the patches of mud he wore, at his filthy shoes.

"Yes, madame. But I believe there may be some people here."

"I don't know. They provide early mass on Saturday and one on Sunday. That's all now. Everyone goes up the hill to St. Augustine. Or elsewhere."

"Yes, madame, but have you seen some children here?"

"Children? What do you want with the children?"

"I believe my son is with them. And my wife. I have just finished working and wanted to meet them here at the chapel. They keep a school here for the children."

"What is your wife's name?"

"Alena. Alena Trnova."

"And what is the name of your son?"

"Aleks. He is eleven but he's tall for that. With dark hair."

"I don't know them. I haven't seen anyone."

"I understand."

"You understand?"

"Yes, madame."

She looked past him and his mud up the stretch of the hill, down the street as a tram squealed to a stop at the corner. No one got off or on.

"They're in the crypt," she said and he bent for her whisper, the mole sprouting at the corner of her mouth two black hairs and a white one that moved with her words. "And they'll hide there. When the Russians come they're going to hide in the crypt."

Trn nodded. Two soldiers in long coats, rifles slung from their shoulders, passed across the street.

"That's my house there." She pointed with the bag at a green house next to a shop with clocks in the window. "From those front windows I see everything that comes and goes in this little square. Have been seeing it for more than twenty years."

"And they told you about the hiding?"

"I've been attending Mass here in this chapel more than two thousand one hundred times. I number them when I can't sleep and I can't sleep any night now so I know. I have the sciatica down to my knee." She gestured with swollen fingers. "So I know. My priest asked me to be one of those who shelter here. A battle is coming, he thinks. Many people do."

"Many people may be right."

She looked upward, groaned at the little clock in the little steeple.

"It's nearly three. They stop at three and come up. A few at a time. A wise practice. That clock has always been a bit behind but they should be coming up."

"I've never seen the crypt here," Trn said. "Is it large?"

"No. Not large." She shook her head. "I should say it is as large below ground as the chapel itself above. Or nearly so." She nodded, lips pursed from her reckoning. "So large enough for a good many women and children," she said. "The faithful."

"And when will you move below?"

"When the priest says. When the battle comes."

"And you have food?"

"We each contribute something that will not perish, little by little, and take it down on Sunday so not to be noticed. We stock the niches. They moved the dead long ago. Not all, not those under the floor. It's damp there. Too damp for the ones in the niches." She leaned the three whiskers toward him, whispered. "But to be sure the Germans have more to watch these days than the handbags of old ladies going to chapel on Sunday."

Trn nodded, smiled at her smile.

"Now I have heard," she whispered, "that the people of Prague can hear the American tanks. If they climb Petřín Hill and are very quiet."

"I have heard this too," Trn said.

"You have heard the tanks?"

"No. But the rumor."

"Do you believe it?"

"No, madame. It is only a rumor. The Americans only crossed the Rhine a few days ago."

"But tanks can go very fast."

"They can, madame. But the Russian tanks are nearer."

A creaking tram clanged a warning and the old woman winked at Trn and nodded.

"So. I must be on my way, young man."

He almost asked her if he looked so young but she was shuffling home, head down, hugging the bag to her side.

The tram labored up the hill toward the city center. A couple walked past talking of a child with fever. Under a molar Trn pressed the swollen gum with the tip of his tongue, shifted the molar itself.

The two soldiers returned and in their long coats watched across the square. The clock read thirteen minutes before the hour. Trn put on his hat and bent toward home, the long steep climb home, mud falling from his shoes as he went.

"I want you to take this," he said, unclasping the watch from his wrist.

"But it's too big," Aleks said.

He made the band fast on the boy's forearm and pulled the sleeve down again and said, "I won't be here when you get back so ask Grandfather to make another hole in the band for you."

The last view before Alena pulled the door was of Aleks on the landing, his dark eyes staring up out of the dark. Trn went to the sitting room, clicked on the radio, sat on the couch, then reached and clicked the radio off again.

"Come, Viktor. She knows you don't approve."

"Of the teaching?"

"Yes, of course. Of the church."

"I'm not bothered by that. Any exercise his mind receives is an addition. I don't object to that. The boy can decide for himself."

"To what then?"

Trn drew his hand down his face.

"When the war comes, and it is coming every day, we should all be in the same place. That's the only way we can be of help to one another."

"Perhaps there's room in the crypt."

"I don't believe so but even if there were I could not go."

"And why?"

"Because I cannot take refuge in war where I would not take refuge in peace. I cannot take the place another might take."

"Another more deserving?"

"Yes, another more deserving. But we shouldn't separate. What's boiling toward us in that smoke on the horizon is chaos and in that chaos we shouldn't divide ourselves. It will be hard enough together. It would be worse apart."

"Don't you believe the crypt would be safer than here?"

"I don't know that any place will be safe."

The old man set his cold pipe on the table.

"What can we do then?"

"I want you to speak to Alena. I would like you to convince her to stay here. To stay with the Steinhardts in the cellar."

"Maybe they're right," Miroslav said. "Maybe they will be more sheltered in the valley than here. On this hillside. If the Germans make a hedgehog defense as they did in Budapest and fight house by house there won't be anything left."

"Do you really think there will be shelter anywhere?"

"No but no doubt some places will be safer than others."

"Do we know where those places are?"

"The crypt might be one of them."

Trn locked his hands together and stared down into their chain.

"What if they demolish the dam? The valley will flood to the lower reaches of the city just as the river used to do."

"Viktor, I can convince her of nothing."

"I think you can. I know you can try."

The old man pulled up the blanket over his paunch.

"Alena is completely out of sympathy with me. We both know that. There is no more feeling there. You heard what she said just now. That it would all be easier if I were gone, would stay gone."

"She couldn't mean that, Viktor."

"She's said it before." He swallowed against a clot rising in his throat. "If they should get into trouble there who will help them? When the running starts who will wait for them, hold his hand toward them? Who will carry Aleks if he falls? When the bullets begin to strike the stone?"

Miroslav picked at the blanket with a thumb and finger. He sighed at the window, dropped his eyes again. "Why should April be so cold?"

"I don't know but this year it is."

"At least Vienna's fallen," the old man said. "We were to be part of the defense of Vienna, I thought. Her northern flank."

"Now it seems we're the center."

Miroslav pinched a handkerchief over his nose.

"I will speak with her, Viktor."

"Thank you." Trn rose and reached a hand to the old man's shoulder, left it there. "Thank you very much."

The old man blinked into his eyes.

"You have been a good son-in-law, Viktor."

Trn shrugged. "But not much of a husband. A poor husband."

"She's like her mother. What can we do? She asked me the other day if you could teach English. Someone had inquired but I told her any damn fool with half an eye to his head could see that Malinovsky is going to beat Patton by two hundred kilometers. And then she wondered if you could teach Russian."

He smiled an aged smile and breathed a chuckle that faded with the breath. They shook hands and the old man peered into Trn's palm.

"You still have blisters from the last time."

"Soon enough I won't have any room left for blisters."

"You can't get blisters on top of callouses. That's what I always heard."

"We'll see. I don't know when I'll be back."

The old man glimpsed his eyes.

"Things will be different, Viktor. After the war."

"I'm sure they will. But even if they are what difference will it make?"

"Maybe just enough."

"I must report. Do you want me to turn on the radio?"

"God no. It's filled with that little bastard's birthday music. The world's gift to him this year is that from his headquarters he can go back and forth between the eastern and western fronts by taxicab. His gift to the world is that the Allies can travel straight down the autobahn to Berlin."

"Goodbye, Miroslav."

The old man nodded and his hand lifted from the blanket as if to bid farewell.

Trn padded in sock feet down the stairs, two alabaster toenails leading the way from the right sock, another from the left. Down the street he looked back once more at the house, the Steinhardts' banner furled over the wall in observance of the nativity. The last commemoration. Because the others with their own bloodred banners were at the gate, the hordes on the march with their own red brassards bearing the hook of another strict religion. Hands in his pockets he turned away and hunched on toward the collection point at the Zentrum.

T hey lay on the crowded ground as if sleep could be had. One filthy blanket for every two men and the wind blew through the flaps on a night cold for April's end even in the seasons of this world. Trn looked up into the dark crown of the tent, his arms for pillows until the feeling went out of both hands. Then he laid his head in his crushed hat and listened.

Artillery thundered to the south, to the east and northeast but mostly tonight to the south. Malinovsky and the Second Ukrainian coming up from Vienna. Long cannonades that went on when the other sectors were quiet, gunners finding their range. So many he couldn't count because the next detonation obliterated the one before. As you dug you could feel the tremors tumble through the earth. The noise deadened the snoring in the tent even though they all snored, breath torn from exhaustion, and Trn was sure that he snored too. They muttered. The blanket departed when the next man twisted and called out to his father and Trn listened for what the father might tell him, what the son might reply. Then he must have slept because clanging metal opened his eyes, the guard at the tent flap beating his truncheon against the blade of a shovel. Some of the men already stood, cloaked like hags in their blankets, barely the light to see them stamping their feet on the crests of mud.

There was nothing to eat now except the tablet of glucose doled out by the guard. "Shovels for breakfast again," a grizzled man grumbled and they took up the handles from the stacks and went down into the ditches where the rifle barrel directed. A silver plane passed. "Only a spotter," the guard called. The men pushed themselves from the ground and the plane lifted and joined another and a third and they flew on to higher clouds, disappeared north while the men picked up their shovels. No one said anything for a moment and then the grizzled man whispered to Trn, "Did you see? Not one shell. If there's no flak and no fighters you have to wonder how much longer they can hold."

"I don't understand," another man stammered, "why we don't, start waving our, hands at them and, let the, Russians dig this, hole for us."

A man digging at their backs said they'd moved all the squadrons and all the batteries to Berlin and another said they should all shut the hell up before some SS heard them and got every fucking one of them shot the hell through the head.

The guard bellowed and beckoned with his arm and Trn with two others slid into a shallow transverse trench behind the first line. With his shovel he faced south, the others north, a drumbeat of artillery rolling over the horizon. The guards stared east where the howl of Katyushas picked up the cadence, rockets in relay dropping somewhere on someone. "Stalin's organs," the next man said and the other said, "Let's hope we don't all get fucked by Stalin's organ."

This went on and then if the bombardment continued in other sectors Trn couldn't hear it for what fell to the east. He couldn't hear the planes either but a series of men in the trench dove at the mud and he did the same, twisting his neck to see. A silver flight of ten or a dozen collected and bore west toward the rear. He scouted the sky for more and through the haze saw only the twin needles of Petr and Pavel on their hilltop. More haze hung to the north and the wind bore the thick smell of smoldering oil.

The mud warmed and stank like the dung of a sty from his boyhood. Men undid their shirts and took off their coats and tried to fling them over the parapet they raised but Trn kept his. Their trench progressed and then they were so deep even the cathedral spires were lost.

A corporal walked their line, hair peppered gray under his cap, gray stubbled jaw. He licked his lips and wiped his mouth with the back of his hand while the storm built its thunder, resettled the strap of the rifle across his shoulder and walked on. They grunted down over their shovels for more mud. You could hear it all progress as the Russians walked their shells up to the front. Each man paused to verify this by looking into another's eyes and then over their heads the air was peeled back from the earth and the ground beyond them burst and when it ceased trembling Trn climbed to peer at the field still smoking a hundred meters away. A second shell screamed over and clods of mud plummeted into the trench where he lay and before the mud stopped raining men were running past him, clambering with hands in the mud walls to get by. A man toppled and tried to claw himself up on Trn's coat. A shovel tripped someone else and the pack piled over and past him. A shell exploded at some unseen distance and when the sound was gone Trn was jogging with others down the trench through the sluice of mud. Some were stopping to kick against the walls to make toeholds and one of these went sprawling when the corporal leaped in on top of him. Voices screamed "Halt!" and Trn reached the end of the trench and climbed out onto ground where two horses lay fallen across the grass in their twisted rigging.

He circled a crater with white smoke still clinging to its lowest reaches. He looked back to see an officer strike a man across the shoulder with a truncheon, the dirt with the blow dusting up from the man's coat. Infantry in gray ran at all angles and collided with knots of men running in shoes gobbed with mud. They cried "Halt!" but there were trees nearby, just beyond a line of trucks drawn up at the foot of the hill, and no one halted. A shot clattered flat across the struggling grass when he was almost to the trucks and then a concussion took him to the ground and he crawled between two tires and lurched on through smoke into the silver of birches. Those already there set their backs against the trunks and coughed, leaned while their throats hacked for air. Another shriek came over and an explosion tossed men running into the air. Planes droned and somewhere he could hear horses screaming. The bark of a tree in his line of sight went to splinters at the level of his eyes. He made his way to the edge of the copse and looked west toward the city. Something north of him was on fire, something large. The silent smoke raged up into a great black column and formed its own weather among the low clouds but in fact all the horizon he could see churned with darkness. Southwest through broken haze he squinted out the cathedral spires pricking the sky and that put the little chapel northwest of him. Rifle shots still cracked behind when he ran out of the trees toward the fires in the distance.

For a time he crossed ragged fields, rough grass to his knees, made his way from one tree line to the next and then into a pine forest that climbed a range of hills. The explosions were all well behind him now. He worried these ridges would be fortified but found only shallow entrenchments, all empty. Not enough men to defend to this depth. Maybe they only meant to make a show of force, a demonstration to slow Malinovsky, then withdraw to the central highlands, but he believed this no longer than it took him to think it. From the summit of the last hill in the range he could see a road snaking west toward the city, disappearing into cedars at the river. Before he descended out of the woods he saw they'd already destroyed the bridge from bank to bank, hulks of concrete shattered into the water stacking white against the wreckage like pilings. He looked at it longer than he needed to. If they were already dropping bridges then eventually they'd blow the dam. Blow the dam and flood the plain into the city, then hide behind the deluge, like Holland. The Russians must have thought of that too.

A whine came traveling, two motorcycles with sidecars. They kept their speed along the road paralleling the far side of the river and disappeared and slowly the whine faded too. The black water ran on in its channel between stone walls. He could climb along the wreckage but could he scale the other side? He listened for another patrol but all he heard was the river and the shelling muted behind him. In any case he had to get across.

He left the trees in a crouch and went over the side, let himself down from the ledge, the muddy toes of his shoes and the tips of his fingers fitted into joints between the courses of stone until he could drop to the first floe of concrete that pitched and settled under him. Before he stepped once a shot ricocheted and he went flat. His hat rolled on its brim to the edge of the slab and the wind carried it over and it rode the swift current up and down before it sank. He scanned the opposite bank, the line of cedars, a stone abutment where the bridge had joined the road.

"I'm Czech." His jaw with a week's beard scraped the concrete when he called out. "I'm going home." Nothing moved that he could see except water and the branches of the cedars. In German he called, "I'm going to stand so that you can see I am a civilian. I'm alone and I don't have any weapons."

He pushed himself up, held his overcoat open.

"Do you see?"

He turned once slowly, hands raised, scanning the trees again as his eyes came about.

"I'm coming over and I'm going to walk down that road and you won't see me again." He said it once more in German. "Verstehen Sie?"

Two plates of the bridge had buckled in the center like a tent and he couldn't climb the side steeped against him so he took off his coat and draped its length over his shoulders, lowered himself into the cold water and handed himself along the downstream side. He made a lunge for the next jagged edge and lifted himself out by the projecting steel, the water rilling off him to splatter the lines painted on the bridge. He felt the ache of water more in his shoulders than his feet and legs. The coat was wet too but he put it on and clamped his jaw against his shivering. As he readied to jump a body bobbed against the fragment he stood on, rested back into the wash and surfaced again. Only the remnant of a man, the face pallid except for bruised eyes, a gold ring crimping a bloated finger, the guts inside the ruined ribs a pale anatomy lesson through which the current ran. Three more bounds and he was staring up the stone wall for toeholds.

"Now I'm coming up," he called. "I'm coming up."

The cement was cracked and loose and he fingered it out where he needed to, expecting at the top to see a gun barrel staring him down. His hand felt the grit on the ledge and with a last effort he rose and crouched, dripping onto the broken road sloping gently into the city. In the gloom under the cedars he saw no one. He stood wincing for a shot that didn't come and the sound of water died as he walked away in squelching shoes. By the shadows he tried to judge the time and the direction he might be going and the direction he should take but all he could tell was that he was in the city again, buildings to each side of the road, houses, a brick school set back in its fenced grounds, the end station of a line with red trams numbered six and thirteen parked behind the fence and that was some help.

He turned through a maze in an empty path of streets he didn't know but reckoned would bear him northwest and then for the first time he heard repeated gunfire in the distance. Out from a haze before him, a local fog at the end of a long straight street, the reports rose. He stooped in the shuttered entry of a shop that had a dusty chrome toaster in the window and he leaned to see as far as he could. Someone yelled and a man in a red sweater sprinted aslant the road and two soldiers came running after. One of the two raised a pistol that jerked his arm upward and blue smoke bloomed and the soldiers ran through it. Trn went on into the burned air, slow steps from doorway to doorway, left down a narrow street then right onto another. He waited, saw no one, went on at a run but the world grew loud again and he stopped. A small square at the end of the street filled with smoke and echoes and he crouched on a doorstep some houses away. A shadow moved across the edge of his eye, a lace curtain parted and a hand opened the window across the way. A boy not so tall as Aleks called, "Are you with the resistance?"

Trn shook his head. Behind the boy a man appeared with a scowl on his face and moved the boy out of the window and shut it, wrenched down the blackout curtain. Trn dashed across and rapped at the window, rapped until the scowling face appeared behind a pane.

"Where is this?" Trn said through the glass.

The man shook his head.

"I'm trying to reach home," Trn said.

"There are a lot of people saying that. Are you in the resistance?"

"No. I've been in a trenching brigade and I'm trying to reach my family. I don't know this quarter. What square is this?"

"A trenching brigade?"

"Yes."

Trn knelt under the window and the man opened it to the width of his mouth.

"Namesti Novi. Where are you trying to get to?"

"Namesti Miru."

"That's a long way. You can't get there."

"Why?"

The man opened the window to lean and look toward the square.

"The resistance has come out because the Germans are falling back. They've taken over parts of the city and they're not allowing any movement until the Red Army comes. The Volkssturm are fighting the resistance and there's infantry. Panzers too."

"How do you know?"

"We've seen them pass. And it's on the radio. The resistance took over the radio. For a while. But the Germans took it back."

The visible square exploded then and trailing the noise a gray dust boiled down the street. Trn shrank as it settled over him, blind debris falling out of the cloud in particles. The world returned slowly, its space choked with powder and shouts in the distance and the rapid stutter of guns. Trn peered out between his arms at the gray street, the window closed and coated with dust.

He sprinted across the lanes toward what he took to be west and three blocks later the sound of gunfire abated. He crossed a broader avenue, moved through the dust still hanging and from the next corner peered out at a rising barricade, civilians crawling over the pile of stone and masonry and splintered timbers, the handle of a buried baby carriage pointing toward him as he made his way forward. With axe and mattock men in shirtsleeves, women in dresses, were prying stones out of the street course by course and handing them forward in line brigades to be thrown onto the crest of the rampart.

At first they didn't any of them look at him till a barechested man with a black armband came up to him, stood before Trn with his fists on his hips. He didn't say anything.

"How far is it to Namesti Míru from here?"

"What have you come for?"

"I'm trying to reach my family, my wife and my son. They're in hiding in Namesti Míru."

"If they're hiding they're safe. We need another man here."

"The Germans have mined the dam and if they demolish it that part of the city will be flooded."

The man glared at him.

"How do you know they've mined the dam?"

"They've mined everything."

The man spat at the ruined road.

"So you won't help then."

"They're in danger. I've got to get to them."

"We're all in danger. We all have families. I've got about thirty men and women at this barricade to stop anything that comes. You would make thirty-one."

Trn surveyed the broken street, the mounting debris across it, a line of men lying along the jagged crest with a few rusted rifles, tin casques from the last war on their heads. On the sidewalk a collection of glass bottles stoppered with rags. Some of the casques bore the painted flag of the old republic. One of them shifted and under it was Dolezal stroking his fat mustache.

"Maybe you've come to see what we're doing here."

With his fists on his hips the man was still staring. He sucked his teeth, spat on the pounded earth where the stone of the road once lay. Two men with picks unbent their backs to listen. The brigades had stopped too, a man with a stone in his hands watching Trn.

"If the Germans blow the dam that district will be flooded. Maybe this one too. I don't know."

"If they do then we'll hold the Germans by the throat till we all drown."

"I only want to get to my family. That man there can tell you. Dolezal."

The casque Dolezal wore turned slowly away.

"Dolezal," Trn called. "Tell him."

"What's your name?" the man said.

Trn gazed over the roadbed and took a step away. A man with a pick dropped it and the handle rang against the cobbles and the man with the stone hurled it at Trn and missed. One long stride and Trn began to run.

Someone called out for him to stop, called for him to be arrested, but he had already vaulted the last heap of the wrecked street and reached the nearest corner when a single shot chased him. He ran on and took the first street without looking back and made the next corner and slid behind a trash can. But no one was coming and he heard nothing except his own lungs bellowing dust through the ache in his throat. He coughed into his hands, breathed under their cover, spat powder. Still no one appeared at the end of the street and he waited on one knee only long enough to reconfigure the way west. Then he stood and went on.

B lock by block what remained of the neighborhoods spread under low skies. He kept a hand or shoulder always to the rough walls and dodged into the next recess when he saw someone, a woman hooded in a black shawl teetering on heels till she pitched suddenly forward, swallowed by the ruin, a jogging file of infantry, three ghosts cloaked in blankets against the gusts of smoke. Over the rooftops, down the alleys came gunfire that he squinted to fix by its echoes off the broken brick. At a cross street the gutter gurgled and ran red into the drain as from a cloudburst on Mars and round the corner he found the source, a man in an overcoat prone on the cobbles with the top of his skull sheared away. The surge diminished while Trn watched but it hadn't stopped when he walked on. The artillery built again in the east and he wondered how much longer the Germans could stand it. When they gave way that's when they'd destroy the dam, when the cannons stopped. They'd have no reason not to.

The open end of the street before him flashed white and the ground trembled so that he reached out and swayed under the loudest blast he'd yet heard or a chain of them as if the detonation of the last lit the next and within that crescendo the crash of all the world's glass. Then like a silent newsreel of disaster the street filled up with slow smoke. In the dark that followed he could feel concussions go on in his chest and in the ground under his knees.

When he took down his hands after the last reverberation he moved into a gloom silent except for the tuning fork someone struck at his right ear that quavered up through the register near and then far and then shimmered again in his left ear. He worked a finger into each ear to restart their drums and the tympany of the world came back with crying and screams and sparks of glass everywhere. He spat on the pavement and found with his tongue crystal briars and spat again. He tasted salt blood. A voice, a man's voice joined by a woman's, was yelling, "Get away from the windows," but when Trn squinted through the smoke he saw no more windows. The walls gaped with jagged fangs of glass and the screams and crying came into the street from the height of six or eight stories.

His sleeves sparkled and he wore glittering epaulettes. He took off the coat and shook it. He thought to feel and his face was powdered in glass and his scalp spiked with it and he licked two bloody fingers and dabbed at his brow, his lids and lashes, his cheeks and lips. A man walked down the sidewalk toward him, glimmering to a halt and shining in his hair.

Trn said "Do you know what happened?" in a voice strange even to himself, as if he were speaking from the other side of a locked door. The man passed on, blood drooling from his ear. Glass daggers cracked beneath Trn's steps and the reek of burning gasoline hung in the street. Another explosion burst, muted, far away it seemed. In the next block a cluster of people watched an orange fire that roared two or three stories against the blackened buildings at the far end and the fire issued a black smoke that tumbled over itself to get into the sky.

A man held onto the cornerstone and blood leaked from the gash on the back of his hand.

"What's this?" Trn said.

The man jerked with surprise. Blood ran into his eye and he smeared it with his bloody hand. "There was a field there," he said looking back, "a field at the end of the street. The Germans kept an ammunition depot there."

A woman with her arms folded, her hair fanning in the heat, didn't look at him, her nose in profile tinged orange. No one watched him leave and it was a long while before the windows had panes again and the smell of gasoline burned away. From the balconies white sheets furled in the smoke even though the SS had warned they'd shoot the owners of houses demonstrating such defeatism. A Wehrmacht convoy crossed him once, covered trucks, seven of them, towing field guns, but they passed quickly and one more bleeding man no concern of theirs. He skewed his course to theirs and kept it for a time but with no watch and no sun to reckon by he didn't know how long. No streets were familiar or named since they'd pulled down all the signs. He had not gone far when the streets ran out and the rubble began, apartment blocks shattered down into their foundations and heaped against their own ruin. He rounded a scree of shattered brick and nearly collided with a man tugging a little girl by the hand. She knuckled her eyes and the man crouched low and took her up in his arms.

"Have you seen a woman?" the man asked. "A woman with a green scarf?"

"No."

"She went to fetch her mother so we could all leave the city but she hasn't come back. My wife. She has a green scarf." The little girl hid her face at his neck and sobbed. "And a brown coat."

"I'm sorry," Trn said. "I haven't seen her."

The man looked at him through dusty glasses that magnified his eyes into vague stains. They blinked as if slowly falling asleep together.

"She wanted to go last week but they wouldn't let me leave the factory. I told her to go."

"What time did she leave for her mother's?"

"I don't know. What day is today?"

"Do you know—" Trn began but the man looked back at him and said, "They're coming here now."

The man looked back the way he had come.

"Hear that? Down there? Russians. We saw them, one of their tanks."

The little girl sobbed, wiped her nose with the back of her hand and wiped her hand over her father's blue shirt and hid her face again.

"You must find a place to hide," Trn said.

"I must find my wife."

"Look, there's the white arrow there, above the door. Do you see? Go into the shelter and wait till this is over and then look for your wife. She may be with her mother. Is it near, where her mother lives?"

"It's gone," the man said. "It's not there anymore." He swallowed so the knot in his throat rode and fell inside his collar.

Trn looked through the dust at his blurred eyes.

"The whole block where her mother lived."

"Would you like me to help you to the shelter? I can carry her."

The man looked in the direction Trn pointed, shrugged the little girl higher onto his shoulder.

"Why don't you give her to me?" Trn reached out his hands. "I can carry her."

"No. No, we can make it."

"Are you sure?"

"Yes. Thank you."

The man knelt and set the little girl on her feet and took up the little hand. She fisted her eye, her blond hair tangled with dust.

"She's tired," the man said.

"I know she is," Trn said. "She can rest in the shelter."

"It's just walls now," the man said. "Where we live is just walls."

Trn nodded and gripped the man's shoulder and faced him toward the arrow.

"Maybe there will be something to eat in the shelter."

"I don't think so," the man said.

He watched them stagger over the blocks of rubble and the man bent once to speak to the little girl and since Trn did not look back that was the last he saw of them.

The next block was worse, strewn with boulders of charred masonry, fallen wire and so much debris that he wasn't walking on road any longer in a district where the Allies had already dropped their brandbombs. An unmade bed hung half out of a broken house. In a room further down a portrait of some soldier tilted on a floral wallpaper and in the exposed bathroom a clawfooted tub fractured in two leaked water through the breach and Trn climbed over the wreckage to cup his hands and drink. Somewhere in the pile a clock wound up toward a dizzy chime. He listened for the hour, drinking from his hands, but it spun on and never struck and then the stutters of machine guns began to duel somewhere beyond the ruined buildings. He stumbled into an alley and handed himself along the crumbling wall to its end, the machine guns louder but he could not tell where.

He peered out into the ruined street. A barricade like he'd seen before heaped with stone and timbers, piping, whatever came to hand, another bathtub upended. At the other end of the street two trams had been derailed and wedged nose to tail to block the way. Men scrounged behind the barrier, others tossed rubble into the trams through their shattered windows. He was turning back when three figures loomed in the way he had come, one of them with a rifle raised.

"Ahoj."

"Ahoj. Are you a communist?"

"I'm not anything."

"Who are you then?"

"I'm trying to get to my home."

"Who are you?"

A door, a rattled collection of planks, was three steps in the wrong direction. With hands raised he started forward as the men did and then dashed against the door that didn't open because his hand missed the knob but the planks burst anyway and he rolled down a flight of stairs that also collapsed step by step into a darkness where everything smelled of black forgotten waters. Some floor jerked him to a stop and he crouched into the dark as far it would take him. The shape of a man blotting the light in the high doorway began cursing.

The rifle barrel rose and behind his elbow and closed eyes Trn could still see the blast. When the concussion had faded the door was an empty rectangle of high pale light hung with smoke in the black wall. The ball of his left shoulder throbbed but he knew that was from the fall and by the dim light from the door he felt his way along a narrow corridor of sweating brick. He could only turn right and that's the way he went, rats crying as they fled his shoes in the dark, his hands proving out the slow walls until his shin struck a board edge at what became another flight of stairs. He tested them each up toward a chink of light that became a trapdoor. His fingers on the cool metal, he listened to the light. He pressed to see out. Another street studded with rubble, gunfire but distant. He tried the next step and shouldered the door higher. The trap was in a sidewalk and he was looking up at a shattered shop window, the remains of a brown book and a black one painted on the remains of glass, the street stretching away till it curved. He was climbing from the weight of the door, grit under his palms, until he looked behind at a black horse dead on its side, its black eye close enough to stare him down.

A man squinted at him over the horse's belly. He had a knife in his hand, a pail between his knees. The man looked down and with his whole torso began sawing at the shank again. The horse lay aslant the tram track, tangled in hoops of wire. A woman in the shreds of a dress was lumbering toward them, the handle of a saucepan in one fist, a butcher knife in the other. The man looked up again, his jaws clamped. "They're not alive," he said, clinking his blade against the wire. "We haven't had electricity for days."

Flies crawled among the hairs of the black snout, over the dark protruded tongue, the black egg of the eye. They rose and zipped above the open belly as the man moved to a new place on the hide and went on sawing. Machine guns chattered again beyond the curve of the street and the man lifted out between his dripping hands a livid mass that ran like a sponge of blood and dropped it in the pail. "Liver," he said. He plunged the blade into its work again then suddenly looked up at a deeper sound that cancelled the machine guns, a low creaking

as in some giant's iron jaw. The man stared into the curve of the
street and without his eyes reached and took up the pail by its wire
and in a crouch hustled away. The woman had also disappeared.

As Trn stood the door of the bookshop opened with a small tin-
kling and a boy leaned out, tall, down on his chin.

"Are you a comrade from our cell?"

"What's your cell?"

"That means you're not." The boy looked up the street, looked
over Trn. "Cohort three, of the northern district."

The creaking came louder and with it round the curve they could
see the barrel of the tank emerge, the bore crank round to face them,
a cluster of men crouching behind, rifles in their hands.

"You better come in anyway," the boy said and the door closed
behind them with the tinny ring of the bell. The shop was dark, lined
with cases of dark books. The boy stooped in broken glass, contem-
plated the street through the broken window.

"We won't be able to see anything here," he said.

"See what?"

"The battle. They've already fought over this street twice. The
Red Army liberated it and then the fascists repelled them. But you
see how the Red Army is returning to the offensive." He put his
hands on his knees, pushed himself to stand. "Let's go upstairs."

Trn looked up at him.

"It's no safer here than there and you can command the whole
street from there."

The wooden staircase groaned and twisted on itself as the boy
leaped the steps by threes. On the first floor he strode past a wooden
desk to a window already opened and put out his head and shoulders.

"Come look," he shouted back at Trn. "They're almost here."

Over the boy's shoulder Trn spied the tank nearly below them
now, the soldiers still moving at a crouch, perhaps twenty helmets
like dull turtleshells shifting as their eyes roamed. The tank churned
over brick that broke into a sudden reddish dust. A soldier's face
tilted up at them and Trn dodged down, pulled the boy away.

"They wouldn't harm us," the boy said.

"They don't know who you are," Trn said. "They may think we're snipers."

"I believe they understand we are one with them in the antifascist struggle."

They could hear the tank grind on amid shouts in the street and then the first shots. The boy jumped to the window, hands gripped on the still.

"A panzer," he called. "Come see."

The Russian tank had stopped, the men behind it scattering to the walls. The boy shouted, "Here comes the panzer." The Russian tank recoiled with a burst and settled in the dust it raised and clanked forward and recoiled again as ricochets echoed in the street. The panzer at the open end of the street was on fire and the boy was yelling until down some angle came a burst that shuddered the Russian tank and the turret exploded upwards as if torn open from the inside. The street erupted into shouts and gunfire and a man with the shoulders of his uniform in flames lay over the rubble beside the burning tank. Soldiers in gray raced past through the black smoke boiling from the turret.

The boy said, "Those bastards." He was pulling out the drawers of the desk. "It's not right. They came down the alley with a panzerfaust. Did you see?" He lifted out a green ball that filled his palm and ran to the window and hurled the ball into the street, calling, "You all will die."

The boy stood at the window with his arms at his sides as the gunfire carried up the street.

"I have to go get it."

"It would be suicide to go out there now."

"I forgot to pull the pin."

Tears started from his eyes and sat on his lashes.

"What's your name?"

"Jirka."

"Where do you live, Jirka?"

The boy motioned out into the street.

"You have family at home there?"

"My mother. Two sisters."

"Why don't you go to them. They need you now."

"They killed my father. In June. They arrested him one night and for five days we didn't know of him until they told us to come get him from the gymnazium. He lay on a table without even a sheet over him. They gave others sheets but my father was there in his under-wear. I could smell him from the corridor. He'd pissed himself. His shorts yellow and his brows so swollen he couldn't see and the flat bone of his nose crooked in front of one eye." The boy slumped at the desk, arms crossed over a torn map of the new Europe still priced at twenty-one crowns. "I can't remember which eye now. I try to remember. And today I forget to pull the pin on the last grenade." He laid his head on his arm.

"Then your mother and sisters need you today more than they've ever needed you."

The boy rubbed his eyes across his sleeve and mumbled.

"A child is the synthesis of the parents. Father, mother: son. I should mark an improvement over them in every way."

"Jirka. Have you heard anything from the other cells?"

"A little."

"Do you have a radio?"

"No. Cadres run dispatches from command to the outposts. But I'm the only one left."

"Do you know if they've destroyed the dam?"

"I don't know."

"Do you know the fastest way from here to Namesti Míru?"

"The Germans wired the dam long ago."

"I know. I'm worried about the flood if they destroy it."

"You're much closer to the dam than you are to Namesti Míru."

"How close?"

"Not more than four kilometers."

Without raising his head the boy waved at a corner of the room.

"Four kilometers?"

The boy nodded and sniffed and Trn looked into the corner.

"Thank you, Jirka." He gripped the boy's shoulder, leaned to find his eyes. "Go home now. To your mother and sisters."

But the boy wouldn't look up, made no move to rise, and Trn left him there, the boards of the stairs aching against their nails as he took them at a run.

In the street the man was back at the horse with his knife and pail, the woman in tatters hobbling to join him as if on broken knees. The soldiers all were dead, one with the tunic burned off his blistered back. Slow flames still fought their way out of the shattered tank and Trn used it as cover, his hand on the armor almost too hot to touch, looking in both directions before he stumbled across the havoc. In the smoke he cast no shadow.

C ivilization ended abruptly. The street quit at the last building and across a field sat an abandoned tram, a number twelve, and he realized now how far he'd strayed from the way he'd set out all those hours ago. He joined the tramline for the course he and Aleks had ridden to school and walked among the trees beside the rails and came to another tram deserted on the inbound track, examined its bloody skin where it had been strafed, then walked on again. In the eastern distance the artillery thudded and once planes drove him flat to the weeds but he kept near the line as it traveled up the valley and joined the road. He leaned a moment with his hand on a flayed birch to watch the river still placid between its banks, then kept his parallel course north through the woods.

Three convoys of varying lengths trucked past towing guns and ammunition, carrying infantry, all moving south, and behind the trees he tried to map in his mind what that might mean. He moved deeper into the shade until the tramline spurred toward the lake and then he went that way. From the last stop he followed through the grass the bare trace of bathers and picnickers from holidays long uncelebrated. In one direction the shoreline ran west and in the other curved north toward the dam. At points the pines grew from the slope nearly to the water's edge and their image wavered on the surface of the lake with the passing clouds. The cannonade strengthened while the water calmly bore the sky. Eventually he could make out the dam from some distance, the rusted catwalk perched over the concrete wall and at the midpoint the plate-metal shack for the control valve like the wheelhouse of a little boat.

He watched the windows and worked down in a crouch to almost the last pine, frightening from a bush a scatter of black birds that chittered and flapped away. Finally a figure in a long gray field coat stalked out of the valvehouse and paced all the way to the gate near the shore and made an about face. Trn could hear the boot steps echo on the grating. The rifle strapped over the man's shoulder jogged beside him. It was still a good run in the open to the gate. That he could jump, it was only waist high, but then what? He dusted bark from his palm, stared through the bush, red berries among the green leaves and thorns. The thunder behind was distancing itself like the storm was passing south.

The soldier reached the far gate, paused and came back. Trn thought he might go in but the soldier stopped and looked down into the lake, hands pale on the railing. Trn calculated the number of strides to the gate and the seconds necessary to take them. The berries were brighter red at the stem. His hand clutched a sprig and he pulled the cluster free and spilled the handful into his coat pocket and to be sure stripped another bough for the other pocket. For the last extremity. The soldier was still at the railing. He wore glasses and scratched in his left ear vigorously, examined what his nail might have dislodged and flicked it into the lake. He brought out a packet of cigarettes and shook one loose and struck a match and put the packet away. He blew smoke in what seemed more a sigh than anything else and watched the match burn down before dropping it into the water.

When he lifted his face toward the bombardment Trn saw that under his cap he was just a boy. The boy walked to the other railing and looked down into the white water rushing away. He took off the cap, ran a sleeve over his brow, and settled the cap again. When he snapped the embering stub into the air, the strap of the rifle slipped to his elbow and he tugged it up and went in the valvehouse. The metal door clanged shut.

Trn counted sixty as slowly as he could and then counted thirty and let go of the pine. He legged himself over the gate, watching the windows of the valvehouse dark and grimed. The door stayed closed. The gauge erected for the lake stood a little over twelve meters. He flattened himself under the railing, the white flume a long drop below him and all that he could hear now. The wires were black, looped round the struts of the catwalk and snaking down the wall rusted and green to the holes drilled for the charges. He reached along the concrete and grabbed at the first wire and pulled but it was bracketed along its descent and much thicker than he had thought it would be. He had to shift his torso further under the railing to wrest the wire free with both hands. Six he could count from here, more beyond the valvehouse. No doubt six there too. Die Symmetrie. The door stood closed. He crawled to the second wire and jerked again so the grating shook under him but when he stilled himself the tremor wasn't his. The boy had already stopped running and the rifle barrel was swinging down to Trn's left eye. The boy's mouth stretched into a yell Trn couldn't hear. The barrel motioned for him to stand and then pointed at his chest and the boy yelled at him again over the water.

"Was machen Sie?"

His face, the thick round lenses hooked behind his large ears, reminded Trn very much of a pale rabbit. The face of a student wandered up before him but he couldn't recall the name, a name with this same rabbit's curl of lip.

"Are you alone here?" Trn said.

The bleary eyes behind the lenses darted at him.

"If you leave," Trn said, "no one will know."

"Stop your mouth," the boy said and the snout of the rifle nosed Trn's heart and prodded him back a step.

"The Russians are surrounding."

"I said shut up."

His voice was deeper than Trn expected.

"Listen. They know the war is lost. Your officers know it can't go on."

The barrel jerked up and struck Trn's chin and clacked his teeth together. He ran a tinge of blood around his mouth and gathered and spat it over the railing into the wash. The back of his hand brought away the blood from his chin where the forward sight had cut. The dark eyes peered through the lenses over the barrel boring him down.

"The war will be over in a few days," Trn said slowly. "You've survived it this long. Don't you want to live?"

"I am a German soldier. I cannot desert my post." A gloved hand wiped quickly under the nose, darted back to the stock. "I take my orders directly from the Führer. No German soldier takes one step backwards."

"Then how did the Russians get here from Moscow?"

The rifle butt swung round and Trn took the shock with his shoulder, stumbled against the railing but didn't fall. When he stood again he didn't raise his arms.

"You have family at home. They want to see you again."

The pink tongue leaped and wet both lips.

"The engineers are coming. I am to wait for them. The patrol will come soon."

"And I know you must want to see your family. Think of your mother. Your father."

"My mother's dead. She died in a fire in Regensburg. In a bombing." The boy's face was red. He swallowed and said, "Get on your knees."

Trn said, "Killing won't bring her back."

"The penalty for sabotage is death. Immediate execution."

"Sabotage is destroying this dam. In an hour or two at the most the Russians are going to come over that ridge. You've heard their artillery and you know it's true."

"Down to your knees."

"You can shoot me but you'll do it while I stand. And the Russians will still come. They'll still take this ground. And you will die but you don't have to."

"Turn around."

"If you're going to shoot me you must have the courage to do it with my eyes on you."

He reached for Trn's arm, clutched the coat sleeve in his fist.

"I told you to turn around."

With his right hand Trn slapped the boy so hard his palm stung as if the cheek had been faced with needles. The boy's glasses vanished from his eyes and his cap fell. Trn braced against the railing and carried the boy across the catwalk against the far rail so the rabbit face jolted back and the rifle clattered butt first and rang down on the grating. The boy stretched for it, Trn still pinning him to the railing until he could kick at the barrel and send the rifle scuttling along the walk. The bolt caught a moment in the grating and then the length of it tipped over the edge into the lake.

The boy slumped in Trn's hands, his head hanging toward the rifle's last visible position.

Trn said, "Do you have the detonator?"

The eyes wouldn't come up.

"Where is the detonator?"

"I don't have it."

"Where is it?"

"The engineers will bring it when they receive their orders."

The boy's face was close under his own, close enough for Trn to see the cleft at the end of his nose.

"The safest route for you," Trn said, "is that way. Walk across the dam and go northwest."

"I cannot be captured. If the Russians find me I'll die." His eyes without the glasses were feeble and the wet lashes blinked. "Or the SS will hang me. I took the oath. I swore by God." His chest heaved under Trn's hands.

"Do you see a god in any of this to swear to?" Trn let him go. "Cross the dam and follow the shore. In less than two kilometers you'll leave the lake and go on northwest. Toward the central highlands. Your army will be there. Tell them you were separated from your company in a counterattack."

The boy looked as Trn pointed.

"I cannot abandon my post."

"Son, you're the one who's been abandoned. Go on now. You've risked your life enough. You ought to be free now."

The boy stood and started slowly down the walk, a hand on the railing before he turned.

"Where are my glasses? I cannot see how to go without my glasses."

Trn found them on the grate, held then out.

"I'm afraid they're mangled."

"I've fixed them before."

He walked away, head bent over the frames, passed the valve-house and began to run with echoing steps, unlocked the gate and as it swung to ran on, his damp hair leaping.

Trn made fists, flexed his fingers and went back to the wires, pulling them all in sequence, wrapping what came away round his left arm as he went. The thunder was coming back before he finished, the wail of rockets overwhelming the sound of the water below, a shriek of planes at the last edge of the afternoon. He looked over the railing at the charges still packed in their holes but surely they wouldn't have time to rewire everything. He stripped the coils from his arm and flung the bundle that seemed to hang a moment in the air before it plummeted to the white water and disappeared. He climbed the rusted gate again and faced home. A long walk south and he'd be done.

He climbed into the hills to avoid the road and at the first crest looked back over the way he'd come, lurched down two steps to wince through the latticed branches at a miniature truck coughing blue smoke on the far shore. Two toy soldiers hauled back the leads of three straining dogs, Alsatians prancing over the catwalk. One leaped and stood its paws on the top rail and bounded down and then Trn heard the faint first barking. Another dog clawed the gate and tried to chew its lead. A bare-headed soldier made to unlock it and one of the figurines raised a tiny rifle that bucked against his shoulder and Trn heard a whistle pass somewhere among the limbs and the air cracked over the lake and the three soldiers set off across open ground as the dogs hurtled on straight toward him.

But the dam stood empty. He stayed to be certain of that. The truck had gone and left nobody on the catwalk, no scurry of climbing engineers. He turned and began to labor up the hill so he couldn't hear his striving breath for the crash of dead leaves under his feet.

He was down the other side and halfway up the next slope when he looked back to sight along the crest behind him. What sun there was lay shrouded in the west so if they were coming at him through the trees he didn't have light to find or silhouette them. What he could see was the jagged trail disturbed among the gray leaffall on the slope he'd come down. Open country would be faster but it would be faster for them too. He climbed on, pulling himself by every tree he could reach.

The sky in the east was bruised past purple and the wound was spreading overhead, over him. Somewhere rockets fell. He came down out of the uneven country to a stream and drank out of his hands as long as he dared and splashed upstream twenty meters and climbed the bank into a field that he slouched across in the weeds. So maybe the dam wasn't so important after all. A static mark on a map in some bunker. But it wasn't their method to omit markers on maps. Their method was obliteration. Even if we cannot conquer we shall drag the rest of the world into destruction with us. The horizon flashed twice and exploded twice as if two phosphorous suns had dawned and died in the same instant and by their glow he saw the tracks of the tramline paralleling the road. Beyond stood a brick warehouse. To his left he heard a truck shift and come on at speed south down the road and while he watched the rising whine of three more trucks gained on the first, the Balkenkreuz on their doors glancing past and lost in a flaring that came over the ridge from the dusk. Three shells dropped in a line from the warehouse to the road and a truck exploded so brightly Trn's eyes clenched. When he looked over his arm a wall of the warehouse had collapsed. By the flames of its interior Trn saw two trucks disappearing south and one that burned in the road at a canted angle, the rear wheel on fire, still spinning.

The bark sounded while he hid there and then a second and on they went till there was no interval between them, as if the three were one dog with an inexhaustible voice. He cut away from the warehouse so he wouldn't be outlined in its fire and crossed the road and followed the tramline because the two would separate soon and the road took mostly open ground. When he looked back he thought he saw the weeds stirring across the field and he ran on. Three white houses were set beside the track in the dark. A fourth was ruined, one corner all that was standing, and here he tried to swallow back his breath to listen, hands on his knees and eyes closed, shoulder to the destroyed wall. It was suddenly colder with no sun and he stank inside the collar of his shirt, could smell himself inside the mud he wore, the powdered glass. In the crypt what did Aleks smell? Along the way he had come more shells exploded and he raised his eyes to see pines burning like matchsticks on the last hill he'd run. They were searching out the range of the road in the night and didn't know they'd found it.

A few steps on and his shoe slid. Another sliding step. Shit. Dogshit. He looked down at his shoes. Then he stepped precisely into all the piles he saw on the gloom of the paving and jogged on between the rails until he could make out the trees of the withered orchard to either side, frail limbs blacker than the falling dark and clawing against the night. The fence ran to both sides. His memory had overlooked that. If they chased him down here he didn't know if he could climb the fence. Something bayed in his mind and he told himself it was only his mind eliding with the howling night, the eastern sky bursting again and somewhere the earth in answer bursting back. He rested, panting in the dark. At any rate you can't take them to your door. Whatever you do you can't do that. When he thrust a hand into the pocket of his trousers his keys were gone. God knows where or how many hours ago. He stumbled over a crosstie and pushed himself up from the gravel. He could see the first painted walls of the city now standing out against nightfall and a fire burning somewhere in the quarter lit up the polished rails curving home.

He ran shrugging off his coat and by the collar flung it on top of a wall yellowed with firelight, unlaced his shoes still damp inside and stinking and knocked them against the base of the wall, tied the laces together and swung them under a bush. As well as he could in sock feet he jogged back down the gravel, left the track searching and slowed in the dark till he found a rift in the fence and close by the steps he was looking for. He took them down to the door of the cellar without a house. The knob gave in his fist and the door creaked mercifully in the night and he shut it behind him. The dank earth breathed a moist dust that he breathed in and out of his body. The floor was packed hard under his toes. His fingers stubbed out a board, a bench or a table, jars of cool glass. He sat slowly and it held.

To vanquish the dark he shut his eyes for more darkness and opened them after a counted minute to four dirty panes in the door. They contained all the light the night would spare. From the black pooled round him he could draw some shelves knocked into the clay walls, some long rags hanging, a hammer and saw hooked from nails, a shovel and a sickle blade standing together. He lifted the hammer, pounded three blows into his palm to tell its weight, turned the handle and tried the claw. He reached for the sickle and set it beside him. Beyond the panes the muffled war went on. Once its wave swelled so the door rattled and a rag fell from the wall. The ceiling salted with dust the back of his neck, the tops of his ears.

He settled into the rough wall, avoided a pain, a root thick as a shoulder in his back, found space and crossed his arms over drawn knees, the hammer weighted in his fist. If they come. If they should come. Then he remembered the berries as he reached for his pockets. Well the coat had its back to the wall now. It's the hammer now. I'll hear the dogs first, that will be my warning, the growls and clawing at the door. He picked the saw from its nail and laid it on the table beside him too. In the crypt they will have candles burning down on the stone ledges but will they have enough to burn all night? And if they do he won't like the shadows leaping on the beaded walls, the whispers. But they'll take the dam by morning. If they haven't already.

The concussions for a time came one upon the next. Miroslav would be in the basement with the Steinhardts and Alena in the crypt would hold the boy close. She'd find the strongest corner for them and hold him in her lap and he'd be fine. He wasn't scared of thunder, even as a little boy no storm disturbed him. They had something to eat, the old lady said so, so he was eating. The planes scared him. They scared Magda too, the planes and the dark. But there were hardly any planes now and he wouldn't hear them down there. Probably wouldn't. A radio might work there if they had one. They must be at targets well to the rear by now. The columns and trains, the bridges. The Il-2s, the Sturmoviks that screamed through the air, the Yak fighters flown by women pilots. Aleks could tell them all. Smart boy. He deserved the whole world. An explosion fell without light and the earth convulsed and then subsided and the shovel slid down the wall with a little clang at the end. He can tell you so many things. So they can't blow it now. Now that the war was over. Now that the war is over there'd be school again and they'd work on friendships, even with Adam Svoboda. They must have gone past with the dogs. Or maybe the shelling had driven them away. So much was his fault. Three dogs and three men for one Czech. That was tying down the enemy's resources. That can go in your report to Pavel. So they can't now but if they do come I have this hammer beside me and these blades and they won't follow me home. In this narrow space and this dark I would have the advantage. He was envisioning such a combat at close quarters, in the darkness, the shouts and flailing arms, when another concussion startled his eyes open again. The hammer was missing from his hand and he reached for it in the gloom, fumbled it up from the table. The four panes were grimed with light. Maybe it was only for a moment. Another explosion carried over the distance, not so loud as a rocket. It thudded again more faintly. A mortar.

He pulled the door and stood in its shadow. He could smell fire but see no flames. Strands of smoke layered like morning mist through the dead trees in the orchard and he climbed the four steps slowly. The withered limbs, the track, the sign beside the fence that said TRAMVAJ, all stood plainly out of the morning twilight. A machine gun chattered away somewhere, joined or answered by another. How could you sleep? The guns went on arguing while he pissed behind a bush by the door, looking up and down the empty rails, careful of the water flowing toward his sock. More machine guns. He closed the door and bent under the broken wire of the fence and walked through wet weeds beside the gravel toward the city, found his coat still on the wall and jumped to snatch it back, the torn lining cold, his arms and shoulders cold within it. The shoes were there and he scraped their soles on the curbstone, stripped off his ruined socks and used them as rags and laced his shoes on bare feet. The tracks curved to join the street and he went on, close to the wall, his eyes already on the long straight view, only a quarter hour's walk on a good day to Namesti Miru.

He dodged along doorway to doorway, sprinted across corners looking left and right. Bodies from both armies sprawled together here. A long stretch of tram wire was down and coiled in the street like a great lazy spring. Two opposed buildings were wrecked, not one window with a sash, the splinters of a door hanging by a single hinge. All the walls were pricked and gouged, the maw of another broken building gaping at him with long yellow teeth of flame eating a corpse cracked and spitting like sausage. More dead were heaped in the next block, Russians in tan crumpled against Germans in field gray, their dead teeth bared for him to see, blue claws grappling with the rubble. Some of the German corpses wore Luftwaffe uniforms. Tanks, no two pointed the same direction, some kind of shattered field piece, heavy machine guns, all of it iron carrion waiting for some great metallic scavenger to descend and peck out its guts like the ravens already perched and hunting for eyes, fats, strings of broken meat. A two-wheeled cart sat unscathed and yoked to a disemboweled mule, the long gray vessels flooding the gutter. A filthy cat crouched under the cart and through the spokes watched Trn pass.

The explosions and gunfire now seemed so distant he wondered if his ears were mute. A stray blast came over the houses from blocks away and he knelt in the entry of a bakery, no bread in the windows, a bakery only by the loaves painted on the miraculously intact glass. He peered ahead, behind, picked up a cartridge case cool in his fingers, the brass when he held it to his nose stinking of rotted acid. Some movement caught him about to rise and he flattened himself against the wall before he searched out a window high across the street, beyond the branches of a decimated tree. An old woman leaned on her sill. In her black kerchief she waved him on. Trn looked at her and she waved him on again, a languid hand. He nodded and she nodded back and at a dash he crossed from corner to corner and from here he could see the rise that climbed into the city center and at the bottom of it the square he needed. Slowly and at an angle the façade of the chapel came into view. He waited for something to stir but it didn't. He walked out slowly through rifts of smoke until all of it stood forth, straight walls and the slates of the roof mostly in place, the clock in the steeple saying six minutes till six. He stepped among the dead to reach it.

The windows were broken out but the wooden doors were still locked. He peered through the dim inside, empty benches, empty altar. He rattled the handle, shouldered the seam between the doors and leaned. They gave but didn't part so he stepped back and drove his weight behind his shoulder. The lock cracked and he nearly fell on the stone floor. He found the stairs to the crypt in the back corner and halfway down the barred door. It creaked open and clanged against the stones and no one rose out of the dark to meet him.

"Alena?"

No light at all and silence below. The acrid smell of wax and old smoke.

"Aleks?"

He took the last steps down to the dead buried under their stones but only the dead were there. Through the dark he kicked a box scuttling across the floor, brought it to the light tripping down the stairs to see a jar of torpid honeycomb, a napkin with breadcrumbs stuck to a wooden spoon, a testament. In the dark he found other boxes but no other sign. On the ledge of a niche he fingered wax cool and hard, the temperature of the stone it clung to. He ran the stairs and examined the chapel, the benches, the stones in the aisles, the wall behind the altar and never a drop that could be blood. He tried to shut the wooden doors but they leaned open. The clock now said seven minutes after six and he had a long hill to go. He didn't recall touching his lips but his mouth tasted of poisoned brass.

He spat and left the square by a lane and remembered the green house next to the shop of clocks only when it was too late to look back. The lane bent and straightened and he stopped, retreated to peer from behind a tree at a tank astride the road, Russian, a T-34, nearer than a shout. Men lay across it, lay on the road, eight he could see. At the twin tailpipes the armor was smoked black and the metal skirt was bent from the track at one corner. The turret was plainly painted 298 in white.

This was the straightest way and he took it, creeping forward along the fences as if taking the morning air, his hands in his pockets. Then he took them out of his pockets and held them open for all to see. A soldier in the small front garden of a house grunted under a bush and pillowed his head on his arm without opening his eyes. Trn stepped over the bottles around them, liberated of all their contents. A man with his neck crooked against the turret snored soundly, his face freckled with mud. Trn looked back at the barrel pointed his way and went on once more with his hands among the pulped berries in his pockets.

A squealing caught him up at the next corner, where the street climbed toward home, and he stood very still while a soldier teetered up on a bicycle. One hand on the bar steered a crooked course and the other hung a bag over his shoulder. His boots kept slipping from the pedals as the bicycle swerved and wobbled. The squealing stopped and without dismounting the soldier tugged twice at the lapel of Trn's overcoat. His eyes were no color at all and he tugged down again and Trn took off the coat and the soldier draped it over the handlebar and tottered on down the lane. Trn had started up the hill when an alarm clock sounded and the soldier dropped the bicycle and flung the bag to the road and drew a pistol. Trn saw him shoot the bag until the ringing stopped and then the soldier put the pistol back into his belt and reassembled himself on the bicycle with the bag and the overcoat and wove off toward his comrades.

When Trn was halfway up the hill the war began again, a solid line of detonations far away but the strongest since the night before. The concussions stalled him a moment, the only man in sight now, his face raised to listen on a hill sloped against him, and then on bruised feet he began to run.

Rounding the long bend onto their street he could see that all looked still except the black smoke at a rolling boil beyond the tower of St. Augustine's. At number five the Hakenkreuz was gone from the Steinhardts' balcony and a white sheet fluttered from Dita's. The gate was locked and he climbed and vaulted the fence and hammered at the front door till the glass shook. He backed away and called to the balcony through the horn of his hands, called them all. He lobbed pebbles from the garden over the balcony wall until Aleks's head peered out—"Daddy!"—and then Alena was peering down at him.

"I'm here."

"Is it safe?" Alena said.

"No. Not yet."

"We didn't know what happened to you."

The door opened and Aleks ran out to him, arms wide.

He stroked the back of the boy's head, both thin shoulders. "Careful," he tried to say. "There's glass." He kissed his neck, his ear, the hair on the crown of his head and stood away to see the boy's face broken with tears and he clutched him and lifted him and whispered to his nape, "It's all right. Everything's all right now. We're all right here."

They went up the stairs wiping their eyes and before the landing Trn said, "Damn," and stooped to take off his shoes.

"Daddy. Where did the glass come from?"

Alena held open the door, Miroslav behind her, behind his rheumy eyes, his hand rising to take Trn's, tears in the runnels of his cheeks as they embraced. Alena's hand was on his shoulder and then on his arm in the dim hall and he looked into her eyes and smiled at the tears standing on her lashes and she smiled too.

Miroslav said, "We wondered when you'd come," and Trn said, "I've been trying to get back to you all night," and then Alena backing away said, "Your clothes. God. Get them off."

"I know," Trn laughed. "I know I'm filthy."

"Throw them out on the stairs. I'll bring you something else."

"What happened out there?" Miroslav said.

Aleks said, "Where are your hat and coat?"

"I think the front collapsed in the night." The damp shirt clung to him and he had to peel off his undershirt. "I had a hard time coming."

He went into the bathroom in his shorts, no water from the tap but the tub was full. From it he filled the basin with his old shaving cup and ladled water over his head and neck so thorns of glass from his hair and behind his ears rilled down with the suds. The soap like grains of salt found a hundred slits in his fingers and hands. Alena put through the door pants, a shirt, socks.

"Hurry," she said. "Do you hear that?"

Through the walls the orchestra was tuning up again, building its crescendo. They were sitting amid the furniture cushions on the floor of the hall when he came out, their backs to the wall, Aleks in the middle, arms around his sharp knees, Alena's skirt gathered under her, Miroslav with the radio in his lap. Trn crouched with them.

"What do they say?"

"That the Germans are counter-attacking. Natürlich. I suppose that's what we're hearing out there too."

Aleks tightened his arms to sit smaller, eyes on the carpet. Alena stared at the opposite wall and Aleks looked around her.

"Will the Germans retake the city, Daddy?"

"It might happen." He reached to feel the boy's hand. "It's happened before but from what I saw the Germans can't hold. They don't have the force any longer. Their strength is almost gone. It's all temporary now and we just have to hold on a little longer, maybe a few days at most, maybe only a few hours, and then it will all be over."

"We thought it would be better to wait here than the sitting room," Aleks said, "in case of the windows."

"That's exactly the best idea."

"It's almost dark with the doors closed," Aleks said. "Wait." He lifted his sleeve and brought Trn's watch down his arm. "Here. It still works."

"Thank you, Aleks. Of course it does."

"Of course the Steinhardts have the cellar," Alena said, "have it and have it locked."

Somewhere a consistent barrage rained, distant but nearing, and in the gloom they listened.

"I went to the chapel."

Alena looked at Aleks who stared down at the carpet again.

"That one," Alena said, "refused to stay at the chapel. So we trooped up the hill in the dark with the whole war falling around us."

"It wasn't quite dark," Aleks said.

"Not last night," Trn said.

"No. Two nights ago."

"Why?"

Alena looked at Aleks again.

"Because he wanted to wait here for you. He rattled the bars of the door until I had to bring him home."

"I think everyone wanted to be home," Aleks said.

Miroslav said, "Listen." The radio broke its static with a weak voice as if the man or his microphone were exhausted. "The signal is very low," Miroslav whispered.

The hammer and sickle had flown from one spire of Petr and Pavel at first light but now the broken cross was there again and you could see the blockwork chip and dust away where the Red Army fired on German spotters in the belfries. But the Soviet flag remained over the castle.

"That was when they proclaimed we'd been liberated," Miroslav told Trn, "when the Russian flag went up over the castle last evening."

The voice gathered speed and relayed what other eyes saw from various windows in the radio building near the train station and what word dispatches brought. A line of cars and the engine were burning on the track where the crew had tried to run them west and two Red Air Force fighters had strafed them. Another train had come into the station already on fire and the smoke obscured much in that direction though large guns could be heard beyond the marshalling yard and sometimes the flash of their muzzles could be seen.

"Is that what we're hearing too?" Aleks said.

"That might be too far away," Trn said.

"So we're hearing another part of the war? The war for our neighborhood?"

They listened to reports of heavy fighting in the district below the castle and civilians were warned to seek shelter wherever they could find it. Miraculously someone had just telephoned from there to say the combat was intensifying.

"The Steinhardts wouldn't let you into the cellar?"

Miroslav leaned to see him in the near dark. "I'm not asking that goddamn German for anything," he said.

"I pounded on the door," Alena said. "I had Aleks ask through the lock. They didn't even answer. They never said a word."

"What about Dita?"

"She's upstairs."

"Shouldn't I get her?" Trn said. "The closer she is to ground the better for her."

"She's under her mother-in-law's bed," Alena said, "and won't come down."

"And Havlicek?"

"I assume he's hunched in his flat smoking and waiting for the end like the rest of us. Probably got a bottle of something, lucky bastard."

"Father," Alena said.

The city center was loud with gunfire now, the broadcaster said, and in their hall they could hear the reports plainly over the radio. The voice said he didn't know how much longer he could broadcast. Just below the window of the radio offices a line of Red Army soldiers staggered and fell, their caps all came off as their heads hit the street, and a panzer mounted a barricade raised by civilians yesterday and rolled over the Russian bodies and out of sight. His name was Vilem Papanek and his family lived in the Komarov district and if they could hear him he loved them. He said a dispatch run in from the castle district reported the fighting there seemed to be over and the observer from the roof of their building said he could see a swastika flying over the castle. Trn looked at Miroslav but Miroslav wouldn't look at him because they huddled now against a wall that was four tram stops and one hill from the castle. Alena's eyes closed and when Trn glanced at Aleks the boy gazed straight into the dark with his jaw clamped tight.

Trn thought that was the end and then the voice of Vilem Papanek came through the silence to say, "I don't. Entering the. Peal to all. Barricades. Terror and."

The voice phased entirely into static as if that were the next natural stage of human speech and that was all that came from the box.

"Can you raise any other signals?" Trn said.

"I'll see. I put the churchillka in there since what difference can it make now." Miroslav shrugged and spanned the spectrum bristling with noise. From Bratislava there was nothing, nothing to be heard from Warsaw. Vienna was in Russian and Trn was able to make out a few words, *peace* and *death* repeated at intervals but they were so close to Czech he didn't need to interpret. The BBC barely carried a bulletin from the Pacific where the Americans were covering slow ground on Okinawa. Trn did translate that. Japanese shipping was being sunk at an accelerating rate. The estimated tonnage lost this month alone. Trn shrugged and told Miroslav to try again but he could raise nothing anywhere and said, "Ach, there's a dozen generals sitting out there on their thumbs who know no more than we do in here."

"Aleks," Trn said, "where is the spyglass?"

"In Grandfather's room. In the desk."

Trn stood.

"What are you going to do?" Alena said.

"Only see a bit of what's happening."

As he closed the kitchen door he heard Alena say, "No, Aleks. No."

On the balcony the war was louder in the waves of smoke gusting through like weather fronts. Thudding mortars, the pop of smaller arms over the trees somewhere beyond the brow of the hill. He panned the lens across the neighborhood. No flag flew from the gymnazium. Through smoked glass he watched three tanks trailing a cluster of infantry. On Gorkeho through the trees he could see two trucks disgorge more soldiers. An officer blew his cheeks around a whistle and the soldiers trotted up the hill. He craned out to look the other way and through a pause in the smoke he could see four tanks, five, wheeling at a bend and churning toward the gymnazium, followed by two yokes of horses, each pulling a gray gun on two wheels. The door opened and Miroslav came out, grimaced to settle himself knee by knee.

Just as Trn put his eye back to the glass the top floor of a house along the crest before him blossomed into dust and shooting timbers and the concussion rained over them as he dodged behind the wall.

"That was the Deutschkron house," Trn said.

"Couldn't happen to besser volk."

"If we take a hit like that."

"What else can you see?"

"Some troops are moving on Zeleneho but they're taking fire at the top of the hill.

Miroslav looked at him. "Do you think we can get through this?"

"And go where?"

"I mean live through it."

"We can," Trn said, and he helped the old man up and followed his stooped back and closed the door on another explosion. In the kitchen he took three gulps of water from the pitcher standing in the sink. In the hall Alena and Aleks lifted their eyes but not their faces.

"Can they stop them?" Alena said.

"I don't know but we should be ready in case they can't. This is high ground. Somebody's going to want it."

"They didn't come through yesterday. It wasn't like this yesterday."

They heard a muted explosion and then another, nearer, louder, that set their shoulders cringing.

"In the night the Russians moved north and south around us, I think. But now they're counter-attacking. The Germans. They're coming back."

"I thought you said their strength was almost gone."

"It is. But not yet. Not all of it."

She frowned at the wall.

"Is it the Red Army coming up the hill?" Aleks said. "I haven't seen a Red Army soldier yet. Are there T-34s?"

"Aleks, you are not going anywhere near that balcony."

"No, it's the Romanians coming up the hill."

"I thought the Romanians were fighting beside the Germans," Aleks said.

"Now they fight beside the Russians."

"How can you tell it's them?"

"Their flag's on the tanks."

"Can we get to the crypt?" Alena said.

Trn looked from her to Aleks and back.

"Is that where you want to go?"

Aleks shook his head. "It's too scary there."

"It may very well become scary here in the next hour," Trn said, "but I don't think it's possible to get you down the hill now. We could move below though, to the ground floor. You and Aleks could go into the storage closet."

Aleks shook his head and Miroslav worked the radio dial again. "I've got something," he said. "Wait." They all bent to listen. The strains of "Deutschland über Alles" grew out of the box and Miroslav frowned in great wrinkles and said, "I'm just going to switch off."

They sat on in the hall growing cold with evening. Alena bit at her chapped lips, her fingernails. Aleks looked down at one hand holding the other in his lap. They all startled from the wall at two quick bursts, the loudest so far, and then a third louder again and something nearby came crashing inside the sound, falling a long way down. Miroslav leaned his brow on the knuckles of his fist. A dry smoke wafted into their dark as if a collection of dust heaps had been set fire around them. Alena fingered a ladder in her stocking, resmoothed her dress.

Aleks said, "I'm hungry." Alena sighed.

"I'll get you something," Trn said.

"There's a little bread in the box," she said.

He closed the kitchen door behind him and went onto the balcony door and knelt behind the wall with the spyglass. A house or what remained of it was billowing thick smoke on the hillside and through it he could hear the battle for their quarter. Voices called out of the haze and he strained for the language but couldn't say. In the end just voices shouting in the burning distance.

When he opened the door to their gloom Alena was whispering, "Little Jesus, I adore You, O Mighty Child, I implore You, save me in this need." Trn handed the bread to Aleks.

"What could you see?" Aleks said.

"Not much."

"You could have been shot," Alena said.

"A tank," Trn said.

"Whose?" Miroslav said.

"Russian. You could see the red star."

"Who's winning? Doesn't that mean the Russians are winning?" Aleks said.

"It certainly means they have reinforcements, which is something the Germans can't say."

They shared a little stale bread. Trn licked his fingertips to take up the crumbs from his shirt. Suddenly their faces lifted at the sound of planes thrumming their power across the sky. Trn got up and moved toward the toilet and Alena said, "Remember to use the pot," and above the ringing of his water against the enamel he heard the hill pounded, his hand pressed to the shaking wall. As he was buttoning a loud explosion shook all the front windows in their casements and back in the hall he heard Aleks whispering to Alena, "It's good you moved all the figurines from the shelf."

They each made their trips to the chamber and for a time the war smoke masked their human smell till Aleks said, "Someone's going to have to dump the pot." Trn took it to a rear window, tilted it into the back garden, but from there he could see nothing except smoke and the fall of evening. He brought in their pillows and more blankets and Aleks crawled across the floor and sat between his outstretched legs and finally slept against his sore ribs. Miroslav snored from his corner and when Trn's head snapped awake Alena's breath was a snore too. He could see nothing of any of them though he felt the weight of Aleks on his chest. It was the first night of the war he'd not pulled the blackout curtains.

The earth still rumbled somewhere over the hill, as if the thunder withered from the storm. He listened to it a long time in their dark and then even it died down. Aleks woke him stirring, twisting to see his face.

"Daddy? Someone's at the door."

A fist rapped again there in Trn's blinking. Alena stretched both arms, rose from her curl on the floor, her fingers combing through her hair.

Miroslav yawned stiffly. "Bad news wouldn't come knocking, would it? Wouldn't it just burst through the door?"

"Viktor?" Another rap, a whisper through the door. "Alena?"

When Alena opened it Dita's hands were wringing one another at her chin.

"You're here?" Her wide eyes searched over theirs in the near dark. "Viktor? You're all here."

Alena said, "I told you we'd all be well in the end."

"But is it the end?" Aleks said.

Dita's face smiled her eyes into wrinkles.

"You haven't been listening to the radio?"

"What's the use?" Miroslav said.

"They've pushed the Germans back twenty kilometers."

"That means it's really only five," Miroslav said. "Or three."

"But they're gone," Dita said. "They're really gone. Listen."

Trn took Aleks's shoulder and pulled him close to hold.

"Does this mean the war is really over?" Aleks said.

"For us," Trn said, "I think it is."

Miroslav shuffled his feet, clapped his hands.

"Father, what in the world was that?"

"That was a jig from my youth, my dear. After fifty years I think it's time to dance it again."

Alena laughed behind her hand as Miroslav performed his dance once more and then stooped for the radio but before he switched it on a bell struck and the quaver carried. They stared through the stale air of the hall as if to see the wave pass over them.

"St. Augustine's," Alena said.

They crowded onto their balcony as others did across the way, sheets still flying as other bells began to peal into the distant morning. Not the brazen clang before the war but the tinny shimmer of their replacements and it clappered on for measure after measure before the first dog howled and then a baying chorus went up over the hillside as if they finally remembered what bells were meant for.

At the kitchen table they all slumped still smiling. Through the balcony door the cool light vibrated with the scent of fire.

"I should like some tea," Aleks said in Trn's lap. "Do we have enough left for weak tea?"

"If we had gas," Miroslav said.

"This is no day for tea," Dita said. "What we need is wine."

"If we had wine," Miroslav said.

Dita smiled and winked and bustled up from the table.

Miroslav rubbed his hands together. "No substitute for kin in the country. I'll bet she has a dozen bottles in her wardrobe."

"And wine for breakfast," Alena said glaring at her father.

"It's the fruit of the vine, my dear, fruit for breakfast. Perfectly natural."

"I wish there were tea," Aleks said. "I'd like tea. Daddy, what happened to your chin? There's a cut."

"I fell. Maybe I could hold the kettle over the flame in the stove. We've a little coal left, haven't we?"

"I don't want the bottom of my kettle scorched," Alena said.

Dita appeared with a bottle in each hand and Miroslav clapped his palms.

"Mrs. Asterova, you are angelic."

"Pay no attention to him, Dita," Alena said.

They poured the wine around in four small glasses and Miroslav offered a toast to the end of the war. All drank. Aleks raised his sip of water.

Miroslav said, "To liberation," and poured again.

Miroslav said, "To dogs and church bells."

"Father, too fast."

"Nonsense. To the Allies."

"Will I see a Sherman now?" Aleks asked.

Trn said, "I wager you will."

"To the Sherman tank."

"If you're going to do this I'm going to stop and sweep this dirty floor."

"To your broom," Miroslav said, his glass upraised.

"No folly like an old man's folly," Alena said.

"To old men."

"Dita, don't let him open the other one. Is your flat all right?"

"I think so. But the Prochazka house is burning."

"The brilliance of this," Miroslav winked to Aleks, "is that you can drink to anything. To church bells."

"You already drank to bells, Grandfather."

"You're drinking by yourself, Father, can't you see that now? No one's joining you."

A shot broke over the clamor and a dog yelped and another report cracked flat across the hillside. Trn winced and stood Aleks from his lap. The bells rang on but fewer dogs contended with them. The five of them crowded on the balcony to see a ragged rank of soldiers coming down their street, more trailing. One of them kicked a gate reeling and he and another soldier wrestled through it. Some used rifles like canes, fists choking the necks of bottles.

"What is it?" Alena said looking over his shoulder.

"I want to see," Aleks said.

"Get back inside," Trn said.

"Why?"

"Go back."

The soldiers broke into small cohorts and one shoved another to the ground to be first through the door of a house where a woman upstairs hurried to shut her window.

Trn shut the door and said, "We have to hide you and Dita."

"I can do that," Dita said and she took Alena's hand.

"You have a place?"

"A very good place, Viktor. In the—"

"Don't tell us."

"Why are they hiding?" Aleks said.

"Because they're coming now." Dita nodded firmly and tugged Alena toward the landing.

"You're certain?" Trn said.

"Entirely." They went up the stairs, Alena looking back at Trn once before they disappeared.

"What are we going to do, Daddy?"

"We are going to be very still and very quiet and wait until this is over," Trn said.

From below a shudder came up through the dark, an impact like an animal kicking at the boards of his stall and then a great crash of splinters and shouting rose from the foot of the stairs.

"Why don't you lock the door?"

"It won't do any good."

"Aren't you at least going to close it?"

"They'll only break it down and tomorrow we'll need it. Go to the sitting room and sit beside Grandfather."

"Can't we hide? Can't we hide our things?"

"It's too late now to hide any more than we've already hidden."

The stairs scuffled with feet and deep voices and Aleks ran for the kitchen, came back with the spyglass. In the sitting room he scanned the shelves frantically and snatched the wooden king where it stood alone and put it in his pocket. The spyglass went into his shirt as he slumped on the couch. Miroslav fell into his chair.

Another sharp crash turned all their faces toward the door and Miroslav said, "There goes Havlicek." They heard rough laughter and stomping and a pause in the voices that went on too long and then steps scraping the carpet in their hall. A broad face appeared at the door and surveyed the sitting room with eyes like black almonds pressed into slits in the skin. He didn't say a word, the rifle in both hands, a bedroll sashed across his chest. He went away and they heard more boots and the soldier came back with a very tall man wearing the same brown tunic. He seemed taller still for his officer's cap and riding breeches.

"Don't say anything," Trn said.

The broad face spoke to the officer with a mouth missing every front tooth and the officer made no reply. Their boots were very high and left tracks in dried mud where they went. The soldier turned his sharp cheekbones, pointed with his chin at Miroslav in his chair and said, "Davai casy."

Miroslav squinted at Trn.

"I think he wants your watch."

"Davai casy suda!"

"I think you should hurry."

Miroslav unbuckled the band, handed up the watch. The soldier slung the rifle and thrust his chin at Trn and Trn offered his watch. Aleks raised his arms to show both bare wrists. The soldier strapped Miroslav's watch on his left wrist and Trn's on his right so that now he wore four on one arm and three on the other. One of the faces lacked a crystal.

The officer was busy in the sideboard, tossing out the table linen, pausing at the lace. From each shelf of the bookcase he routed the books with sweeps of his arm and sent them to the floor spine by spine. His companion had moved on to Miroslav's room. The old man closed his eyes while the desk drawers slid out and hit the floor in sequence. "That old desk was my grandfather's," Miroslav said. "God it was hard to get up these stairs forty years ago." The soldier came back to the sitting room with the bedclothes gathered in his arms and disappeared into the hall.

A shriek came from far away, from the stairwell. Trn stood to listen and it came again as if through the walls. A crash fell against the ceiling. He moved into the hall and Aleks said, "Daddy?" but the officer caught at Trn's arm and pinned him to the wall with a shoulder. A broad pinkish scar stretched along his jaw to his chin and the stubble of his beard didn't grow there.

With a breath like vinegar the officer called into the stairwell and another soldier came stamping and stopped in their door. He had a dirty bandage wrapping his head as if to soothe a toothache, a patch of blood above one ear, and after the officer spoke to him he remained at the door with his rifle dropped like a crossbar, staring at Trn while the officer went into the bedroom. Trn slid down the wall and sat where he'd passed the night, his head in his hands, staring at his sock feet.

"Where?" the officer said in German.

When Trn looked up through the bedroom door the officer was tossing clothes from the wardrobe, fingering out a white dress and a blue one to show Trn.

"Where?"

Trn shook his head.

"Frau," the officer said.

"Mrtva," Trn said.

The officer narrowed his eyes and Trn looked at the floor, at the clothes on the floor and said again, "She's dead." It was more than close enough. It was nearly the same word in either tongue. The officer crossed himself and threw an armload of clothes on Trn's bed and opened the window and made a bundle of the clothes with the bedding and dropped it all into the garden.

The one with almond eyes opened the door to the chamber and the odors of the pot wafted into the hall but he had discovered the toilet. He stooped over it, removed his cap, began to cradle with his hand water from the bowl over his scalp. The one in the door murmured to him and the first came out with water rilling down his brow and they stepped over Trn's feet and exchanged places. The wounded man stood his rifle in the corner beside the toilet and produced a sliver of soap from his pocket and unwound his bandage and on his knees washed his hands and face and close-cropped head.

The breaking went on in the kitchen where the officer had gone. He opened and rifled all the cabinets, pulled the crockery to the floor just as he had the books. His long black boots trod over the fragments and half a teacup popped and burst. A bottle of rape-seed oil rolled under the table. The shriek came back past the soldier at the door, shriveled, farther away, as if the pain nailed to the flesh unraveled from the throat. His head in his hands, Trn's eyes wandered over boot scuffs in the carpet, mud from the steppes, the swamps, mud churned with blood. As if the men who had destroyed the Wehrmacht could ever stop destroying.

"Daddy, he's got the radio."

The officer blocked the whole frame of the kitchen door and Aleks was reaching for him, reaching up for the radio clutched in the officer's arms. The two of them crowded together in the doorway. Trn came between them, pushing the radio out of Aleks's grasp as the scar reddened and stretched over the officer's jaw and he unbuttoned his holster. In the one instant he had left Trn saw it was a luger before the dimensions of the hall narrowed to blast and smoke. Trn felt a kick at his side and got another at his back that sharpened his breath, then the boots were stamping down the stairs. He lay on the floor, Aleks surrounded in his arms. Blue torsions of smoke twisted over him and rose toward the ceiling of the hall.

"Are you all right?" He winced, tried to lift the boy. "You aren't hurt, are you?"

"He took our radio."

"We'll have another radio."

Aleks stared. "Look at the hole."

Miroslav was staring at it too, the white plaster of the wall cracking away from the impact.

"It's like a crater," Aleks said.

"I might have been standing there," Miroslav said.

"Are you all right?"

"Yes, I'm all right."

"Daddy, where are you going?"

"I have to find your mother."

He took the stairs two at a time, cradling his ribs, but Alena and Dita were already peering from the door.

"We heard a shot," Dita said.

"It's all right. They didn't find you? I heard screaming."

Dita shook her head. "It wasn't us. They upended everything but it wasn't us." She and Alena glanced at one another and then Alena said, "It must have been Mrs. Steinhardt in the cellar."

The cameramen in their Red Army uniforms, the black boxes at their eyes, watched the residents of the city line up to hand back the stones from the ramparts and array them into streets again after the transit of Mars. As if a reel from the war ran backwards except now they smiled into the lenses, reaching for the next stone coming down the line, drew their wrists over their brows for spring had come. They stood in line for bread, for sour cucumbers, a few leeks, what there was to be had. Lines of people mustered on their packed cases in the street, swastikas chalked on their bags, on the backs of the coats they wore, the backs they turned to the cameras. Their children sagged in their laps, their infants cried, sometimes for days. They whispered behind their hands, heads lowered, and were shouted at to shut up.

The very day the rumor passed that Hitler was dead in Berlin red placards were pasted up across walls and pillars inviting the quarter to the Russian camp in the park on the hill. Some wreckage was cleared for the occasion. The children climbed a panzer hulk flanked by T-34s that the tankers petted and posed beside with grimy smiles. Shell holes deeper than a grown man were explored to the bottom of the mud while parents peered over the edge and mothers recalled their boys clambering from the pit. An army band blared brass at one end of the field and at the other on short stringed instruments and accordions and harmonicas soldiers played tunes that their comrades danced to, shouting and kicking on a platform of laid boards, slapping the soles of their black boots, in linked arms circling one direction and then the other while the boards bent under their swaying weight and the cameras rolled. They waltzed with smiling female soldiers in tight brown skirts and reached to take the hands of local women into their dance. At the mouth of his tent an officer brewed a cube of sugar in a steaming cup and sucked from the cube between his lips and grinned as they walked by. He had a blackened eye and black teeth. He greeted them and raised his cup and Alena turned away.

"We'll never be able to understand these fellows," Miroslav said. "They eat all their vowels back in their molars."

Aleks said, "May I go see the tanks?" and Alena nodded after him. "But don't get lost."

A line of riflemen under command shouldered their rifles before the sledding hill and demonstrated their skill at twenty or twenty-five meters into a line of cutout targets depicting Hitler and his hierarchy.

"The famous Russian snipers, I suppose," Miroslav said, "about whom we've heard so much."

Alena said, "I don't know why I came at all. These brutes. Look how few women are here."

"These are different brutes," Miroslav said. "They can hardly be said to be brutes at all. Look at that one there lighting the wrong end of his cigar. That other gang is busy liberating Prague now."

"Hitler's dead a week and they're still fighting," she said. "What sense does that make?"

"About as much sense as anything in the last seven years, I suppose."

"I'm sure all the women of Prague will be eternally grateful for their liberation. Their kitchens smashed and their linen stolen. I'll never get all that mud out."

A voice from the crowd called Trn and Ivan emerged, laughing.

"You wouldn't happen," Miroslav asked, "to have the correct time, would you?" and Ivan examined his bare wrist. "I think it's time to get another watch," he said. He clapped Trn on the back.

"Did they take your faucets? They sawed off every one of mine. It's going to be a clever sight when they get back to Siberia and hammer them into their walls and open the taps. You know they had a film in the cinema the other night, got it going already. And they showed something about Stalin at Yalta and he's walking up to Churchill with his hand out and someone in the audience shouts 'Davai casy!' and the seats erupt and they put on the lights and the military police questioned everyone but no one had any idea who said it."

A string of black horses tethered at the trees was for show and Aleks went running for them. Ivan told Trn he needed more than a trim and shook hands and they went after the boy so Trn could lift him to see better. Aleks reached and the animal snarled its black lips and shied, mane jumping.

Alena said, "Do you want to be bitten?"

"Careful," Trn whispered. "He's a draft horse, a work animal. He won't be used to petting."

"Look at his nostrils," Aleks said. "So big and hairy. And his huge teeth."

"Look how he has more teeth than his master." Miroslav nodded good day at the soldier standing by the string, a child himself who gummed a smile.

At various tents, around their fires, the hosts offered skewered meat, soups with potato in battered tin cups, square cakes with no sugar. "That Hitler, what a marksman," someone bellowed. "What a soldier! Fires one shot the whole war and it's a perfect bull's eye." The crowd roared. Down a line of civilians came an open jar passed on to them. Aleks sniffed at it, examined the white label.

"That's not Russian. I know it's not German."

"It's English," Trn said.

"What does it say?"

"Peanut butter."

"What is peanut butter?"

"I'm not sure," Trn said. "Some kind of paste, from America. USA, see? Shall we try it?"

"What do you do?"

"I think you spoon it onto your finger."

They watched it lumped there, glistening with oil, sniffed again. Aleks licked it and his eyes widened on Trn. He put his whole finger in his mouth and gulped to swallow.

"I like peanut butter," he said.

"I do too," Trn said. "Let's have another finger."

He held the jar toward Alena, Miroslav, but they declined and Alena pinched up her watch and said, "I'm going now. I don't know why I came in the first place."

"Look." Aleks took his finger from his mouth to point at a dog, a small white dog leaping and barking, racing across the grass after some children. "May I go see the dog?"

"No, Aleks. We're going home now."

"But he's so small."

"He probably belongs to the soldiers," Miroslav said. "Their mascot."

They walked across the broken ground and Aleks picked up a cartridge case from the mud. "I have a souvenir from the war," he said, his nose wrinkling at the smell of it. "But I didn't see Peter. I thought you said after the war Peter would come back. But those other people are still in his house."

Trn rested a hand on the boy's neck.

"We must be patient with time," he said. "We must wait and see what it brings us."

They left by the place where the stone gate lay shattered, started down the hill past St. Augustine's missing all its glass.

"When will the war be over really? When Peter comes back?"

"It must be over soon," Trn said. "Nothing goes on forever."

He set the old blanket that Aleks now slept under in the sun of the window sill and when he turned she glanced away, sitting at her table brushing the night from her hair.

"I want to speak to you."

She stood and came round to sit on her bed, smoothed the folds in her robe, crossed her legs.

"Now the war is over I want you to leave."

"You want me to leave."

"Yes. Leave Father's flat."

He sat on his bed, elbows on his knees.

"We've known it was coming to this for a long time. And now that the war is over it's time for you to leave. It's no good your staying here."

"Two nights ago we talked about getting a bigger flat. So Aleks could have his own room and your father could come with us."

"You talked about a bigger flat," she said.

Trn took a breath and looked at the round outline on the wall where her mirror had been and then at her straight lips.

"What is his name?"

Her eyes darted to the floor, drifted away to the wall.

"It doesn't matter."

"That's true but I want to know."

"Antonin."

"Antonin what?"

"Antonin Klicek."

"And you've fallen in love with him."

"For some time now. Yes."

"For some time." He nodded. "What about Aleks?"

"He will stay here with me of course, with his mother."

Trn said, "I'm not leaving my son."

"But that's not part of the problem, you see."

"What do you mean?"

"Aleks is not your son."

"You're lying."

"No," she said. "I'm not."

"You're only saying that to make me leave. You think it will make me mad, drive me away. But you're wrong."

"No. It's true. Aleks is not yours."

"Whose then if not mine? Antonin Klicek's?"

"It doesn't matter now. Someone before. When I thought you weren't coming back from England. There was someone else."

"So why did you marry me?"

She stared down at her bare foot kicking there between them.

"I still don't believe you."

"What you believe or don't believe makes no difference now but ask Father if you like. He's known all this time."

"That can't be true."

"Ask him."

Trn took hold of his brow, gazed over the old patterns of wood under his feet, the broken and missing inlays.

She said, "He's the one who said you'd marry me."

Trn shook his head.

"You always told me that Aleks had my eyes."

"I never meant it."

"I suppose you only meant to make me believe he was mine." He took a deep breath, looked down at his coupled hands. "How long has your father known?"

"I told you. From the beginning."

"But about Klicek. How long has he known that?"

"A long time. From early in the war."

"Does Aleks know?"

"No. Of course not."

"He's never met this man?"

"I told you."

"Has he ever been here?"

"Why? It's not your house."

"Has he ever been here?"

"Yes. But Aleks was always away."

"But your father was here."

She said nothing, sitting on her bed, her palm running a caress across the robe.

"So much for mother church."

"How dare you, of all people, to speak to me of the church. After so much unhappiness who can sit in judgment of me now? After years of unhappiness and misery. Certainly not you."

"No. Certainly not me."

"After you'd get off me I stank like a fish. I hated that smell, your spume across my stomach."

"And how does Klicek leave you smelling?"

Her hand shot through the space between them but only her fingers managed to slap him.

Trn looked back at her.

"You bastard. This is Father's flat and you will leave it."

"And who will pay your father's rent?"

"Bastard." She rubbed her knuckles. "Tonik has money. He has a job."

"Unlike me."

"Yes. Unlike you in every respect."

Trn passed a hand down his face.

"So," he said. "Tonik. Who am I to stand between you and Tonik. But understand that I am not leaving my son. Do you understand that? I am not leaving Aleks. I will see him."

She scowled at something between the beds.

"Do you understand that?"

"Yes," she sighed. "I suppose you can see him. Some afternoon."

"I will see him more often than that."

She uncrossed her legs, hooked them the opposite way. "We can discuss that after you go."

"I've never gone more than three days of his life without seeing him. Until the war."

With two whisks of the back of her hand she brushed some stranded lint from her robe. Her fingers joined over her knee.

"I don't know how long it will take me to find a flat in this chaos. But when everything is settled I will leave. But I will see Aleks."

She rose and went back to her table and picked up her brush and put it down and lifted her compact and began to dab very lightly under her eyes as if the mirror were still there.

"I thought you would have fought harder," she said to the wall.

Trn stood. "I guess in this war we've all learned what's worth fighting for."

In the sitting room Aleks said, "Will we have leeks again for dinner tonight?"

Trn saw him there, a book in his lap.

"Yes," Trn said. "I suppose we will."

"I don't care for leeks," Aleks said.

"I know."

"I'm a bit of a malcontent when it comes to leeks."

Trn nodded.

The boy raised the book toward him. He said, "Can I show you something?"

Miroslav put down the one page of the paper and said since there was no more radio he was going to nap on his bundle of blankets since there were no more mattresses. Aleks pointed to a picture in a collection of old photographs of the city, some of the pages torn after their sacking. Trn listened to him discuss the ruins that were to be pulled down and the design of the buildings to come. "What do you think, Daddy?" Trn nodded and reached an arm around the boy's shoulders and in his drawing book Aleks showed him the sketches of an entirely new architecture he had begun towards the reconstruction until Trn shifted toward her calls even before she reached their landing. When he opened the door she stood panting, a hand cupped over her nose.

"What is it, Dita?"

"Do you smell it, Viktor? It's very strong upstairs."

"I do. I hadn't before but now that the door's open. Is it stronger above than on this floor?"

"I think so. And strongest in the stairs."

"Do you have your windows open?"

"I had to. It's suffocating."

He called to Aleks but the boy was at his elbow.

"Open all the windows. Get Grandfather to help if you can."

"What is it?"

"A gas leak. Dita, can you go down and see Mr. Havlicek? We don't need him lighting a cigarette. I'll go up. Is your door open?"

"Yes."

"Better prop the front and rear doors while you're downstairs. Aleks, close this door after me and roll a towel across the bottom of it. What about the Steinhardts?"

Dita said, "I haven't seen them since." She looked down at one set of fingertips hooking the other. "I came straight to your door."

The gas was stronger with each flight into the climbing dark. In Dita's kitchen he listened at the stove and the oven, the water heater there and in the bathroom. He climbed the stairs toward the Steinhardts' door, his nose in the crook of his elbow. The door was splintered at the knob and he had only to push it to see the ruin inside. The hall was a wreckage of papers, a smashed secretary, the telephone in pieces. He called out still hiding behind his arm, their sitting room nothing but more debris, all the cushions gutted, torn books strewn across the floor, no picture left on the walls, the only order two chairs upright. He put open the windows there and in their bedroom, a mayhem of feathers and shredded clothes, a pier glass just shards in its frame.

It was warmer here under the roof and he was already dizzy and sweating when he discovered a hiss like a snake's in the kitchen where the Steinhardts lay. They had swept a space among the glass and crockery, spread their red flag on the tiles. Together they lay with their necks crooked under the open oven door, brows nearly touching. Mrs. Steinhardt used a hand for pillow.

Trn closed that valve and the others and opened the balcony door and all the other windows in the flat. Pinned to the flag between them, their knees drawn up as they huddled, were Mrs. Steinhardt's two Mother's Crosses. In their skeletal faces their lips and closed eyelids were a deepening blue.

He met Dita coming up to her flat.

"I think it's not so strong now, Viktor. What's the matter?"

"The Steinhardts have killed themselves."

She reached back for the railing. It was still hard to breathe. Trn nodded and after another moment, with widening eyes, she said, "And were they trying to kill the rest of us too?"

✳
✳

The warm morning of the victory parade in June Havlicek was led away by three policemen, his wrists cuffed before him. He limped down the walk and through the gate still twisted from its hinges and he stood by the black sedan while they opened its rear door, his gray beard concentrating on the place of his next hobbled step. Dita looked over her balcony at them on theirs and called down, "I told you it was so."

Miroslav shook his head and said, "Under our very floor. An informer."

Strollers on the street stood still and a woman stopped flapping sheets through her window to gape.

Aleks said, "What about the rabbits?"

"He killed them all yesterday," Dita said. "They were screaming all evening."

Aleks stared after the puttering car and Trn said, "If we don't leave now we may miss the best of the review."

In the crowded square many of the women wore hats against the sun, some smiling in bright lipstick held back for the occasion. Men hung their coats on their shoulders, traded rumors on the sidewalk. The woods were full of Wehrmacht werewolves. But Stalin himself was sending Zhukov to round them up. A train of twenty-three cars would be arriving tonight with cattle and hogs on the hoof. Children of a certain height leaned between the legs of the adults so they could peer down the street while others rode their fathers' shoulders but Aleks could see for himself now. He stood in front of Trn, glancing to comment under the cheering while Trn leaned to listen, nodded though he didn't understand. The crowd swayed with chatter and anticipation from foot to foot and cheering here among them perhaps was Klicek. Though doubtless Klicek had elsewhere to be.

In their leather helmets with ear flaps buckled a marching file of tankers followed the T-34 leading them. Ranks of infantry filed past, each rifle with its bayonet angled at the nape of the soldier marching before, whole companies of women in straitened army skirts, fat cheeks smiling. A cloud slowed and shaded out the entire square before the sun came back. With each contingent a salute of raised fists. Raised palms at the beginning, raised fists at the end. "Where are the Romanians?" someone shouted. "Where are our liberators?" Laughter jostled with the jeers in the crowd and then the wits were shouted down. A great truck passed with a Katyusha launcher perched over the cab, guns pulled by horses and some pulled by small tractors on treads. In the lagging moments between formations boys would dash to their friends on the other side or start and heel back as their friends came faster. A phalanx of prancing horses clicked over the cobbles to the flash of cameras. A long gap followed during which those in suits and uniforms under the tent on the reviewing stand leaned to share their confidences and the cameraman on the raised platform rested from winding his machine. A rustle went through the crowd that maybe the parade was over, then the prisoners liberated from the gymnazium and castle arrived, those who could walk and some on crutches and ten at the rear in chairs wheeled by nurses brightly dressed with white caps in their hair and afterward a cadre of pilots leading an actual silver plane, a Sturmovik, Aleks said, towed on its landing gear by a truck chugging smoke. "Look at its cockpit with the rear gun," Aleks whispered. "It's a two seater. The first models were made to hold only a pilot."

A group of workers in blue factory overalls, right fists raised high, sang about the Red Front and when they had passed a group of Komsomol youth marched by in tight uniforms, shouldering wooden rifles. Last to great cheers came the heroes of the resistance in berets and bowlers, overcoats and glasses. Trn looked for Pavel but found only Dolezal in his drooping mustache, hiking up his trousers while smiling grandly and waving to both sides. The microphone opened with a piercing squawk and buzzed to scattered applause. Some pigeons decamped from undamaged roofs. The first drops of rain fell as the speeches boomed. Trn shifted his weight in his crumbling shoes and once nearly fell backwards when Aleks suddenly leaned against him.

The few spectators who had them raised umbrellas against the rain that fell into a shower. Finally after the microphone clicked off and after the last of the clapping fluttered to a halt the brass of the band struck up again and the reviewing party began to congratulate themselves, sporting their brassards and prominent ears, the breasts of the officers well panoplied with decorations, two generals with stars on their shoulder boards. Trn put up his collar under the brim of his hat and he and Aleks made their way from the square in the river of people dammed along the medieval street, one shuffling step and then another under the little spears of rain that shattered off hats and shoulders and stone. In the press of the crowd Trn looked down at the boy's pale neck, the pink shells of his ears. He needed a hat. He was old enough now. A fedora with a little green feather. The rain streaked his hair. The feet before them moved on, the shoes in the puddles, heels worn up to the leather.

Finally at the curb they paused, a scurry of coats and skirt tails crossing the wide avenue before a car with flags flying blew its horn, tires skirling up the rainwater.

"Is that the dog from the camp?" Aleks said.

The animal paced over the far curb, ears flapping to glance into human faces, sniffing at passing toes, barking once and leaping to paw a man's knee.

"I think it is," Aleks said. "He's going to be hurt."

"I don't know," Trn said.

"He's such a little dog and he's so wet already. There he goes into the gutter."

As Trn stepped from the curb a blurred shape started out from the dark corner of his vision, the crowd in the avenue parting with it. He retreated just as Aleks's fingers slipped from his own and the boy's course slanted toward a drab truck stinking of diesel, swerving, clashing its horn, sliding over the stones to intercept Aleks and take him up by its grill and carry him a length of street before dropping him underneath its rolling carriage. The horn shrilled away into the silence as Trn knocked apart two women clutching shrieks in their hands. Aleks's shadow lay prone under the truck but he couldn't pull the boy out because a tire rested on Aleks's left hand. He couldn't even lift him over because there wasn't space but he had just enough light in the stinking gloom to see the grease and grit spread over the boy's face and the twin bloods starting from his nose. Trn whispered "No no no no" as blood began to cry from the corner of the boy's eye. He yelled over the stones in the road, past the stone in his throat, for them to move the truck, move the goddamn truck, and then they were clawing him out over the cobbles by his heels and his coat so they could.

1948

From summer's drought the shops still suffered. Behind the dusty windows shelf on barren shelf and in the glass his image passing, hands knotted in his old coat pockets, hatted head bearing down against March rasping past his ears. The loudspeaker fixed to the pole finished its song and announced production figures in Czech and then in Russian and began another song but a blue army of railroad men came marching down the street and their song was louder, the stomping of their boots in time.

He went on up the hill, the bell tower of St. Augustine standing taller with every step. A rattling tram overtook him. Through the stone gate he watched the boys fly kites in the park. One spooled out string as fast as his winding hands would let him and the kite lost all shape in the high distance, was nearly lost to sight.

At the end of the street he stopped as always at the gymnazium to read the stone.

THEIR BLOOD IS STILL IN THE BRICKS OF THIS WALL, THEIR BONES BENEATH THE GROUND HERE, HIDDEN TESTIMONY OF PEOPLE WHO PLACED THE STRUGGLE FOR THE LIBERATION OF THEIR COUNTRY ABOVE THEIR OWN LIVES.

The house when he looked back into the wind was graying through the spruce, the paint peeling, dark windows reflecting swift clouds.

He turned onto the Avenue-Marshal-Stalin. Trams clanged and drew to their stops but he walked on. Women still in mourning trudged to the end of long queues for Tuesday dinner behind little children mumbling up to their mothers. So many children. The fruit of two thousand nights without stars.

At Minska he turned and pushed against the door and climbed the stone stairs to the office. He was about to knock when the door opened and a man putting on a fur astrakhan smiled from his beard and said, "After you, comrade."

Trn nodded and behind the counter the clerk looked up from her heavy face.

"Comrade Trn. I didn't expect to see you again so soon."

She raised her arm and pounded down a rubber stamp on the first page of a ream of documents. She inked a second stamp and pounded the page again, then closed the file.

"You finished that batch already?"

"No, Mrs. Kranova. But I'm nearly done."

"I saw that you didn't have your case."

"I should be done by tomorrow. I was wondering if you had anything else."

She laid the stamp in the wooden box with her other stamps, closed the tin lids over her inks, red and black. She frowned.

"It's not permitted, Comrade, to pass you other work until the last has been returned."

The heavy cheeks drew themselves down and she leaned into the window, blew into her hands, cast her eyes about the empty room. "But there may be something coming soon," she whispered. "They captured all the records of the Ninth Army at the end and I hear there's talk they want them put into Czech so we can all read what they did."

"Do you know when those documents will be available, Mrs. Kranova?"

"Impossible to say." She shrugged. "Maybe never. Just come back."

"Thank you, Mrs. Kranova. I will. Do you have any more paper?"
Her lip frowned and shook with her jowls.

"Thank you, Mrs. Kranova."

He went back through a warren of old houses by streets lined with dead stumps, the scuff of his steps the only sound in the empty wind. Across the way the walls of two houses listed open to all weathers, snow in patches on the rubbled block, on the naked laths of what roof remained, on floors of mud. Between them a cratered lot. He went through the gate at number eleven and slowly turned the key, pushed the door to quietly.

"Mr. Trn."

He looked back at her from the gloom of the well, fists on her hips.

"Mr. Trn. The rent is now two weeks due."

"Yes, Mrs. Peskova. I will be paid tomorrow."

"Are you certain?"

"As certain as I am of anything."

She grimaced with the half of her wrinkled face he could see through the shadows. Her radio was making a speech broken by rapt applause. Each stair cracked under him and the boards of the hall floor and finally he heard her door shut over the speech. In his room he hooked his coat and hat and sat at the table and lifted the dictionary to squint at the top sheet of the stack. He wrote, consulting the dictionary twice in the midst of a long subsection, looking from the mimeo typescript to the cheap page grazed under his hand, the ink staining the length of his little finger till the pen ran dry. He inspected the gummed nib, from the drawer took up the dropper and the almost empty bottle, wiped his fingers each one on a handkerchief already blued, replaced the bottle in the drawer between a smashed tin toy and the wooden king. When he reached the end of the page he parted the curtains for a little more light, thumbed for the number of pages left. Six. A woman with a child by the hand walked the gray street, her coat clutched at her throat by the other hand. She hurried the bundled child toddling against the wind.

From a beam of the shattered roof a rook watched them pass the first destroyed house, the bare mud of the crater, his beak following them out of sight. With his hoarse cry he called through the wind. Trn held a palm to feel the cold ray in at the sill, the pen cold in his hand while he scratched out the last words, tried another version.

He laid the dictionary on the stack and the bed springs whinged under him, above him the cracked plaster, its stains like rusted clouds. Like old blood leaked from the attic. From the walls the paper flayed as if it were museum parchment, sepia maps of ancient lands lost beneath a long ago sea, or an undiscovered world yet to die. The panes rattled in their frame again and the curtains shivered and the relic of winter whistled down into the dead grate. Someone shuffled across the hall and the floorboards ached under some slow feet. To finish he needed ink and paper. In his pocket he felt eleven crowns. In his coat pocket he found two more and his handkerchief and blew his nose.

Passing Mrs. Peskova's door he quickened his steps to get into the cold street. On Minska again he turned toward the center, more widows in their queues at the empty shops, other children chirping at their mothers with upturned bird mouths. Barometers of hope in a blustery world. More men in blue came chanting down the very crown of the road, black caps, black rifles, red rags knotted round the biceps of their swinging arms, eyes entranced by their own swelling voice. The traffic stalled to the curb. A young couple scurried round a corner. Behind his white beard a man leaned on his cane to see them by, the thrust of their jaws almost wolfish. They halted at the flugelmann's call and the files made an about face and marched toward the square again, pivoting sharply to disappear down the next street, their cadence present long after they were gone. In their wake the loudspeaker declaimed "With the Soviet Union into Eternity" among other things and the glass behind him tapped. Trn looked back and Ivan rapped again, waved him to the door. The bell rang.

"I wasn't sure it was you," he said, bald head gleaming.

"I'm not so sure myself."

"Nonsense. Take off that hat and let me see what I'm up against today."

"I have to get to Vagner's before he closes."

Ivan looked at his watch, at the two empty chairs, the angled mirror.

"I'll have you done in plenty of time." He snipped his scissors smartly at the air. "You know me, Viktor. How about a shave too? Make you feel like a new man."

"I hadn't planned on a visit to the barber today, Ivan."

Ivan gathered him by the shoulder.

"Old friends don't need to plan, Viktor."

"But I need ink." He showed his stained hand.

"We'll see that you make it. Take off that coat. Today's on the business."

"I can't do that, Ivan."

"But I can. Now sit down. You've been cutting it yourself again, haven't you?"

Trn shrugged under the cape.

"Seen the paper?"

"No."

"Then you don't know we're marching gloriously into paradise."

"I hadn't understood that was our destination."

"You don't listen to the loudspeakers?"

"I never understand what they say."

"I have to listen to this one all day. Here, read this." The point of the scissors dented the page. "See where it says we're on the direct road to a human heaven?"

The scissors worked as Trn glanced over the headlines, noticed the byline of another column. "Paradise Rising." By Pavel Novotny. He handed the paper back and Ivan tossed it on the counter amid his combs.

"They say we won't have any more empty shelves." The scissors began again. "It's as bad as at the end of the war."

"While they're at it," Trn said, "I don't see why the party

shouldn't expropriate the sun so we'll never have to worry about another drought. Maybe the whole sky. We'll all celebrate eternal spring with only perfected rain."

"Can't you feel it warming up outside already?" Ivan said.

"I definitely feel the temperature rising but I don't think it's spring."

Ivan came round the chair, leaned to squint at either side of Trn's head.

"I'll get to keep the shop here," he said. "It's under the limit. And of course my wife and I'll get to keep our little flat. That's under the limit too. And rents will go down. They say. That will help my old father." He ran a comb over Trn's scalp. "Do you think you'll go back to the university?"

"I didn't sign. You can't teach if you don't sign. If I didn't sign in forty-five when the students demanded a pledge I certainly can't now when the party does."

Ivan swiveled the chair, revolved it back, tsked and shook his head.

"If it weren't for me, Viktor, you'd need a bigger hat."

Another chant approached and drew their eyes to the window.

"At least you hear them coming," Ivan sighed. "You get that much warning."

Their tramp came on with their song of the Red Banner and they dominated the window, the street, rank by rank marching past, banded arms and rifles in line, a longer file now as if others had joined or perhaps this was a different set.

Ivan whispered over his scissors, "I don't like those people."

Trn nodded.

"In the beginning, maybe," Ivan said, "right after the war when everybody fretted about werewolves hiding in the woods, but now they've cleared out the rifle factory and put one in the hand of every shockworker who fists a wrench. Who knows what they'll do?"

"No one knows," Trn said. "That's why they call them shockworkers."

"When we didn't know what the Germans would do, that was a different thing." Ivan lifted his scissors. "When do they work? I'd like to know that."

"They give them time to march."

"How much does it pay to march, I wonder."

Trn shrugged up the cape again.

"Hear our president on the radio last night?"

"No. It always sounds like the air escaping from a slow puncture."

"I listened for a bit," Ivan said.

"What did you learn?"

"I don't know. Not much. We're living in a different country now, that's what Gottwald says. A different world."

"The Germans extinguished the Jews," Trn said, "and we expelled the Germans. It will never be the same country again."

"Now we're all just good Slavs living in harmony together, like these fellows in the streets with their guns."

"A month ago we had alternatives," Trn said. "We could prefer. We had a parliament with many wills. Today no one has a voice but the loudspeaker."

"Still," Ivan said, "it could be worse, I suppose." The brush whisked over Trn's nape. "I think about the Poles." The cape snapped smartly and Ivan shook it out.

"What do you think, Viktor? They stood up and look what it cost them. Not one factory left, not one bridge. They got their cocks cut off. We didn't and look how many more of us survived. So now we're all in the same pot while Father Stalin shovels the coals onto the fire. We arrived at the same place but we have more blood in us. I'd say that's better, wouldn't you? We endured it. For them not one family untouched. And how many dead? Tell me that. They won't be able to count them all once they dig them up."

"One in five," Trn said. "So they say." He stared into the clasp of his hands. "Maybe no matter what we did then we would think it was a mistake now." His hands let go of one another. "But sometimes if you can count to one that's loss enough."

Ivan stopped his broom so it stood on its straw.

"I'm sorry, Viktor. I wasn't thinking."

"It's not your fault, Ivan."

"I'm very sorry. To talk that way." His eyes dropped to the heap of hair. "I'm sorry, Viktor."

"I know, Ivan."

"Don't you want to see?" Ivan held up the hand mirror.

"I know it's as close to perfection as you can come on an imperfect head, Ivan."

He had on his coat. He put on his hat. Ivan stood there with the mirror in his hand.

"Thank you, Ivan. It's very kind of you."

"What about the shave? Warm towel on a cold day, you know? I'll have that stubble off and give you your old face again."

"Why would I want that old face? Thanks for the cut though. I needed it."

"Now don't wait so long till next time."

They shook hands and Trn went out into the wind. The bell over the door rang behind him. In his pocket the cupped coins were warm in his fingers by the time he reached the site, stood at the curb as he often did. Less often now. A tram drew up and the others scowled and shouldered past him standing there and then he could see the cobbles again, the tarred stones without a trace of what had happened here, what had spilled. It was possible to construct a plausible history, from newspapers, photographs, the new books, to build up a long assembly line in a place called Michigan, to rig and bolt and weld the Studebaker carried by flat car to Camden New Jersey or Newark or Hoboken where it was craned into the hulk of a liberty ship bound for ice and the White Sea. Or out of Murmansk it came behind a locomotive spitting cinders and ash to the yards of Moscow and then Voronezh where it joined a transport detail. So many times it could have been strafed to destruction. Dodging shells while the Third Battle of Kharkov raged, during the Battle of Kursk when the grim driver stood in the cab to depress the accelerator so he wouldn't be shot. Perhaps into Bessarabia and up the slow Carpathians where it might have broken down but was overhauled to the last gear and put back into service. Probably Ruthenia after that and through the Dukla Pass. With a little knowledge, you could erect any chronicle to a certain point and tell it to yourself, but always only after the fact and by then it was too late. That was history.

As so often he wanted to kneel here, to touch the stones. But another tram was drawing up and others were looking.

Head down he crossed the avenue and jostled an older couple on the corner who glared back at the man who went on muttering through the door at the stationer's to look over the paper and buy the ink for seven crowns. The man who would write in smaller characters from now, majuscule the size of miniscule and miniscule more minor still.

The wind swept the dust in billows from the gutters as he made his way north toward home, home now, the ink bottle of heavy glass cool and cylindrical in his palm. A man and a woman came from a shop door, a dog squatting at the woman's heel while the man locked up. When he heard boots on the march the man reversed the key and the woman tugged at the leash and they all three went in again to miss the four blue files that advanced into the narrow street. Across the way a woman pushed her baby into an entry. Trn kept close against the wall but the vanguard shoved him anyway and the next stomped a heel on his toes. The march eddied round him hobbled there until a man glowered down and the whole column dragged to a halt. Under his cap the man had blue eyes and one of them crossed and wandered off to gaze at the wall over Trn's shoulder.

"What are you doing there?"

"I was going home."

Trn tried to press past but a rifle rose to bar the way.

"And where would that be? A fine house, I bet. One you're going to lose now."

"A room off Slovakova."

The leader if such he was sneered and thumbed back the cap from his red hair while one eye glared at the wall and the other at Trn. "What are you looking at?" he said.

"Nothing."

"What's in your pocket you keep holding to, you toffee-nosed bastard?"

Trn withdrew the ink.

"Ask him what he did in the war," a voice shouted from the rear.

"What's that? What are you writing?"

"I translate."

"Translate? Translate what?"

"Captured documents."

"Captured from whom?"

"The occupation."

"Do the authorities know that? Does the party?"

"I suspect they do."

"What did he do in the war?"

"His pants were full," the leader said over his shoulder. "You can tell that looking at him. He spent the war changing them. Often."

The laughter was general.

"Collaborator," a voice yelled from the siege of scowls. "Translating German."

"At least I didn't manufacture weapons for them."

"What did he say?"

"You heard what I said."

The rifle butt shot forward with such precision that the single blow buckled the bone of his nose and burst a lip. He slid against the wall and took a boot to the stomach that crumpled him like a wad of burning paper. Through his blood he could smell the smears of dog shits and the tang of urine and then another stamp drove his head against the paving and the world out of a new darkness flared. The scowls he could see stretched into jeers and he shot the bottle of ink at the nearest gaping mouth and the man covered his face with both hands. A great howl pitched up. Trn tried to roll against the wall, arms over his head, knees drawn, but the boots still split his skin.

He thought he heard a baby crying before something shattered over his ear and drove his skull into the pavement again.

Somehow one of them had kicked two pebbles past his clenched teeth and then he tasted that they were the salty teeth themselves that rested in his cheek. The paving was cool against his temple, then the flare in his mind went off again. His side erupted in sudden spikes and his crotch warmed. Blood seeped and soaked his clothes that chilled in the wind. His throat throbbed for water. Through a slit a dirty boot came scuffling forward, the slow and dirty sole, then he lost the sight even of that.

The men in blue tramped on, filling the square with a song he couldn't hear. Through windows faces peered at the man out there bent and writhing on the paving stones, swathed in blood. Eyes widened to see him rise to his knees, blind and groping, astonished that he could struggle still to stand against the wall.

ACKNOWLEDGEMENTS

You hold this book because of the generous help of many hands. Indeed, the trail of my indebtedness runs through two continents.

Betsy Teter at Hub City Press took a risk with this project. I'm grateful for her passion about writing in general and her reassuring enthusiasm about this book in particular. I'm thankful too for the editorial powers of Mike Curtis, whose keenness of mind and pencil lessened the risk. The whole production could not have gone forward without the expertise of Meg Reid, Kate McMullen, Megan DeMoss, and Kalee Lineberger.

In the Czech Republic I owe more crowns than I could ever count to Europe's best and most gracious landlady, Markéta Nováková, and to her gracious parents, Jaroslav Novák and Irena Nováková. To Lenka Bělková and her father Zdeněk Čecháček and to Luboš Bělka and his father Stanislav Bělka. To Tomáš Pospíšil, his aunt Marta Brandlová, and his daughter Tereza Kubíčková. To Kateřina Prajznerová, to Jeff Vanderziel, and to my vibrant students at Masaryk University, many of whom shared their own family stories of the war with me. Without the sponsorship of the U.S. Fulbright Commission and the Czech Fulbright Commission I would never have had the opportunity to begin listening to the voices that led me to these pages.

In the United States a host of readers over many years heartened and enlightened me, including Richard Combes, Kendall Henderson (my worthy assistant), and Alan Chalmers. Richard Predmore made an essential suggestion about the story's opening. I am also grateful to Janet Barnes McConnell, Jane Addison, and L.L. Pierce.

Peter Turchi awarded an early version of the story a prize ten years ago that encouraged me to go on.

At the University of South Carolina Upstate my colleagues in the Division of Languages, Literature and Composition, in the College of Arts and Sciences, on the Committee for Faculty Excellence, and on the staff of the university library offered help and nerve. The university's Office of Sponsored Awards and Research Support funded invaluable research assistance.

My mother, my brother, and my sister cheered me with affection and laughs. In the midst of the writing they also saved my life.

And finally, Bram, who lived with this story through much of his adolescence and who without a single sigh fielded all my questions about arms, armor, armaments, and much else. His knowledge of and curiosity about the world have long guided and sustained me and guide and sustain me still.

Thank you all.

HUB CITY
PRESS

HUB CITY PRESS is a non-profit independent press in Spartanburg, SC that publishes well-crafted, high-quality works by new and
established authors, with an emphasis on the Southern experience.
We are committed to high-caliber novels, short stories, poetry, plays,
memoir, and works emphasizing regional culture and history. We
are particularly interested in books with a strong sense of place.

Hub City Press is an imprint of the non-profit Hub City Writers
Project, founded in 1995 to foster a sense of community through the
literary arts. Our metaphor of organization purposely looks back-
ward to the nineteenth century when Spartanburg was known as the
"hub city," a place where railroads converged and departed.

RECENT HUB CITY PRESS TITLES

Whiskey & Ribbons • Leesa Cross-Smith

Ember • Brock Adams

Strangers to Temptation • Scott Gould

Over the Plain Houses • Julia Franks

Minnow • James E. McTeer II

Pasture Art • Marlin Barton

The Whiskey Baron • Jon Sealy

In the Garden of Stone • Susan Tekulve

Baskerville 11.3 / 14.9